CONTENTS

BOOK 1:	1
BOOK 2:	10
BOOK 3:	19
BOOK 4:	30
BOOK 5:	47
BOOK 6:	57
BOOK 7:	65
BOOK 8:	73
BOOK 9:	86
BOOK 10:	99
BOOK 11:	110
BOOK 12:	123
BOOK 13:	133
BOOK 14:	143
BOOK 15:	155
BOOK 16:	168
BOOK 17:	179
BOOK 18:	193
BOOK 19:	203
BOOK 20:	217
BOOK 21:	227

BOOK 22:	235
BOOK 23:	246
BOOK 24:	255

BOOK 1:

Tell me, Muse, about that clever hero who traveled all over the world after he destroyed the famous city of Troy. He visited many cities and learned about many different peoples and their ways. He faced a lot of challenges at sea while trying to save his own life and bring his men back home. But no matter what he did, he couldn't save them because they made a foolish mistake by eating the cattle of the Sun-god Hyperion. Because of this, the god made sure they never made it home. Tell me all about these events, oh daughter of Jove, from any source you know.

Now, everyone who survived the battles or shipwrecks had safely returned home except Ulysses. Even though he wanted to go back to his wife and homeland, he was held captive by the goddess Calypso, who had him in her large cave and wanted to marry him. After many years, the gods decided that he should go back to Ithaca. However, even when he was finally among his own people, his troubles weren't over yet. All the gods began to feel sorry for him except Neptune, who continued to make his life hard and wouldn't let him return home.

Neptune had gone to the Ethiopians, who live at the ends of the earth, one part looking West and the other East. He was there to receive a sacrifice of sheep and oxen and was enjoying himself at their festival. Meanwhile, the other gods gathered in the house of Olympian Jove, and he spoke first. He was thinking about Aegisthus, who had been killed by Agamemnon's son, Orestes. He said to the other gods:

"Look how men blame us gods for what is really just their own mistakes. Take Aegisthus, for example; he fell in love with Agamemnon's wife and killed Agamemnon, even though he knew it would cost him his life. I sent Mercury to warn him not to do either of those things, knowing Orestes would want revenge when he grew up and returned home. Mercury warned him out of good will, but he didn't listen, and now he has paid the price."

Then Minerva replied, "Father, King of kings, Aegisthus got what he deserved, and anyone else who does the same will too. But Aegisthus isn't the issue; my heart aches for Ulysses when I think of his suffering on that lonely island, so far away from his friends. It's a forested island in the middle of the sea, and a goddess lives there, the daughter of the magician Atlas, who supports the ocean floor and holds up the pillars that separate heaven and earth. This daughter of Atlas has trapped poor Ulysses and tries everything to make him forget his home, so he's tired of living and only thinks about seeing the smoke from his own chimneys again. You, sir, don't seem to care about this, even though Ulysses made many sacrifices to you when he was at Troy. Why then do you remain so angry with him?"

Jove replied, "My child, what are you saying? How could I forget Ulysses? There's no one more capable than him, nor anyone who offers more to the gods in heaven. But remember, Neptune is still angry with Ulysses for blinding the Cyclops Polyphemus, who is Neptune's son. That's why he doesn't kill Ulysses outright; instead, he torments him by keeping him from getting home. Still, let's think together about how we can help him return. If we all agree, Neptune won't be able to oppose us."

Minerva said, "Father, if the gods have decided Ulysses should return home, we should first send Mercury to the island to tell Calypso that he is to go back. Meanwhile, I will go to Ithaca to encourage Ulysses' son, Telemachus. I'll inspire him to call the Achaeans together to speak to the suitors of his mother, Penelope, who keep eating his sheep and oxen. I will also take him to Sparta and Pylos to see if he can learn anything about his father's return, which will help his reputation."

With that, she put on her shining golden sandals, which allow her to fly like the wind over land and sea. She took her strong bronze spear, with which she can defeat heroes who anger her, and she swiftly flew down from the highest peaks of Olympus. Soon, she arrived in Ithaca, at Ulysses' house, disguised as a visitor named Mentes, the chief of the Taphians, holding a bronze spear. She found the suitors lounging on the hides of the oxen they had killed, playing games in front of the house. Servants were busy waiting on them, mixing wine with water, cleaning tables, and preparing large amounts of meat.

Telemachus saw her before anyone else. He was sitting among the suitors, feeling gloomy and thinking about his brave father and how he would drive them out of the house if he returned and was honored like before. While he sat lost in thought, he noticed Minerva and quickly went to the gate, annoyed that a stranger had to wait. He took her hand and asked for her spear. "Welcome to our house," he said. "After you eat, you can tell us why you've come."

He led her inside, and Minerva followed. Once inside, he took her spear and set it in the stand next to many others belonging to his father. He led her to a beautifully decorated seat and laid a cloth on it. He also provided a footstool for her and a seat for himself, away from the suitors, so she wouldn't be bothered while eating, and so he could ask her more about his father.

A maid brought them water in a lovely golden pitcher and poured it into a silver basin for them to wash their hands. She set a clean table beside them. An upper servant brought them bread and offered them many delicious dishes from the house. The carver served plates of all kinds of meat, and a manservant brought them wine and poured it out for them.

Then the suitors came in and took their places. Immediately, servants poured water over their hands, maids passed around bread, and pages filled bowls with wine and water. They dug into the food in front of them. When they had eaten enough, they wanted music and dancing to make the feast more enjoyable, so a servant brought a lyre to Phemius, whom they forced to sing. As soon as he started playing, Telemachus quietly spoke to Minerva, leaning close so no one else could hear.

"I hope you won't be upset with what I'm about to say," he said. "Singing is easy for those who don't pay for it, and all this is happening at the expense of someone whose bones are rotting in some faraway place or being crushed in the waves. If these men saw my father return to Ithaca, they would wish they had longer legs rather than more money, because money won't help them now; he has suffered a terrible fate, and even when people say he is coming, we no longer believe them. We will never see him again. Now, please tell me the truth: who are you, and where do you come from? Tell me about your town and parents, how you arrived here, and what kind of ship brought you to Ithaca. Surely you didn't come by land. Also, tell me honestly if you are a stranger to this house or if you visited in my father's time. We had many visitors back then, as my father traveled a lot."

Minerva answered, "I will tell you everything honestly. I am Mentes, son of Anchialus, and I am the King of the Taphians. I came here with my ship and crew, traveling to foreign lands to trade iron for copper. My ship is over there, anchored away from the town at the harbor Rheithron, near the wooded mountain Neritum. Our fathers were friends long ago, as old Laertes will tell you if you ask him. They say he doesn't come to town anymore and lives alone in the country, struggling with an old woman to take care of him and prepare his meals when he returns from working in his vineyard. I heard your father was home, which is why I came, but it seems the gods are still holding him back. He's not dead, but he's likely on some distant island or held captive by savages against his will. I'm not a seer and don't know much about signs, but I'm telling you what I feel from the gods, and I assure you he won't be gone much longer. He's resourceful enough that even if he were in chains, he'd find a way to get back home. But tell me, is it true that Ulysses has such a handsome son? You look just like him around the head and eyes; we were good friends before he left for Troy with the best of the Achaeans. Since then, we've never seen each other again."

"My mother tells me I'm Ulysses' son," replied Telemachus, "but it's wise to know your own father. I wish I were the son of someone who grew old on his own land, because, since you ask, there's no one more unfortunate than he who they say is my father."

Minerva said, "You don't have to worry about your family dying out while Penelope has such a fine son like you. But tell me the truth: what's all this feasting about, and who are these people? Is there a celebration or a wedding? No one seems to have brought any food of their own. And look at the guests! They're behaving horribly, making a mess of the whole house. It would disgust any decent person who sees them."

"Sir," Telemachus replied, "when my father was here, everything was fine for us and our home. But the gods have made things different, and they have hidden him away more than anyone has ever been hidden before. I could accept it better if he had died bravely in battle, or surrounded by friends when the fighting was over; then the Achaeans would have built a tomb for him, and I would have inherited his glory. But now the storm winds have taken him away, and we don't know where he is. He has disappeared without a trace, and all I have left is sadness. My troubles don't stop with missing my father; the chiefs from all our islands—Dulichium, Same, and the wooded island of Zacynthus, along with the main men of Ithaca—are eating me out of house and home under the excuse of courting my mother. She won't say outright that she won't marry, nor will she finish things with them. So they are destroying my home, and soon they will ruin me too."

"Is that so?" Minerva exclaimed. "Then you really want Ulysses to come back. Give him his helmet, shield, and a couple of lances, and if he is the man he was when I first knew him, having fun in our house, he would take care of these rascally suitors right away if he stood once more at his own door. At that time, he was coming from Ephyra, where he had gone to get poison for his arrows from Ilus, son of Mermerus. Ilus was afraid of the gods and wouldn't give him any, but my father did, because he liked Ulysses a lot. If Ulysses is still the same man he was, these suitors won't have a chance at a happy ending.

"But it's up to the gods to decide if he will return and take his revenge in his own home. However, I urge you to get rid of these suitors right away. Take my advice: call the Achaean heroes together for an assembly tomorrow morning. Lay your case before them and ask the gods to witness. Tell the suitors to leave, each going to his own home. If your mother wants to marry again, let her return to her father, who can find her a husband and provide her with the gifts a dear daughter should have. As for you, I encourage you to take the best ship you can find, with a crew of twenty men, and go search for your father who has been missing for so long. Someone might tell you something, or maybe you'll hear a message from the gods. First, go to Pylos and ask Nestor; then go on to Sparta and visit Menelaus, who was the last of the Achaeans to return home. If you find out that your father is alive and on his way home, you can tolerate the waste these suitors will cause for another twelve months. But if you learn of his death, come back immediately, hold his funeral with all the honors, build a tomb in his memory, and let your mother marry again. Then, after all this, think carefully about how you can get rid of these suitors in your own home. You're old enough to stop pretending you're just a child; haven't you heard how people praise Orestes for killing his father's murderer, Aegisthus? You are a fine-looking young man; show your strength and make a name for yourself. Now I must return to my ship and my crew, who will be getting anxious if I keep them waiting. Think about what I've said."

"Sir," Telemachus replied, "thank you for speaking to me like I am your own son. I will do everything you say. I know you want to continue your journey, but please stay a little longer until you can take a bath and refresh yourself. After that, I will give you a gift, a beautiful keepsake like dear friends give to each other."

Minerva answered, "Don't try to keep me; I want to leave right away. As for any gift you wish to give me, keep it until I come again, and I will take it home with me. You shall give me a fine gift, and I will give you one of equal value in return."

With those words, she flew away like a bird into the sky, but she had given Telemachus courage and made him think more about his father. He felt the change, wondered about it, and knew that the stranger had been a god. So, he went straight to where the suitors were sitting.

Phemius was still singing, and the listeners sat quietly as he told the sad story of the return from Troy and the troubles Minerva had caused the Achaeans. Penelope, daughter of Icarius, heard his song from her room upstairs and came down the grand staircase, accompanied by two of her maids. When she reached the suitors, she stood by a post that supported the roof of the cloisters, with a serious maid on either side of her. She held a veil before her face and was crying bitterly.

"Phemius," she called out, "you know many stories of gods and heroes that poets love to sing about. Sing something else for the suitors, and let them drink their wine in silence, but stop this sad tale, for it breaks my heart and reminds me of my lost husband, whom I mourn constantly. His name was great throughout Greece and the middle of Argos."

"Mother," Telemachus answered, "let the bard sing what he wants. Bards don't create the troubles they sing about; it's Jove, not they, who brings good and bad upon people as he pleases. This man means no harm by singing about the unfortunate return of the Danaans; people always enjoy the latest songs the most. Accept it and endure it; Ulysses is not the only man who never came back from Troy; many others met the same fate. Now go back inside and focus on your daily tasks—your loom, your distaff, and managing the servants—because speaking is a man's job, and mine above all, for I am the master here."

She went back into the house, thinking about what her son had said. Then, going upstairs with her maids into her room, she mourned her dear husband until Minerva made her fall into a sweet sleep. But the suitors were noisy in the covered cloisters, each hoping to be her next partner.

Then Telemachus spoke, "Shameless and disrespectful suitors, let's enjoy our feast in peace and avoid any fighting, for it's rare to hear a man with such a beautiful voice as Phemius has. But tomorrow, gather in assembly so I can formally tell you to leave and take turns feasting at each other's houses at your own expense. If you choose to continue taking advantage of one man, heaven help me, but Jove will hold you accountable, and when you fall in my father's house, there will be no one to avenge you."

The suitors bit their lips as they heard him, amazed by his boldness. Then Antinous, son of Eupeithes, said, "The gods seem to have taught you how to talk tough; may Jove never let you become the chief of Ithaca like your father was."

Telemachus answered, "Antinous, don't argue with me, but, god willing, I will be chief too if I can. Is this the worst fate you can think of for me? It's not bad to be a chief; it brings wealth and honor. But now that Ulysses is dead, there are many great men in Ithaca, both young and old, and someone else may take the lead among them. Still, I will be the chief in my own house and rule over those whom Ulysses has won for me."

Then Eurymachus, son of Polybus, said, "It's up to the gods to decide who will be chief among us, but you shall be master of your own house and possessions. As long as there's a man in Ithaca, no one will harm you or steal from you. Now, my good fellow, I want to know about this stranger. Where does he come from? What family does he have, and where is his home? Did he bring news about your father's return, or was he on some business of his own? He seemed well-off, but he left so quickly that we didn't have time to learn much about him."

"My father is gone," Telemachus answered, "and even if I hear rumors, I don't believe them anymore. My mother sometimes calls for a soothsayer to ask questions, but I don't listen to his prophecies. The stranger was Mentes, son of Anchialus, chief of the Taphians, an old friend of my father's." But in his heart, he knew it had been the goddess.

The suitors returned to their singing and dancing until evening, and when night fell, they went home to bed, each in his own place. Telemachus's room was high in a tower that looked out onto the courtyard. He went there, deep in thought. An old woman named Euryclea, daughter of Ops, the son of Pisenor, went ahead of him with two blazing torches. Laertes had bought her when she was young, paying the worth of twenty oxen for her, and he treated her with as much respect as his wife, though he didn't take her to bed for fear of his wife's anger. She lit Telemachus to his room, loving him more than any of the other women in the house because she had nursed him as a baby. He opened the door to his bedroom and sat down on the bed. As he took off his shirt, he handed it to the old woman, who folded it neatly and hung it over a peg by his bedside. After she left, she pulled the door shut with a silver catch and secured it with a strap. But Telemachus, lying under a woolen blanket, kept thinking all night about his planned voyage and the advice Minerva had given him.

BOOK 2:

When rosy-fingered Dawn appeared, Telemachus got up and got dressed. He put on his sandals, strapped his sword across his shoulder, and left his room looking like a god. He sent messengers to call the people for an assembly, and they gathered quickly. When everyone was there, he went to the assembly place with a spear in hand, and he wasn't alone; his two dogs followed him. Minerva gave him a divine beauty that made everyone marvel at him as he walked by, and when he took his father's seat, even the oldest men moved aside for him.

Aegyptius, an old man with a lot of experience, was the first to speak. His son Antiphus had gone with Ulysses to Ilius, the land of noble horses, but the fierce Cyclops had killed him when they were trapped in the cave, cooking his last meal. He had three other sons, two of whom still worked their father's land, while the third, Eurynomus, was one of the suitors. Yet, Aegyptius couldn't get over losing Antiphus and was still weeping when he began his speech.

"Men of Ithaca," he said, "listen to me. Since Ulysses left us, we haven't had a meeting until now. Who is it that has called us together, whether old or young? Has he heard of an enemy coming, and does he want to warn us? Or is there something else important to discuss? I'm sure he is a good person, and I hope Jove will grant him what he desires."

Telemachus took this as a good sign and stood up, eager to speak. He stepped forward in the assembly, and the herald Pisenor handed him a staff. Turning to Aegyptius, he said, "Sir, I have gathered you here because I am the most troubled. I have not heard of any approaching enemy to warn you about, nor do I have a public matter to discuss. My grievance is personal, based on two great misfortunes that have come upon my house. The first is the loss of my excellent father, who was a leader among you all and like a father to everyone here. The second is much worse and is leading to the ruin of my estate. The sons of all the chief men among you are pestering my mother to marry them against her will. They are afraid to go to her father, Icarius, to ask him to choose one of them and provide gifts for his daughter. Instead, they keep hanging around my father's house, slaughtering our oxen, sheep, and fat goats for their feasts, without considering how much wine they drink. No estate can survive such reckless behavior; we no longer have Ulysses to protect us, and I can't fight them off. I will never be as good a man as he was, but I would defend myself if I could. I can't tolerate this treatment any longer; my house is being ruined. So I urge you to respect your own conscience and public opinion. Fear the wrath of the gods, lest they become angry with you. I pray to Jove and Themis, who guide all councils, not to leave me alone in this—unless it is because my brave father Ulysses wronged the Achaeans, and you wish to take it out on me by supporting these suitors. If I must lose everything, I'd rather you did the eating yourselves, so that I could at least take action against you and get paid back, instead of having no way to fight back now."

With that, Telemachus threw down his staff and began to cry. Everyone felt sorry for him, but they all remained silent, not daring to respond angrily except for Antinous, who said:

"Telemachus, you insolent braggart, how dare you blame us suitors? It's your mother's fault, not ours. She is a very cunning woman. For nearly four years now, she has been driving us mad by encouraging each one of us and sending messages without meaning a word. Then there was that other trick she played on us. She set up a big loom in her room and began working on a huge piece of fine needlework. She said, 'Sweethearts, Ulysses is indeed dead, but do not pressure me to marry again right away.

11

Wait until I finish this pall for the hero Laertes, so it will be ready when he dies. He is very wealthy, and the women will talk if he is laid out without a pall.'

"This is what she said, and we agreed. We could see her working on her great web all day, but at night she would take the stitches out by torchlight. She fooled us like this for three years, and we never caught her. But as time went on and she was nearing her fourth year, one of her maids who knew what was going on told us, and we caught her in the act of undoing her work. So she had to finish it, whether she wanted to or not. The suitors, therefore, say this: both you and the Achaeans should understand—'Send your mother away, and tell her to marry whoever she and her father choose.' I don't know what will happen if she keeps teasing us with her airs and the skills Minerva has given her. We've heard of famous women like Tyro, Alcmena, and Mycene, but none were like your mother. It's not fair for her to treat us this way, and as long as she continues to act as she does, we will keep eating up your estate. I don't see why she should change; she gets all the honor and glory, while you're the one who suffers. Understand that we will not leave until she makes her choice and marries one of us."

Telemachus replied, "Antinous, how can I drive away the mother who bore me? My father is gone, and we don't know if he is alive or dead. It will be hard for me to pay Icarius the large sum I must give him if I insist on sending his daughter back. Not only will he be harsh with me, but heaven will also punish me, for my mother will call on the Erinyes to avenge her when she leaves. Besides, it wouldn't be honorable, and I won't do it. If you're offended, then leave my house and feast at each other's homes at your own expense. But if you choose to continue to take advantage of me, heaven help me, Jove will deal with you, and when you fall in my father's house, there will be no one to avenge you."

As he spoke, Jove sent two eagles from the mountaintop, flying side by side on the wind. When they were directly over the assembly, they circled above, beating the air with their wings and glaring down at those below. Then, fighting fiercely, they flew off to the right over the town. The people were amazed and wondered what it meant, and then Halitherses, the best prophet among them, spoke up:

"Hear me, men of Ithaca, especially you suitors, for I see trouble coming for you. Ulysses will not be away much longer; indeed, he is near to bring death and destruction, not just to you but to many others living in Ithaca. Let's be wise and stop this wrongdoing before he arrives. Let the suitors act on their own; it will be better for them. I am not prophesying without reason; everything that has happened to Ulysses I foretold when the Achaeans set out for Troy. I said that after enduring many hardships and losing all his men, he would return home in the twentieth year, and that no one would recognize him. Now all of this is coming true."

Eurymachus, son of Polybus, replied, "Go home, old man, and prophesy to your own children, or it may be worse for them. I can read these omens better than you; birds are always flying around somewhere, but they seldom mean anything. Ulysses has died in a distant land, and I wish you had died with him, instead of prattling on about omens and adding to Telemachus's anger, which is already fierce enough. You probably think he'll reward you, but I assure you that when an old man like you, who should know better, encourages a young man, he'll only suffer for it. He will gain nothing, because the suitors will stop this, and we will lay a heavier burden on you than you'll like, and it will be hard on you. As for Telemachus, I warn him in front of you all to send his mother back to her father, who will find her a husband and provide all the gifts that a dear daughter deserves. Until then, we will continue to bother him with our courtship, for we fear no one, and we care nothing for him or for your fortune-telling. You can preach all you want, but it will only make us hate you more. We will keep eating up Telemachus's estate without paying him until his mother stops torturing us by making us wait and hope for her. We cannot pursue other women we might marry because of how she treats us."

Then Telemachus said, "Eurymachus and you other suitors, I won't say any more or plead with you further, for the gods and the people of Ithaca know my story now. Give me a ship and a crew of twenty men to take me here and there, and I will go to Sparta and Pylos in search of my father, who has been missing for so long. Someone might tell me something, or maybe a message from the gods will guide me. If I hear that he is alive and on his way home, I can endure the waste you suitors will cause for another twelve months. But if I hear of his death, I will return right away, celebrate his funeral with all the proper honors, build a tomb for him, and let my mother marry again."

With these words, Telemachus sat down, and Mentor, a friend of Ulysses who had been left in charge of everything, rose to speak. He addressed the assembly plainly and honestly:

"Hear me, men of Ithaca. I hope you never find a kind ruler again, nor one who will govern you justly; I hope your leaders from now on will be cruel and unfair. Not one of you remembers Ulysses, who ruled you like a father. I am not as angry with the suitors, because if they choose to act badly and wager their lives that Ulysses will not return, they can do as they please and consume his estate. But I am shocked at how you all sit idly by without trying to stop these disgraceful actions. You could if you wanted to, for you are many and they are few."

Leiocritus, son of Evenor, responded, "Mentor, what nonsense is this? How can one man fight many over food? Even if Ulysses himself were here trying to push us out while we feast in his house, his wife, who longs for him, would not be pleased, and he would have no one to blame but himself for fighting such great odds. There's no sense in what you're saying. Now, go about your business, and let his father's old friends, Mentor and Halitherses, help this boy on his journey, if he goes at all—which I doubt, because he is more likely to stay here until someone tells him something."

With that, he ended the assembly, and everyone went back to their homes, while the suitors returned to Ulysses' house.

Telemachus went alone to the seashore, washed his hands in the gray waves, and prayed to Minerva.

"Hear me," he cried, "you goddess who visited me yesterday and told me to sail the seas in search of my father, who has been missing for so long. I want to obey you, but the Achaeans, especially the wicked suitors, are stopping me from doing so."

As he prayed, Minerva appeared to him in the form and voice of Mentor. "Telemachus," she said, "if you are made of the same stuff as your father, you will not be a fool or a coward from now on, for Ulysses never broke his word or left a task unfinished. If you take after him, your voyage will not be in vain. But if you do not have the blood of Ulysses and Penelope in your veins, I doubt you will succeed. Sons are seldom as good as their fathers; they are usually worse, not better. Still, as you will not be a fool or coward from now on and have some of your father's wisdom, I have hope for your journey. Just make sure you don't ally yourself with those foolish suitors, for they lack sense and virtue and do not consider the death that awaits them all. Your voyage will not be delayed; your father was a dear friend of mine, so I will find you a ship and come with you myself. Now, go home and start preparing for your journey. Gather provisions for the trip; see that the wine is stored in jars and the barley meal, the staff of life, is packed in leather bags. Meanwhile, I will go around the town and gather volunteers. There are many ships in Ithaca, both old and new; I will check them for you and choose the best. We will get it ready and set sail without delay."

Thus spoke Minerva, daughter of Jove, and Telemachus quickly followed her advice. He went home, feeling down, and found the suitors butchering goats and roasting pigs in the outer court. Antinous approached him and laughed as he took his hand, saying, "Telemachus, my fine fire-eater, let go of any bad feelings, and eat and drink with us like you used to. The Achaeans will provide you with everything—a ship and a select crew—so you can sail to Pylos and learn about your noble father."

"Antinous," Telemachus replied, "I cannot eat in peace or enjoy myself with men like you. Was it not enough that you wasted so much of my father's property while I was still a boy? Now that I am older and wiser, I am also stronger, and whether here among you or by going to Pylos, I will do all I can to hurt you. I will go, and I will not go in vain—though, thanks to you suitors, I have no ship or crew of my own, and must be a passenger, not the captain."

With that, he pulled his hand away from Antinous. The other suitors continued preparing dinner in the buildings, taunting him as they did.

"Telemachus," said one young man, "thinks he will bring friends to help him from Pylos, or perhaps from Sparta. Or will he go to Ephyra to get poison to put in our wine and kill us?"

Another said, "Maybe if Telemachus goes on board a ship, he will be like his father and die far from his friends. In that case, we could divide up his property among us. As for the house, we can let his mother and her new husband have that."

This is how they spoke. But Telemachus went into the high, spacious storeroom where his father's treasures of gold and bronze lay piled on the floor, along with linens and spare clothes kept in open chests. There was also a supply of fragrant olive oil and casks of aged, fine wine, unblended and fit for a god, stored against the day when Ulysses might return. The room had well-made doors that opened in the middle, and the faithful old housekeeper Euryclea, daughter of Ops, son of Pisenor, was in charge both night and day. Telemachus called her to the storeroom and said:

"Nurse, pour me some of the best wine you have, after what you're saving for my father, in case, poor man, he escapes death and finds his way home again. I want twelve jars, and make sure they all have lids. Also, fill some well-sewn leather bags with barley meal—about twenty measures in all. Get these things ready quickly and say nothing about it. I will take everything away tonight after my mother goes upstairs. I am going to Sparta and Pylos to see if I can find out anything about my dear father's return."

When Euryclea heard this, she began to cry and spoke to him fondly, "My dear child, what has given you such an idea? Where do you want to go, you who are the one hope of the house? Your poor father is gone in some foreign land, and when you are gone, these wicked suitors will plot to get rid of you and take all your possessions. Stay among your own people and do not go wandering on the barren ocean."

"Fear not, nurse," answered Telemachus, "my plan has heaven's support; but swear to me that you will say nothing about this to my mother until I have been gone for ten or twelve days, unless she asks about my absence. I don't want her to ruin her beauty with tears."

The old woman swore she would not, and once she had made her oath, she began pouring the wine into jars and packing the barley meal into bags while Telemachus returned to the suitors.

Then Minerva thought of another task. She took on Telemachus' appearance and went through the town, telling each member of the crew to meet at the ship by sundown. She also approached Noemon, son of Phronius, asking him to lend her a ship, which he was happy to do. When the sun set and darkness covered the land, she got the ship into the water, put all the gear on board, and stationed it at the harbor's edge. Soon the crew arrived, and the goddess encouraged each of them.

Furthermore, she went to Ulysses' house and put the suitors into a deep sleep. She made their drinks intoxicating, causing them to drop their cups, so instead of lingering over their wine, they returned to the town to sleep, their eyes heavy with drowsiness. Then she took on the form and voice of Mentor and called for Telemachus to come outside.

"Telemachus," she said, "the men are on board and at their oars, waiting for you to give your orders, so make haste and let us leave."

With that, she led the way, and Telemachus followed. When they reached the ship, they found the crew waiting by the water. Telemachus said, "Now my men, help me get the supplies on board; they are all prepared in the storeroom, and my mother knows nothing about it, except for one maid."

With these words, he led the way, and the others followed. After they brought the supplies as he instructed, Telemachus went on board, with Minerva taking her seat in the stern while he sat beside her. The men untied the ropes and took their places on the benches. Minerva sent them a favorable wind from the west that whistled over the deep blue waves. Telemachus told them to grab the ropes and hoist the sails, and they did as he commanded. They set the mast in its socket, raised it, and secured it with the stays, then hoisted the white sails with twisted oxhide ropes. As the sail filled with the wind, the ship sped through the deep blue water, the foam hissing against her bow as she raced onward. They secured everything on the ship, filled the mixing bowls to the brim, and made drink offerings to the immortal gods, especially to the gray-eyed daughter of Jove.

Thus, the ship sped on her way through the night from dark until dawn.

BOOK 3:

As the sun rose from the beautiful sea into the sky to bring light to both mortals and immortals, Telemachus and his crew arrived at Pylos, the city of Neleus. The people of Pylos were gathered on the shore to offer sacrifices of black bulls to Neptune, the lord of the Earthquake. There were nine groups, each with five hundred men, and each group had nine bulls. While they ate the inner parts of the animals and burned the thigh bones as offerings to Neptune, Telemachus and his crew arrived, furled their sails, anchored their ship, and went ashore.

Minerva led the way, and Telemachus followed her. She said, "Telemachus, don't be shy or nervous; you've taken this journey to find out where your father is buried and how he met his end. Go straight up to Nestor so we can learn what he knows. Ask him to speak the truth, and he will tell no lies, for he is a good man."

"But how can I, Mentor," Telemachus replied, "approach Nestor? How should I address him? I am not used to long conversations with others, and I feel embarrassed to ask someone so much older than me."

"Some things, Telemachus," answered Minerva, "will come to you naturally, and heaven will guide you; for I am sure the gods have been with you since your birth."

She then moved on quickly, and Telemachus followed her until they reached the place where the Pylian people were gathered. There they found Nestor sitting with his sons while his companions prepared dinner, putting pieces of meat on spits while other pieces were cooking. When they saw the strangers, they crowded around them, taking their hands and inviting them to take their places. Nestor's son Pisistratus offered his hand to each of them and seated them on soft sheepskins on the sand near his father and brother Thrasymedes. He then served them their portions of meat and poured wine for them into a golden cup, giving it to Minerva first and greeting her.

"Pray, sir," he said, "to King Neptune, for it is his feast you are joining. After you have prayed and made your offering, pass the cup to your friend so he can do the same. I am sure he will also lift his hands in prayer, for no man can live without God in this world. Still, he is younger than you, so I will give you precedence."

As he spoke, he handed her the cup. Minerva thought it was very proper of him to have given it to her first; she then began to pray earnestly to Neptune. "O thou," she cried, "who encircleth the earth, grant the prayers of those who call upon thee. Especially send down thy grace on Nestor and his sons; also reward the rest of the Pylian people for the fine hecatomb they are offering you. Lastly, grant Telemachus and me a happy outcome in respect of the matter that has brought us in our ship to Pylos."

When she finished her prayer, she handed the cup to Telemachus, who prayed as well. Soon, when the outer meats were roasted and taken off the spits, the carvers served each man his portion, and they all enjoyed a fine dinner. After they had eaten and drunk enough, Nestor, the knight of Gerene, began to speak.

"Now," he said, "that our guests have finished dinner, it is best to ask them who they are. Who are you, strangers, and from what port have you sailed? Are you traders, or do you roam the seas with your hands against every man, and every man's hands against you?"

Telemachus answered boldly, for Minerva had given him the courage to ask about his father and gain a good name.

"Nestor," he said, "son of Neleus, honor to the Achaean name, you ask where we come from, and I will tell you. We come from Ithaca, under Neritum, and I seek news of my unfortunate father Ulysses, who is said to have sacked the city of Troy alongside you. We know what fate befell each of the other heroes who fought at Troy, but as for Ulysses, heaven has hidden from us even the knowledge that he is dead. No one can tell us where he perished, whether he fell in battle on the mainland or was lost at sea in the waves. Therefore, I plead at your knees if you would be pleased to tell me about his sad end, whether you saw it with your own eyes or heard it from some traveler. He was a man born to trouble. Please do not soften the truth out of pity for me; tell me plainly what you saw. If my brave father Ulysses ever did you loyal service, either by word or deed when you Achaeans were harassed among the Trojans, remember that now and tell me truly."

"My friend," replied Nestor, "you remind me of a time filled with sorrow, for the brave Achaeans suffered much at sea while privateering under Achilles and while fighting before the great city of king Priam. Our best men fell there—Ajax, Achilles, Patroclus, who was like a god in counsel, and my dear son Antilochus, who was swift of foot and valiant in battle. But our suffering was even greater; no mortal tongue could tell the whole story. If you stayed here and asked me questions for five or six years, I could not tell you everything the Achaeans endured, and you would grow weary of my tale before it ended. For nine long years we tried every kind of strategy, but heaven was against us; during that time, there was no one who could compare with your father in cleverness—if indeed you are his son—I can hardly believe my eyes—and you speak just like him, too. No one would guess that people of such different ages could sound so alike. He and I never disagreed from beginning to end, neither in camp nor council, but with a single heart and purpose we advised the Argives on how to do their best.

"When we had sacked the city of Priam and were setting sail as heaven dispersed us, Jove chose to trouble the Argives on their return journey. They had not all been wise or understanding, and thus many met a bad end due to the anger of Jove's daughter, Minerva, who caused a quarrel between the two sons of Atreus.

"The sons of Atreus called a meeting, but it was not as it should have been, for it was sunset, and the Achaeans were heavy with wine. When they explained why they had gathered, Menelaus wanted to sail home at once, which displeased Agamemnon, who thought we should wait until we offered hecatombs to appease Minerva's anger. Foolish as he was, he should have known he would not prevail with her, for when the gods make up their minds, they do not change them lightly. So the two exchanged harsh words, and the Achaeans sprang to their feet with a cry that shook the air, torn between what they should do.

"That night we rested and nursed our anger, while Jove plotted mischief against us. In the morning, some of us drew our ships into the water and loaded our goods with our women on board, while about half stayed behind with Agamemnon. We —the other half—embarked and sailed; our ships went well, for heaven had calmed the sea. When we reached Tenedos, we offered sacrifices to the gods, longing to return home. But cruel Jove did not yet intend for us to do so and stirred up another quarrel, during which some among us turned back and sailed with Ulysses to make peace with Agamemnon. I, however, and all the ships with me pressed forward, for I sensed mischief brewing. The son of Tydeus sailed with me and his crew. Later, Menelaus joined us at Lesbos, where we were deciding our course—for we didn't know whether to go outside Chios by the island of Psyra, keeping that to our left, or inside Chios, facing the stormy headland of Mimas. So we asked heaven for a sign, which indicated we would be safest if we crossed the open sea to Euboea. We did just that, and a fair wind arose, giving us a swift passage during the night to Geraestus, where we offered many sacrifices to Neptune for helping us so far on our journey. Four days later, Diomed and his men reached Argos, but I continued on to Pylos, and the wind never died down from the day heaven first made it fair for me.

"Therefore, my young friend, I returned without hearing anything about the others. I do not know who made it home safely or who was lost, but as duty compels me, I will give you all the news I have received since I have been here in my own house. They say the Myrmidons returned home safely under Achilles' son Neoptolemus; so did the brave son of Poias, Philoctetes. Idomeneus lost no men at sea, and all his followers who escaped death in battle made it back to Crete with him. You have certainly heard of Agamemnon and the terrible end he came to at Aegisthus' hands—and Aegisthus paid a fearful price for it. It is good for a man to leave a son behind, as Orestes did, who killed false Aegisthus, the murderer of his noble father. You too—because you are a tall, good-looking fellow—show your courage and make a name for yourself in history."

"Nestor, son of Neleus," replied Telemachus, "honor to the Achaean name, the Achaeans praise Orestes, and his name will live forever because he avenged his father so nobly. If only heaven would grant me the chance to take similar vengeance on the insolence of the wicked suitors, who are mistreating me and plotting my ruin! But the gods have no such happiness in store for me or my father, so we must endure it as best we can."

"My friend," Nestor said, "you remind me that I have heard your mother has many suitors, who are treating you badly and ruining your estate. Do you accept this quietly, or does public opinion and the voice of heaven stand against you? Who knows but that Ulysses may return and take revenge on these scoundrels, either alone or with a force of Achaeans? If Minerva were to take as much liking to you as she did to Ulysses when we were fighting before Troy—because I have never seen the gods take so much interest in anyone as Minerva did in your father—if she would care for you as she did for him, these suitors would soon forget their wooing."

Telemachus answered, "I cannot expect such things; it would be too much to hope for. I dare not allow myself to think of it. Even if the gods themselves willed it, such good fortune could not come to me."

Minerva then said, "Telemachus, what are you saying? Heaven has a long reach if it intends to save a man; if it were me, I would not care how much I suffered before getting home, as long as I was safe when I arrived. I would prefer that to returning quickly and then being killed in my own house, as Agamemnon was by Aegisthus and his wife. Still, death is certain, and when a man's hour comes, not even the gods can save him, no matter how fond they are of him."

"Mentor," Telemachus replied, "let's not talk about this anymore. There's no chance my father will ever come back; the gods have long since decided his fate. However, there is something else I would like to ask Nestor, for he knows much more than anyone else. They say he has ruled for three generations, making it feel like you're talking to an immortal. So, tell me, Nestor, and tell me truly: how did Agamemnon die? What was Menelaus doing? How did false Aegisthus manage to kill a man so much better than himself? Was Menelaus away from Achaean Argos, traveling elsewhere, so that Aegisthus felt bold enough to kill Agamemnon?"

"I will tell you the truth," Nestor replied. "You've guessed how it happened. If Menelaus had returned from Troy to find Aegisthus still alive in his house, there wouldn't have been a tomb for him; instead, he would have been thrown outside the city for dogs and vultures to eat, and no woman would mourn him, for he committed a great wickedness. But we were over at Troy, fighting hard, while Aegisthus, who was lounging around in Argos, flattered Agamemnon's wife, Clytemnestra, with endless praise.

"At first, she would have nothing to do with his evil plan because she had a good heart, and Agamemnon had left a bard with her to keep guard over his wife. But when the gods plotted her downfall, Aegisthus kidnapped the bard and left him on a deserted island for crows and seagulls to feed on, after which she willingly went to Aegisthus' house. He then offered many burnt sacrifices to the gods and decorated temples with beautiful tapestries and gold, for he had succeeded beyond his expectations.

"Meanwhile, Menelaus and I were making our way home from Troy, on good terms with each other. When we reached Sunium, the point of Athens, Apollo killed Phrontis, the steersman of Menelaus' ship, with his painless arrows. No man knew better how to handle a vessel in rough weather, and he died right there with the helm in his hand. Menelaus, although eager to move on, had to wait to bury his comrade and give him proper funeral rites. Afterward, when he could sail again and had gone as far as the Malean headlands, Jove brought more trouble upon him and caused a strong wind to blow, creating high waves.

"Here he divided his fleet and took half of them toward Crete, where the Cydonians live by the waters of the river Iardanus. There is a high headland that juts out into the sea from a place called Gortyn, and along this coast, the sea runs high with a south wind. After Phaestus, however, the coast is more sheltered, as a small headland can provide great protection. This part of the fleet was driven onto the rocks and wrecked; the crews barely managed to save themselves. As for the other five ships, they were blown by winds and waves to Egypt, where Menelaus gathered much gold among the people who spoke a different language. Meanwhile, Aegisthus was plotting his evil deed back home. For seven years after he killed Agamemnon, he ruled in Mycene, and the people obeyed him. But in the eighth year, Orestes returned from Athens to take his revenge and killed Aegisthus, the murderer of his father. Then he held a banquet to honor the people of Argos for the funeral rites of his mother and false Aegisthus, and on that very day, Menelaus came home with as much treasure as his ships could carry.

"So take my advice: do not wander far from home, nor leave

your property in the hands of such dangerous people; they will consume everything you have, and you will have gone on a fruitless errand. Still, I encourage you to visit Menelaus, who has just returned from a journey among distant peoples, a journey so treacherous that no man could hope to return once the winds had carried him so far from home; even birds cannot fly that far in a year. Go to him by sea, and take your own men with you. Or, if you prefer to travel by land, I can provide you with a chariot and horses, and my sons will escort you to Lacedaemon where Menelaus lives. Ask him to tell you the truth, and he will do so, for he is a good man."

As he spoke, the sun set, and darkness fell. Minerva said, "Sir, all you have said is wise; now, order the tongues of the victims to be cut, and mix wine for drink-offerings to Neptune and the other immortals. Then, let us go to bed, for it is bedtime. People should leave early and not keep late hours during a religious festival."

Thus spoke the daughter of Jove, and they obeyed her. The servants poured water over the hands of the guests, while pages filled the mixing bowls with wine and water, handing it out after each man made his drink offering. They threw the tongues of the victims into the fire and stood up to make their offerings. After they made their offerings and drank as much as they wished, Minerva and Telemachus prepared to return to their ship, but Nestor stopped them.

"Heaven and the immortal gods," he exclaimed, "forbid that you leave my house to go back to your ship. Do you think I am so poor that I have too few cloaks or beds for my guests? Let me assure you I have plenty of rugs and cloaks, and I will not allow the son of my old friend Ulysses to sleep on the deck of a ship—not while I live, nor will my sons after me; they will keep an open house as I have done."

Then Minerva replied, "Sir, you have spoken well, and it would be better for Telemachus to follow your advice. He shall return with you and sleep at your house, but I must go back to give orders to my crew and keep them encouraged. I am the only older person among them; the rest are young men, Telemachus' own age, who took this voyage out of friendship, so I must return to the ship and sleep there. Tomorrow, I have to go to the Cauconians where I have a large sum of money long owed to me. As for Telemachus, now that he is your guest, send him to Lacedaemon in a chariot, and let one of your sons go with him. Please provide him with your best and fastest horses."

When she finished speaking, she flew away in the form of an eagle, and everyone marveled at what they saw. Nestor was astonished and took Telemachus by the hand. "My friend," he said, "I can see you are destined to be a great hero one day, since the gods attend to you in this way while you are still so young. This must be one of those who dwell in heaven, the formidable daughter of Jove, who showed such favor to your brave father among the Argives. Holy queen," he continued, "please send your grace upon me, my good wife, and my children. In return, I will sacrifice a yearling heifer, unbroken and never yoked by man. I will gild her horns and offer her up in sacrifice to you."

Thus he prayed, and Minerva heard him. He then led the way to his own house, followed by his sons and sons-in-law. When they arrived and took their seats on the benches, he mixed them a bowl of sweet wine that had been aging for eleven years when the housekeeper opened the jar. As he mixed the wine, he prayed and made drink offerings to Minerva, daughter of Aegis-bearing Jove. Then, when they had made their drink offerings and drunk as much as they wished, the others went home to sleep in their own houses, but Nestor put Telemachus to sleep in the room over the gateway along with Pisistratus, his only unmarried son. Nestor himself slept in an inner room of the house, with his wife, the queen, by his side.

When rosy-fingered Dawn appeared, Nestor left his bed and took his seat on the white polished marble benches in front of his house. Here sat Neleus, peer of gods in counsel, but he was now dead, gone to the house of Hades; so Nestor sat in his seat, scepter in hand, as guardian of the public good. His sons gathered around him as they left their rooms—Echephron, Stratius, Perseus, Aretus, and Thrasymedes; the sixth son was Pisistratus, and when Telemachus joined them, they made him sit with them. Nestor then addressed them.

"My sons," he said, "hurry to do what I ask. I wish first to honor the great goddess Minerva, who showed herself to me during yesterday's festivities. Go, one of you, to the plain and tell the stockman to find me a heifer, and come back here with it at once. Another must go to Telemachus' ship and invite the crew, leaving only two men in charge of the vessel. Someone else should fetch Laerceus the goldsmith to gild the heifer's horns. The rest of you stay here; tell the maids in the house to prepare a fine dinner and gather seats and logs of wood for a burnt offering. Tell them also to bring me some fresh spring water."

At this, they hurried off to carry out their tasks. The heifer was brought in from the plain, and Telemachus' crew arrived from the ship. The goldsmith brought his anvil, hammer, and tongs to work the gold, and Minerva herself came to accept the sacrifice. Nestor provided the gold, and the smith gilded the heifer's horns for the goddess to enjoy their beauty. Stratius and Echephron brought her in by the horns; Aretus fetched water from the house in a decorated ewer, holding a basket of barley meal in his other hand. Strong Thrasymedes stood by with a sharp axe, ready to strike the heifer, while Perseus held a bucket. Nestor began by washing his hands and sprinkling the barley meal, offering many prayers to Minerva as he threw a lock of the heifer's hair onto the fire.

When they finished praying and sprinkling the barley meal, Thrasymedes struck the heifer down with a blow that severed the tendons at the base of her neck, and the daughters and daughters-in-law of Nestor, along with his venerable wife Eurydice, screamed with delight. They lifted the heifer's head from the ground, and Pisistratus cut her throat. After she bled and was dead, they butchered her. They removed the thigh bones, wrapped them in two layers of fat, and set pieces of raw meat on top of them. Then Nestor laid them on the wood fire and poured wine over them while the young men stood near him with five-pronged spits. Once the thighs were burned and they had tasted the inner parts, they cut the rest of the meat into small pieces, put them on the spits, and roasted them over the fire.

Meanwhile, lovely Polycaste, Nestor's youngest daughter, washed Telemachus. After she washed him and anointed him with oil, she brought him a fine mantle and shirt, making him look like a god as he came from the bath and took his seat beside Nestor. When the outer meats were finished, they took them off the spits and sat down to dinner, waited on by worthy servants who poured wine into gold cups. Once they had eaten and drunk enough, Nestor said, "Sons, harness Telemachus's horses to the chariot so he can leave at once."

Thus he spoke, and they did as he said, yoking the swift horses to the chariot. The housekeeper packed them provisions of bread, wine, and sweet meats fit for the sons of princes. Then Telemachus climbed into the chariot, while Pisistratus gathered the reins and took his seat beside him. He urged the horses on, and they flew eagerly into the open country, leaving the high citadel of Pylos behind them. They traveled all day, swaying the yoke upon their necks until the sun set and darkness fell. Then they reached Pherae, where Diocles lived, who was the son of Ortilochus and grandson of Alpheus. Here they spent the night, and Diocles entertained them well. When rosy-fingered Dawn appeared again, they yoked their horses and drove out through the echoing gatehouse. Pisistratus urged the horses on, and they sped forward eagerly; soon they reached the open fields, and in due time completed their journey, so well did their steeds carry them.

BOOK 4:

When the sun set and darkness covered the land, Telemachus and Pisistratus reached the low-lying city of Lacedaemon. They drove straight to Menelaus' home and found him hosting a feast with many clansmen in honor of his son's wedding and his daughter's marriage to the son of the brave warrior Achilles. He had promised her to him while he was still at Troy, and now the gods were bringing the marriage about. Menelaus was sending her with chariots and horses to the city of the Myrmidons, where Achilles' son reigned. For his only son, he had found a bride from Sparta, the daughter of Alector. This son, Megapenthes, was born to him of a bondwoman, as heaven allowed Helen no more children after she bore Hermione, who was as beautiful as golden Venus herself.

Menelaus' neighbors and relatives were feasting and enjoying themselves. There was also a bard singing to them and playing his lyre, while two tumblers entertained them as the music played.

Telemachus and the son of Nestor stopped their horses at the gate. Eteoneus, a servant of Menelaus, came out, and upon seeing them, hurried back inside to inform his master. He approached Menelaus and said, "Menelaus, some strangers have come, two men who look like sons of Jove. What should we do? Shall we take their horses out, or tell them to find friends elsewhere?"

Menelaus was quite angry and said, "Eteoneus, son of Boethous, you never used to be foolish, but now you speak like one. Of course, take their horses out and show the strangers in so they may have supper. You and I have often stayed at others' houses before we returned here, where I hope we can rest in peace from now on."

So Eteoneus rushed back and called the other servants to join him. They took the sweating horses from under the yoke, secured them in the stables, and fed them a mix of oats and barley. Then they leaned the chariot against the wall of the courtyard and led the way into the house. Telemachus and Pisistratus were amazed by the house's splendor, which shone like the sun and moon. After admiring everything, they went into the bath and washed themselves.

Once the servants had washed them and anointed them with oil, they brought woolen cloaks and shirts, and the two took their seats beside Menelaus. A maid brought them water in a beautiful golden ewer, pouring it into a silver basin for them to wash their hands, and she set a clean table beside them. An upper servant brought them bread and offered many delicious things from the house, while the carver served plates of various meats and set golden cups by their side.

Menelaus then greeted them, saying, "Dig in, and welcome. After you finish supper, I will ask who you are, for the lineage of men like you cannot be unknown. You must be descended from a line of kings, for common people do not have sons like you."

He handed them a piece of fat roast loin, which had been set near him as a prime part, and they eagerly reached for the good things before them. Once they had eaten and drunk enough, Telemachus leaned close to Pisistratus and whispered, "Look, Pisistratus, my dear friend, see the gleam of bronze and gold—of amber, ivory, and silver. Everything is so splendid that it's like seeing the palace of Olympian Jove. I am completely awestruck."

Menelaus overheard him and said, "No one, my sons, can compare to Jove, for his house and everything around him is immortal; but among mortal men, there may be another who has as much wealth as I do, or there may not. However, I have traveled much and endured many hardships. It took me nearly eight years to return home with my fleet. I journeyed to Cyprus, Phoenicia, and Egypt; I also visited the Ethiopians, Sidonians, Erembians, and Libya, where lambs have horns as soon as they are born, and sheep give birth three times a year. Everyone there, whether master or servant, enjoys plenty of cheese, meat, and good milk, for the ewes produce year-round. Yet while I was traveling and accumulating riches among these peoples, my brother was secretly and horrifically murdered through the treachery of his wicked wife, so I find no joy in being lord of all this wealth. Whoever your parents are, they must have told you about my heavy loss in the ruin of a grand and magnificently furnished home. I wish I had only a third of what I now possess so I could have stayed at home, and all those who perished on the plain of Troy, far from Argos, were still alive. I often grieve as I sit here in my house for them all. Sometimes I cry out in sorrow, but then I stop, for crying brings little comfort, and one soon tires of it. Yet I mourn for one man more than for all the others. Just thinking of him makes me lose my appetite for food and sleep, so miserable does he make me, for no one of all the Achaeans worked so hard or risked so much as he did. He received nothing in return and has left me a legacy of sorrow. He has been gone for a long time, and we do not know if he is alive or dead. His old father, his long-suffering wife Penelope, and his son Telemachus, whom he left behind as an infant, are plunged in grief because of him."

As Menelaus spoke, Telemachus felt a deep yearning for his father. Tears fell from his eyes as he listened, so he held his cloak in front of his face with both hands. When Menelaus noticed this, he was unsure whether to let Telemachus choose his own moment to speak or to ask him directly about it.

While he hesitated, Helen came down from her high vaulted and perfumed room, looking as lovely as Diana herself. Adraste brought her a seat, Alcippe brought a soft wool rug, while Phylo fetched her the silver workbox that Alcandra, wife of Polybus, had given her. Polybus lived in Egyptian Thebes, the richest city in the world. He gifted Menelaus two silver baths, two tripods, and ten talents of gold; in addition, his wife gave Helen beautiful gifts, including a golden distaff and a silver workbox that ran on wheels, with a gold band around the top. Phylo now placed this by her side, full of finely spun yarn, and a distaff charged with violet-colored wool was laid upon it. Helen took her seat, rested her feet on a footstool, and began to question her husband.

"Do we know, Menelaus," she asked, "the names of these strangers who have come to visit us? Should I guess right or wrong?—but I cannot help saying what I think. I have never seen anyone, man or woman, who resembles someone else as closely as this young man resembles Telemachus, whom Ulysses left as a baby when you Achaeans went to Troy because of my shameless self."

"My dear wife," Menelaus replied, "I see the likeness just as you do. His hands and feet are like Ulysses', as is his hair, the shape of his head, and the expression in his eyes. Moreover, when I was speaking about Ulysses and recounting his hardships on my account, tears fell from his eyes, and he hid his face in his cloak."

Then Pisistratus said, "Menelaus, son of Atreus, you are correct in believing this young man is Telemachus, but he is very modest and ashamed to speak to someone with such an interesting conversation as yours. My father, Nestor, sent me to escort him here because he wanted to know if you could offer him any counsel or advice. A son always struggles at home when his father is away and has left him without support; this is the situation Telemachus finds himself in now, for his father is absent, and there is no one among his own people to support him."

"Bless my heart," Menelaus said. "So, I'm getting a visit from the son of a very dear friend who went through a lot for me. I always wanted to treat him with great honor when we returned safely from our travels. I should have built him a city in Argos and made him a house. I should have helped him leave Ithaca with all his belongings, his son, and his people. I could have taken some nearby cities for him. Then we could see each other all the time, and only death could keep us apart. But I guess the gods didn't want us to have that happiness, because they stopped him from ever getting home."

As he spoke, everyone began to cry. Helen cried, Telemachus cried, and Menelaus cried too. Pisistratus also couldn't help but tear up when he thought about his brother Antilochus, who was killed. He then said to Menelaus,

"Sir, my father Nestor always told me how wise you are. So, if you can, please do what I ask. I don't like crying while I'm trying to eat. In the morning, I'll cry for those who are gone. That's all we can do for them—shave our heads and wipe our tears. I had a brother who died at Troy; he was a good man, and you must have known him—his name was Antilochus. I never saw him myself, but they say he was very fast and brave in battle."

"You're wise for your age," Menelaus replied. "It's clear you take after your father. It shows when a man is the son of someone the gods have blessed, like Nestor, who has had a good life and a happy family. Let's stop this crying and get back to our meal. Let's wash our hands and eat. Telemachus and I can talk in the morning."

Then Asphalion, one of the servants, poured water over their hands, and they started to eat the delicious food before them.

Next, Helen thought of something else. She added a special herb to the wine that made all sadness go away. Whoever drinks this wine can't shed a tear for the whole day, even if their parents die or they see a brother or son get hurt. This powerful herb was given to Helen by Polydamna, the wife of Thon, from Egypt, where many herbs grow—some good and some poisonous. Everyone there is also a great doctor because they are descended from Paeeon. After Helen added the herb to the wine and told the servants to serve it, she said:

"Menelaus, son of Atreus, and you, my good friends, sons of honorable men (as the gods want), enjoy your feast and listen to a story. I can't remember every single thing Ulysses did, but I can tell you about what he did during the troubles at Troy. He covered himself in wounds and rags and snuck into the enemy's city, looking like a beggar. No one recognized him except for me, but he was too clever for me. After I cleaned him up, gave him clothes, and promised not to tell the Trojans until he got back to his camp, he shared everything the Achaeans planned. He defeated many Trojans and learned a lot before he returned to the Argive camp. The Trojan women mourned, but I was glad because I was starting to miss home, and I felt unhappy that Venus took me away from my country, my girl, and my husband, who is not lacking in either looks or smarts."

Menelaus replied, "What you said is true, my dear wife. I've traveled a lot and met many heroes, but I've never seen anyone like Ulysses. His bravery and strength were remarkable, especially when he was hiding in the wooden horse with the bravest Achaeans waiting to strike the Trojans. You came to us then, and a god must have urged you to do so, with Deiphobus by your side. You circled our hiding place three times, calling each of our names and imitating our wives. Diomed, Ulysses, and I listened inside, debating whether to jump out or answer you, but Ulysses stopped us. Anticlus almost replied, but Ulysses covered his mouth to keep him quiet. This is what saved us because Minerva took you away."

"How sad," Telemachus said, "that none of this was enough to save him, nor his bravery. But now, sir, please send us to bed so we can enjoy the gift of sleep."

Helen then told the maidservants to make beds in the room by the gate, using nice red rugs and covering them with warm cloaks for the guests. The maids went out with a torch and prepared the beds, which a servant led the guests to. So, Telemachus and Pisistratus slept in the forecourt, while Menelaus rested in an inner room with lovely Helen by his side.

When the rosy-fingered Dawn appeared, Menelaus got up and dressed. He put on his sandals, fastened his sword, and came out looking like a god. He sat near Telemachus and asked,

"What brings you to Lacedaemon, Telemachus? Are you here on business? Tell me everything."

"I've come, sir," Telemachus answered, "to see if you know anything about my father. My home is being ruined, my estate is wasted, and my house is full of suitors who keep killing my sheep and oxen to win my mother. I'm here asking for your help, hoping you can tell me how my father met his end, whether you saw it or heard it from someone else. He was a man who faced many troubles. Please tell me plainly, without pity for me, what you know. If my brave father Ulysses ever helped you when the Achaeans were struggling against the Trojans, please remember that now and be honest with me."

Menelaus was shocked to hear this. "So," he said, "these cowards want to take a brave man's place? A doe might as well leave her newborn in a lion's den and wander off; when the lion comes back, he'll take care of both of them—and so will Ulysses with these suitors. By father Jove, Minerva, and Apollo, if Ulysses is still the man he was when he wrestled Philomeleides in Lesbos, they would be in big trouble if he were to show up now. As for your questions, I won't hide the truth from you. I'll tell you exactly what the old man of the sea told me.

"I was trying to get here, but the gods kept me in Egypt because they weren't satisfied with my sacrifices, and the gods are very particular about that. Off Egypt, there's an island called Pharos—it has a great harbor where ships can get water before going out to sea. The gods kept me there for twenty days without a single breath of wind to help me move. We would have run out of food, and my men would have starved if a goddess hadn't taken pity on me—Idothea, daughter of Proteus, the old man of the sea, liked me a lot.

"One day, when I was alone, she came to me, for my men were fishing all over the island to find something to eat. 'Stranger,' she said, 'it seems you don't mind starving, as you stay here day after day without trying to leave, while your men are dying.'

"'Let me tell you,' I replied, 'whoever you are, I'm not here by choice but must have angered the gods. Tell me who is stopping me and how I can sail home.'

"'I'll explain everything,' she said. 'There's an old immortal under the sea named Proteus. He's Egyptian, and they say he's my father. He's Neptune's right-hand man and knows everything about the sea. If you can catch him and hold on tight, he will tell you about your journey, what path to take, and how to sail home. He will also share everything that has happened at your house while you've been away.'

"'Can you help me catch this old god without him noticing?' I asked. 'Gods are not easily caught by mortals.'

"'I'll make it clear,' she said. 'When the sun is high, the old man comes up from the waves, announced by the West wind. He'll lie down and fall asleep in a sea cave, surrounded by seals. Tomorrow morning, I'll take you there and hide you. Choose your three best men to join you, and I'll show you the tricks the old man will play.

"He will count his seals and then go to sleep among them, like a shepherd with his sheep. When he's asleep, grab him and hold on tightly, because he will try to escape. He will change into many creatures, and even become fire or water, but you must hold him tight until he speaks to you and returns to his true form. Then you can let him go and ask which god is angry with you and how to get home.

"After saying this, she dove back into the sea, and I returned to my ships. My heart was heavy with worry as I walked. When I reached my ship, we prepared supper since night was falling, and we camped on the beach."

When the rosy-fingered Dawn appeared, I took three men I could really trust and went down to the seaside, praying earnestly to the gods. Meanwhile, the goddess brought me four seal skins from the ocean, all freshly skinned, because she wanted to trick her father. She dug four pits for us to lie in and sat down to wait for us to arrive. When we got close, she made us lie down in the pits one by one and covered us with seal skins. The smell was terrible, like fishy seals, and nobody wants to sleep next to a sea monster! But the goddess helped us by putting ambrosia under our noses, which smelled so nice that it covered up the awful seal smell.

We waited all morning, doing our best to make the time pass, watching hundreds of seals come up to bask in the sun until noon, when the old man of the sea finally appeared. After counting his fat seals, he lay down to sleep without suspecting a thing. That's when we jumped on him with a shout and grabbed him. He immediately started using his tricks, changing into a lion with a huge mane, then a dragon, a leopard, a wild boar, then running water, and finally a tree. But we held on tight and never let go until he was finally worn out and asked, "Which god helped you catch me? What do you want?"

"You already know, old man," I replied. "Don't think you can get away from me. I've been stuck on this island for so long, and I'm losing hope. Tell me which god is stopping me from leaving and how I can sail home."

Then he said, "If you want to get home quickly, you must offer sacrifices to Jove and the other gods before you set sail. It's been decided that you won't return to your friends or home until you go back to Egypt and make offerings to the immortal gods there.

Once you do that, they will let you finish your journey."

I was heartbroken when I heard I had to go all the way back to Egypt, but I replied, "I will do everything you've told me. But please tell me if all the Achaeans Nestor and I left behind in Troy made it home safely or if any of them had a bad end during their journey."

"Son of Atreus," he answered, "why ask me? You might not want to know what I have to tell you because it will make you cry. Many of those you're asking about are dead, but some are still alive, and only two of the main Achaeans died on their way home. As for the battles, you were there yourself. One Achaean leader is still out at sea, but he can't return. Ajax was shipwrecked because Neptune smashed him against the rocks of Gyrae; however, he got out of the water safely. Despite Minerva's anger, he would have survived if he hadn't boasted that the gods couldn't drown him. When Neptune heard him bragging, he took his trident and split the rock of Gyrae in two. The part Ajax was sitting on fell into the sea, and he drowned.

"Your brother and his ships made it home because Juno protected him. But just as he was reaching the high land of Malea, a strong storm blew him back out to sea, sending him to the area where Thyestes used to live, and where Aegisthus was living then. However, it seemed like he would return home after all, because the gods changed the wind direction, and he finally reached his homeland. When Agamemnon stepped onto his native soil, he shed tears of joy to be back in his own country.

"Now, Aegisthus had a watchman he had promised two talents of gold to. This man had been keeping watch for a whole year to make sure Agamemnon didn't sneak away to start a war. When he saw Agamemnon pass by, he hurried to tell Aegisthus, who then began to plot against him. He gathered twenty of his best warriors and hid them on one side of the cloister, while on the other side, he prepared a feast. He sent his chariots and horsemen to invite Agamemnon to the banquet, but he intended to trick him. Agamemnon arrived unsuspecting of the danger, and Aegisthus killed him after the feast, just like butchering an ox. None of Agamemnon's followers survived, nor did any of Aegisthus's men; they were all killed there in the cloister."

As Proteus spoke, my heart sank. I sat down on the sand and cried, feeling like I couldn't bear to live or see the sunlight again. After a while, when I had cried enough, the old man of the sea said, "Son of Atreus, stop wasting time crying. It won't help you. Get home as fast as you can, because Aegisthus may still be alive, and even if Orestes has already killed him, you might still attend his funeral."

Despite my sorrow, I found some comfort and said, "Now I know about these two; please tell me about the third man you mentioned. Is he still alive and stuck at sea, or is he dead? Tell me, no matter how much it may upset me."

"The third man," he answered, "is Ulysses, who lives in Ithaca. I can see him on an island, grieving in the house of the nymph Calypso, who is keeping him prisoner. He can't return home because he has no ships or sailors to help him. As for you, Menelaus, you won't die in Argos. The gods will take you to Elysium, which is at the end of the world. There, fair-haired Rhadamanthus rules, and life is easier than anywhere else. In Elysium, it doesn't rain, hail, or snow. Instead, the West wind from Oceanus sings softly from the sea, bringing fresh life to everyone. This will happen to you because you married Helen and are Jove's son-in-law."

After he spoke, he dived under the waves, and I returned to my ships with my companions, my heart heavy with worry. When we reached the ships, we prepared supper as night fell and camped on the beach. When rosy-fingered Dawn appeared again, we drew our ships into the water, set up our masts and sails, and boarded our ships, taking our places on the benches. I sailed my ships back to the Egypt's stream and offered plenty of hecatombs. After making peace with the gods, I raised a mound in memory of Agamemnon so that his name would be remembered forever, after which I had a quick journey home because the gods sent a fair wind.

"And now for you—stay here for ten or twelve more days, and I will send you on your way with a great gift: a chariot and three horses. I'll also give you a beautiful cup so that whenever you make a drink-offering to the gods, you can think of me."

"Son of Atreus," replied Telemachus, "please don't make me stay longer. I would love to remain with you for another twelve months because I enjoy your company so much, but my crew is waiting for me in Pylos, and you're keeping me from them. As for any gift you want to give me, I would prefer a piece of silverware. I don't want to take horses back to Ithaca; I'll leave them to beautify your stables, since you have plenty of flat land for them to roam in, with lots of lotus, meadow-sweet, wheat, barley, and oats. But in Ithaca, we have no open fields or racecourses; it's more suited for goats than horses, and I actually prefer it that way. None of our islands have much flat ground for horses, and Ithaca has the least."

Menelaus smiled and took Telemachus's hand. "What you say shows you come from a good family," he said. "I can and will make this exchange for you by giving you the finest and most precious piece of silverware in my house. It's a mixing bowl made by Vulcan himself, made of pure silver except for the gold inlay around the rim. Phaedimus, king of the Sidonians, gave it to me when I visited him on my way home. I will give it to you as a gift."

As they talked, guests kept arriving at the king's house, bringing sheep and wine, while their wives packed bread for them to take. They were busy preparing their dinners in the courtyard.

Meanwhile, the suitors were throwing discs and aiming with spears at a target in front of Ulysses' house, acting as arrogantly as ever. Antinous and Eurymachus, the leaders among them, were sitting together when Noemon, the son of Phronius, approached Antinous and said, "Do we know when Telemachus will return from Pylos? He took my ship, and I need it to go to Elis, where I have twelve brood mares with yearling mule foals. I want to bring one of them back to break."

The suitors were shocked to hear this because they thought Telemachus had stayed in the city and hadn't gone to see Neleus. They assumed he was just off on the farms with the sheep or swineherd. Antinous asked, "When did he leave? Who did he take with him? Were they free men or his own slaves? Did you lend him the ship willingly, or did he take it without your permission?"

"I lent him the ship," Noemon replied. "What could I do when someone like him said he needed help? I couldn't refuse. The young men who went with him are the best we have, and I saw Mentor go on board as captain—or maybe it was a god who looked just like him. I'm confused because I saw Mentor here just yesterday morning, and now he's off to Pylos."

Noemon then went back home, but Antinous and Eurymachus were very angry. They called the others to stop playing and come join them. When everyone gathered, Antinous spoke in a rage, his heart filled with anger. "This trip of Telemachus is serious. We thought it wouldn't happen, but he managed to get away with a good crew. He'll cause us trouble soon; may Jove take him before he grows up. Get me a ship with twenty men, and I'll wait for him in the straits between Ithaca and Samos. He'll regret setting out to find news of his father."

The others agreed with him, and they all went inside.

Not long after, Penelope learned what the suitors were plotting. A servant named Medon overheard their plans while he was outside the court and went to tell her. As he entered her room, Penelope asked, "Medon, why have the suitors sent you here? Are you here to tell the maids to leave my son's matters and prepare dinner for you? I wish they would stop wooing and dining here altogether, for they waste my son's estate. Didn't your fathers tell you when you were children how good Ulysses was? He never acted unjustly or spoke harshly to anyone. Kings may favor one person over another, but Ulysses never did wrong to anyone. You show bad hearts and a lack of gratitude."

Then Medon replied, "I wish it were just that, Madam, but they are planning something much worse—may heaven stop their plot. They plan to murder Telemachus when he returns from Pylos and Lacedaemon, where he went to learn about his father."

Hearing this made Penelope's heart sink. She was speechless for a long time, her eyes filled with tears. Finally, she said, "Why did my son leave me? What business did he have to sail off in ships like sea-horses? Does he want to die without leaving anyone to keep his name alive?"

"I don't know," Medon answered. "Maybe a god urged him to go, or maybe he went on his own to find out if his father is dead or alive and coming home."

He then went downstairs, leaving Penelope in deep grief. There were plenty of seats in the house, but she couldn't sit anywhere. Instead, she threw herself on the floor of her room and cried, and all the maids, both young and old, gathered around her, crying too. In her sorrow, she exclaimed, "My dear friends, heaven has tested me with more suffering than any other woman my age and in my country. First, I lost my brave husband, who was the best of men and whose name was honored all over Hellas and middle Argos. Now my darling son is at the mercy of the winds and waves, and I haven't heard anything about him leaving home. None of you thought to wake me up, even though you all knew when he was leaving. If I had known he was taking this voyage, he would have had to give it up, no matter how determined he was, or I would have been left with his corpse. Now, go and call old Dolius, whom my father gave me when I married, and who is my gardener. Tell him to go and inform

Laertes. Maybe he can come up with a plan to get sympathy for us against those who want to destroy his family and Ulysses'."

Then the old nurse, Euryclea, said, "You may kill me, Madam, or let me stay in your house, but I will tell you the truth. I knew all about it and gave him what he needed in bread and wine. But he made me promise not to tell you anything for ten or twelve days, unless you asked or found out he had left, because he didn't want you to spoil your beauty with tears. Now, Madam, wash your face, change your dress, and go upstairs with your maids to pray to Minerva, daughter of Aegis-bearing Jove, for she can save him even if he is in danger. Don't worry about Laertes; he has enough trouble already. Besides, I can't believe the gods hate the family of the son of Arceisius so much. There will be a son left to inherit the house and fields around it."

With these words, she helped her mistress stop crying and dried her tears. Penelope washed her face, changed her dress, and went upstairs with her maids. She put some bruised barley into a basket and began praying to Minerva.

"Hear me," she cried, "Daughter of Aegis-bearing Jove, unweariable. If ever Ulysses burned the fat thigh bones of sheep or heifers for you, remember me now and save my darling son from the suitors' wickedness."

She cried out as she prayed, and the goddess heard her. Meanwhile, the suitors were making noise in the cloister, and one of them said, "The queen is preparing to marry one of us. She doesn't know that her son is doomed to die."

They said this, not knowing what was about to happen. Then Antinous said, "Comrades, let's keep our voices down so no one hears us inside. Let's quietly do what we all agreed on."

He chose twenty men, and they went down to their ship at the seaside. They pulled the vessel into the water and put the mast and sails inside. They secured the oars to the thole-pins with leather thongs, spread the white sails, and gathered their armor.

Then they anchored the ship a short distance out, came ashore to eat supper, and waited for night to fall.

But Penelope lay in her room upstairs, unable to eat or drink, worried about whether her brave son would escape or be overpowered by the wicked suitors. Like a lioness caught in a trap with hunters closing in, she thought and thought until she fell asleep, lying on her bed without thought or motion.

Then Minerva thought of something else and created a vision that looked like Penelope's sister Iphthime, daughter of Icarius, who had married Eumelus and lived in Pherae. The vision was sent to Ulysses' house to comfort Penelope and make her stop crying. It entered her room through the door and hovered over her, saying, "You are asleep, Penelope. The gods will not let you weep and be so sad. Your son has done them no wrong, so he will come back to you."

Penelope, dreaming sweetly, answered, "Sister, why have you come here? You don't visit often, but I guess that's because you live so far away. Am I to stop crying and put aside all the sadness that tortures me? I, who have lost my brave husband, who had every good quality, and whose name was great all over Hellas and middle Argos? Now my darling son is gone off on a ship—he's foolish, and not used to hardship, nor to mingling with men. I worry about him even more than I did about my husband. I tremble when I think of him, worried that something might happen to him from the people he's with or on the sea, as he has many enemies plotting against him, determined to kill him before he can return home."

The vision replied, "Take heart and don't be so afraid. There is one with him whom many would be glad to have at their side—Minerva; she is the one who has compassion for you and sent me with this message."

"Then," said Penelope, "if you are a goddess or have been sent by one, tell me about the other unhappy one—is he alive or already dead and in the house of Hades?"

The vision replied, "I can't say for certain whether he is alive or dead, and there's no use in idle talk."

Then it vanished through the door, and Penelope woke up refreshed and comforted, for her dream had been so vivid.

Meanwhile, the suitors went on board and sailed over the sea, intent on murdering Telemachus. There is a rocky islet called Asteris, not very large, in the channel between Ithaca and Samos, with a harbor on either side for a ship to rest. There, the Achaeans set their ambush.

BOOK 5:

As Dawn rose from her bed beside Tithonus, bringing light to both mortals and immortals, the gods gathered for a meeting. Among them was Jove, the king of the gods. Minerva began to speak about the many sufferings of Ulysses, feeling sorry for him stuck in the house of the nymph Calypso.

"Father Jove," she said, "and all you other gods who live in happiness, I hope there will never be a kind and fair ruler again. From now on, I hope they are all cruel and unjust because none of the people left care about Ulysses, who ruled them like a father. He lies in pain on an island with Calypso, who won't let him leave. He can't get home because he has no ships or sailors to take him. To make things worse, wicked people are trying to kill his only son, Telemachus, who is returning from Pylos and Lacedaemon, where he went to find news of his father."

"What are you talking about?" Jove replied. "Didn't you send him there yourself to help Ulysses get home and to punish the suitors? Besides, you can protect Telemachus and see him safely home while the suitors hurry back without having killed him."

After Jove spoke, he turned to his son Mercury, saying, "Mercury, you are our messenger. Go tell Calypso that we have decided Ulysses can return home. He will travel alone, without gods or men, and after a dangerous twenty-day journey on a raft, he will reach fertile Scheria, the land of the Phaeacians, who are close to the gods and will treat him like one of us. They will send him home with more bronze, gold, and clothes than he would have brought back from Troy, even if he had made it back safely with all his prize money. This is how we have decided he shall return to his country and friends."

Mercury, the guide and protector, did as he was told. He put on his shiny golden sandals, which allowed him to fly like the wind over land and sea. He took the wand that could put people to sleep or wake them and flew over Pieria, descending through the sky until he reached the sea, skimming over the waves like a cormorant fishing. He flew over many waves, and when he finally reached the island, he left the sea and walked on land until he arrived at the cave where the nymph Calypso lived.

Calypso was at home. A large fire burned on the hearth, and the pleasant scent of burning cedar and sandalwood filled the air. She was busy at her loom, weaving and singing beautifully. Around her cave grew a thick forest of alder, poplar, and fragrant cypress trees, where many birds had made their nests—owls, hawks, and chattering sea-crows. A vine heavy with grapes grew at the entrance of the cave, and there were four streams of water flowing close together, watering the beds of violets and lush grass. Even a god would be enchanted by such a beautiful place, so Mercury paused to admire it before going inside.

Calypso recognized him immediately because all the gods know each other, no matter how far apart they are. But Ulysses was not there; he was by the shore, gazing out at the empty ocean with tears in his eyes, grieving deeply. Calypso offered Mercury a seat and asked, "Why have you come to see me, Mercury? You are always welcome, but you don't visit often. Tell me what you want, and I will do it right away if I can. But come inside and let me prepare some food for you."

As she spoke, she set a table with ambrosia beside him and poured some red nectar. Mercury ate and drank until he was satisfied, then said:

"We are speaking as gods, and you ask why I'm here. I'll tell you the truth: Jove sent me; I didn't want to come all this way over the sea, where there are no cities or people to honor me with sacrifices. But I had to come because none of us gods can go against Jove's orders. He says you have the most unfortunate man who fought for nine years at King Priam's city and finally made it home in the tenth year after sacking it. On the way, he angered Minerva, who stirred up winds and waves against them, causing all his brave companions to perish, and he alone was brought here by the winds. Jove commands you to let this man go at once because it is decreed that he shall not die here, far from his people, but will return to his home and see his friends again."

Calypso was furious when she heard this. "You gods should be ashamed of yourselves," she exclaimed. "You're always jealous and hate seeing a goddess fall in love with a mortal and live with him. When rosy-fingered Dawn loved Orion, all of you were angry until Diana killed him. When Ceres fell in love with Iasion and gave herself to him in a plowed field, Jove found out and killed Iasion with thunderbolts. And now you're angry with me because I have a man here? I found him alone on a broken ship after Jove struck it with lightning and sank it, drowning all his crew while he washed up on my island. I grew fond of him and cared for him, hoping to make him immortal so he would never grow old. Still, I can't go against Jove, so if he insists, I will let him go; but I can't send him anywhere myself since I have no ships or crew. However, I can offer him advice to help him return home safely."

"Then send him away," said Mercury, "or Jove will be angry with you and punish you."

With that, he took his leave, and Calypso went to look for Ulysses, having heard Jove's message. She found him sitting on the beach, tears streaming down his face, overwhelmed with homesickness. He was tired of Calypso, and although he was forced to sleep with her in the cave at night, it was she who wanted it. During the day, he sat on the rocks by the shore, weeping and longing for home. Calypso approached him and said:

"My poor fellow, you will not stay here grieving any longer. I will send you away willingly. Go cut some wood and make a large raft with an upper deck to carry you safely over the sea. I will provide bread, wine, and water for you, so you won't starve. I will also give you clothes and send a fair wind to help you home, if the gods in heaven will allow it, as they know better than I."

Ulysses shuddered at her words. "Now, goddess," he replied, "there is something suspicious about this. You can't truly want to help me if you're asking me to put to sea on a raft. Even a well-built ship with a good wind couldn't survive such a long journey. I won't board a raft unless you promise me, with a solemn oath, that you mean no harm."

Calypso smiled and gently touched him. "You know much, but you are mistaken. Let heaven and earth be my witnesses, along with the waters of the river Styx—and this is the most solemn oath a blessed god can take—that I mean you no harm and am only advising you to do what I would do in your place. I am being straightforward; my heart is not made of iron, and I truly feel sorry for you."

After she spoke, she led the way, and Ulysses followed her into the cave, where he took the seat Mercury had just vacated. Calypso set out food and drink for him, while her maids brought ambrosia and nectar for herself, and they all enjoyed the meal together. When they were finished, Calypso said:

"Ulysses, noble son of Laertes, so you wish to go home immediately? Good luck to you, but if you only knew how much suffering awaits you before you reach your homeland, you would choose to stay with me and let me make you immortal, regardless of how much you long to see your wife. I flatter myself that I am just as tall and beautiful as she is; after all, a mortal woman cannot compare to an immortal."

"Goddess," Ulysses replied, "please don't be angry with me. I know my wife Penelope is not as tall or beautiful as you. She is just a mortal woman, while you are immortal. Still, I want to go home and think of nothing else. If some god wrecks me at sea, I will endure it as best I can. I have already faced countless troubles both on land and sea, so I'll accept this as part of my journey."

As the sun set, darkness fell, and Ulysses and Calypso went to bed in the cave.

When morning came, Ulysses put on his shirt and cloak, while the goddess wore a light, graceful dress, adorned with a golden girdle and a veil. She began to think about how to help Ulysses on his journey. She gave him a large bronze axe that fit his hands perfectly; it was sharp on both sides and had a sturdy olive-wood handle. Calypso also provided him with a sharp adze and led him to the far end of the island where the biggest trees grew—alder, poplar, and pine that reached high into the sky. These trees were dry and seasoned, perfect for making a raft.

After showing him the best trees, Calypso left him to cut them down. Ulysses quickly finished, chopping down twenty trees in total. He shaped the wood neatly, making it suitable for building. Meanwhile, Calypso returned with some augers, and he used them to bore holes and fit the timbers together with bolts and rivets. He built the raft as wide as a skilled shipbuilder would make the beam of a large vessel, added a deck on top, and constructed a gunwale all around it. He also made a mast with a yardarm and a rudder for steering. To protect the raft from the waves, he fenced it in with wicker hurdles and loaded it with extra wood. Later, Calypso brought him some linen to make sails, which he crafted expertly, securing them with ropes. Finally, with the help of levers, he lowered the raft into the water.

In four days, Ulysses completed all the work, and on the fifth day, after washing him and giving him clean clothes, Calypso sent him away. She provided him with a goat skin full of wine, a larger one filled with water, and a wallet of provisions. She also created a warm, favorable wind for him. Ulysses spread his sail and skillfully steered the raft with the rudder. He kept his eyes fixed on the Pleiades, the late-setting Bootes, and the Bear —also known as the Wain, which revolves and never dips into the ocean—remembering Calypso's advice to keep it to his left. He sailed for seven days and ten nights, and on the eighteenth day, he finally saw the faint outlines of the mountains on the Phaeacian coast rising like a shield on the horizon.

But King Neptune, returning from the Ethiopians, spotted Ulysses from the Solymi mountains. Seeing him sailing across the sea made Neptune furious. He shook his head and muttered, "The gods have changed their minds about Ulysses while I was away in Ethiopia, and now he's close to the Phaeacians, where it's decided he will escape his troubles. Yet, he will face many hardships before it's all over."

With that, Neptune gathered his clouds, took his trident, stirred the sea, and summoned the winds, plunging earth, sea, and sky into darkness. Winds from the East, South, North, and West struck him all at once, raising a terrible storm that made Ulysses' heart sink. "Oh no," he thought in despair, "what will become of me? Calypso warned me I would face troubles at sea before returning home, and now it's all coming true. The sky is dark with Jove's clouds, and the winds are churning the sea into chaos. I'm sure to perish. Blessed were the Danaans who died before Troy fighting for the sons of Atreus. I wish I had been killed when the Trojans pressed me around Achilles' dead body. At least then I would have had a proper burial and my name would be honored among the Achaeans. Now, it seems I will meet a pitiful end."

As he lamented, a huge wave crashed over him with such force that it knocked him off the raft and into the water. He lost hold of the helm, and the hurricane was so strong that it broke the mast halfway up, sending the sail and yard into the sea. Ulysses was submerged for a long time, struggling to surface due to the heavy clothes Calypso had given him. But he finally broke the surface, spitting out the salty water streaming down his face. Despite his troubles, he did not lose sight of the raft. He swam as fast as he could toward it, grasped it, and climbed back aboard, desperate to avoid drowning. The sea tossed the raft around as autumn winds whirl thistledown along the road, as if the South, North, East, and West winds were all playing with it.

In his plight, Ino, daughter of Cadmus, also known as Leucothea, saw him. She had once been a mortal but was now a marine goddess. Seeing Ulysses in such distress, she felt compassion for him. Rising like a sea-gull from the waves, she took her place on the raft.

"My poor man," she said, "why is Neptune so angry with you? He is giving you a lot of trouble, but he will not kill you. You seem wise; listen to me: strip off your clothes, leave your raft to be driven by the wind, and swim to the Phaeacian coast where better luck awaits you. Here, take my veil and tie it around your chest. It is enchanted, and as long as you wear it, you will come to no harm. When you reach land, take it off and throw it back into the sea as far as you can, then go on your way." With that, she removed her veil and handed it to him before diving back into the deep waters.

Ulysses was unsure of what to do. "Oh no," he thought in despair, "this might be a trap by the gods, tempting me to my doom by advising me to leave my raft. I won't do it just yet; the land she spoke of seems far away still. I will stick with the raft as long as it holds together, but if it breaks apart, then I will swim for it. That seems like the best choice."

Just then, a massive wave crashed down on him, smashing the raft into pieces like dry chaff tossed by the wind. Ulysses managed to grab hold of a plank and ride it like a horse. He removed the clothes Calypso had given him, secured Ino's veil around his arms, and plunged into the sea, intending to swim ashore. Neptune watched him and shook his head, muttering, "Now swim as best you can until you reach people of good fortune. I doubt you'll say I've let you off too easily." With that, he drove his horses to Aegae, where his palace is.

Meanwhile, Minerva decided to help Ulysses by calming all the winds except one, making them lie still. She stirred up a strong north wind that would lay the waters until Ulysses reached the Phaeacian land and safety.

Ulysses drifted for two nights and two days, battling a heavy swell and staring death in the face. But on the third day, the wind died down, and there was a dead calm without even a whisper of air. As he rose with the swell, he eagerly looked ahead and saw land close by. Just like children rejoice when their father begins to recover from a long illness, so was Ulysses filled with gratitude upon seeing land and trees. He swam with all his strength, eager to set foot on dry ground. However, as he approached, he heard the thunder of surf crashing against the rocks. The waves pounded them with a loud roar, and everything was covered in spray; there were no harbors or shelter, only cliffs, low-lying rocks, and mountain peaks.

Ulysses' heart began to sink as he said to himself, "Oh no, Jove has allowed me to see land after swimming so far, but I can't find a place to land. The coast is rocky and rough; the smooth rocks rise sharply from the sea, with deep water close beneath them, making it impossible to climb out. I'm afraid a huge wave will sweep me away and smash me against the rocks, giving me a painful landing. If I swim further to look for a beach or harbor, a storm might carry me back out to sea against my will, or some great monster from the deep might attack me, for Amphitrite breeds many such creatures, and I know Neptune is angry with me."

As he was caught in this dilemma, a wave struck him with such force that it threw him against the rocks, nearly smashing him to pieces. If Minerva hadn't shown him what to do, he would have been lost. He grabbed hold of the rock with both hands, groaning in pain until the wave receded. However, it soon returned, pulling him back into the sea, tearing his hands just like the suckers of a polypus tear away when someone pulls it from its bed, bringing the stones up with it. The rocks scraped his strong hands, and the wave pulled him deep underwater.

Poor Ulysses would have surely perished despite his fate if Minerva hadn't helped him keep his wits about him. He swam out to sea again, beyond the reach of the surf pounding the land, while still looking toward the shore for a haven or a beach to escape the waves. After some time, he found the mouth of a river. This seemed like the best option, as it had no rocks and offered shelter from the wind. Feeling a current, he prayed inwardly:

"Hear me, O King, whoever you may be, and save me from Neptune's anger, for I come to you humbly. Anyone who has lost their way can appeal to the gods, so in my distress, I come to your stream and cling to your knees. Have mercy on me, O king, for I declare myself your suppliant."

The river god calmed his waters and stilled the waves, making everything peaceful before Ulysses, guiding him safely to the river's mouth. At last, Ulysses' knees and hands gave out, for the sea had completely exhausted him. His body was swollen, and water poured from his mouth and nostrils, preventing him from breathing or speaking, and he lay fainting from sheer exhaustion. Eventually, when he caught his breath and regained his strength, he removed the scarf that Ino had given him and threw it back into the salty river, where Ino received it from the wave that carried it toward her. After that, he left the river and lay down among the rushes, kissing the rich earth.

"Oh no," he lamented to himself, "what will happen to me? If I stay here on the riverbank through the night, I'm so exhausted that the cold and damp may finish me off—especially with the sharp wind blowing from the river at dawn. If I climb the hillside, find shelter in the woods, and sleep in a thicket, I might escape the cold and get a good night's rest, but I could be attacked and eaten by a wild beast."

In the end, he decided it was best to head into the woods. He found one on high ground not far from the water, crept beneath two olive shoots that grew from a single root—one a wild sucker and the other a cultivated one. No wind, no matter how strong, could break through their cover, nor could the sun's rays or rain penetrate them. Ulysses settled beneath the trees and started to make a bed from the thick layer of dead leaves around him —more than enough to keep him warm even in the winter. He was relieved to find this, so he lay down and piled leaves around himself. Just as a person living alone in the country hides a brand in the ashes to save himself from having to light a fire, Ulysses covered himself with leaves, and Minerva sent sweet sleep upon his eyes, closing his eyelids and helping him forget his troubles.

BOOK 6:

Ulysses fell into a deep sleep, exhausted from his struggles, while Minerva went to the land of the Phaeacians. The Phaeacians once lived in the beautiful town of Hypereia, near the lawless Cyclopes. The Cyclopes were stronger and plundered them, so their king Nausithous moved them to Scheria, far from everyone else. He built walls around the city, constructed houses and temples, and divided the land among his people. However, Nausithous had passed away and now King Alcinous, who was wise and inspired by the gods, reigned. Minerva went to Alcinous' home to help Ulysses return.

She entered the beautifully decorated bedroom where Nausicaa, the lovely daughter of King Alcinous, was sleeping. Two maidservants, both very pretty, slept nearby on either side of the doorway, which was closed with finely made folding doors. Minerva took the form of Dymas's daughter, a close friend of Nausicaa, and approached the girl's bedside like a soft breeze. She hovered over Nausicaa's head and said:

"Nausicaa, what can your mother be thinking, allowing you to be so lazy? Your clothes are all in disarray, and you're about to be married! You should not only look good yourself but also have nice clothes for your attendants. This is how to earn a good reputation and make your parents proud. Let's make tomorrow a washing day, starting at dawn. I will come help you so you can get everything ready quickly, since all the best young men among your people are courting you. You won't be a maid much longer. Ask your father to have a wagon and mules ready for us at daybreak to carry the rugs, robes, and girdles. Riding will be much nicer for you than walking, especially since the washing basins are a ways from town."

After delivering her message, Minerva returned to Olympus, the eternal home of the gods. Olympus is a place where no rough winds blow, and rain or snow never falls; it remains in everlasting sunshine and peace, where the blessed gods shine forever. This is where the goddess went after advising Nausicaa.

Morning soon came and woke Nausicaa, who began to ponder her dream. She went to find her parents and tell them all about it. She found her mother by the fireside, spinning purple yarn with her maids around her. She caught her father just as he was heading out to attend a meeting of the town council called by the Phaeacian leaders. She stopped him and said:

"Papa, could you get me a good wagon? I want to take our dirty clothes to the river to wash them. You're the chief here, so it's only right you should have a clean shirt when you attend the council. Plus, you have five sons at home—two are married, and the other three are handsome bachelors; they all like to have clean linen for dances. I've been thinking about all this."

She didn't mention her own wedding plans because she was shy about it, but her father understood and replied, "You shall have the mules and anything else you need. Off you go, and I'll have the men prepare a strong wagon that can carry all your clothes."

He gave his orders, and the servants brought out the wagon, harnessed the mules, and attached them. Nausicaa then brought the clothes down from the linen room and placed them on the wagon. Her mother prepared a basket with a variety of delicious food and a goat skin full of wine. Nausicaa climbed into the wagon, and her mother gave her a golden flask of oil for her and her maids to use. Then Nausicaa took the whip and reins, lashed the mules, and they set off, their hooves clattering on the road. The mules pulled the wagon steadily, carrying not only Nausicaa and her laundry but also the maids accompanying her.

When they arrived at the riverside, they went to the washing basins, where there was always enough clean water to wash any amount of linen, no matter how dirty. They unharnessed the mules and let them graze on the sweet grass by the river. They took the clothes out of the wagon and began to wash them, treading them in the water to remove the dirt. Once they had finished washing and the clothes were clean, they laid them out on the beach, where the waves had created a high bank of pebbles. They then washed themselves and anointed their bodies with olive oil. After eating lunch by the stream, they waited for the sun to dry the clothes. Once lunch was over, they removed their veils and began to play ball while Nausicaa sang for them. Just like the huntress Diana when she goes to hunt wild boars or deer, with the wood nymphs, daughters of Jove, joining in her fun—then Leto feels proud seeing her daughter stand a head taller than the others and outshine even the prettiest—so did Nausicaa shine among her maids.

As it was time to head home, they started folding the clothes and putting them back into the wagon. Minerva thought about how Ulysses should wake up to see the beautiful girl who would help him reach the Phaeacians. At that moment, Nausicaa threw a ball at one of her maids, but it missed and fell into the deep water. The splash made them all shout, and their noise woke Ulysses, who sat up on his bed of leaves, wondering what was happening.

"Alas," he said to himself, "what kind of people have I come among? Are they cruel and savage, or hospitable and kind? I hear the voices of young women, sounding like the nymphs who haunt the mountains, river springs, and green meadows. I must try to see them."

He crawled out from under the bushes, broke off a leafy branch to cover his nakedness, and moved toward the sound. He looked like a lion roaming the wilderness, proud of his strength and undaunted by wind or rain, searching for food like oxen, sheep, or deer, daring to enter even a well-guarded homestead. Such did Ulysses appear to the young women as he approached, completely naked and desperate. The other maids scattered away, retreating to the points that jutted into the sea, but Nausicaa stood firm, filled with courage by Minerva, who took away her fear. She positioned herself in front of Ulysses, who hesitated, unsure whether to approach her, fall at her feet, and grasp her knees as a supplicant, or stay at a distance and ask her for clothes and directions to the city. In the end, he decided it was better to speak to her from a distance in case she took offense at his closeness. So he addressed her in sweet and persuasive words.

"O queen," he said, "I beg for your help. But tell me, are you a goddess or a mortal woman? If you are a goddess living in heaven, I can only guess that you are Jove's daughter Diana, for your beauty resembles no one else's. If you are a mortal who lives on earth, how fortunate your parents must be! How proud they must feel when they see such a lovely daughter going out to dance! Most fortunate of all will be the man whose wedding gifts are the finest, the one who takes you to his home. I have never seen anyone as beautiful as you, and I am in awe of you. You remind me of a young palm tree I saw at Delos near Apollo's altar when I was there on a journey that has caused me much suffering. No young plant ever grew as beautifully as that one, and I admired it just as I admire you now. I don't want to touch your knees, but I am in great distress; yesterday marked my twentieth day adrift on the sea. The winds and waves have brought me from Ogygia, and now fate has cast me upon this coast to endure more suffering, for I sense that I still have many trials ahead.

"Now, O queen, have pity on me, for you are the first person I have encountered here, and I know no one else in this land. Show me the way to your city and lend me something to wrap my clothes in. May heaven grant you all that your heart desires —husband, house, and a joyful home; for there is nothing better in this world than for a man and wife to be of one mind in a household. It brings joy to their friends, frustrates their enemies, and they understand one another better than anyone else."

Nausicaa replied, "Stranger, you seem sensible and well-mannered. We cannot predict luck; Jove gives prosperity to both the rich and poor as he sees fit. You must accept what he has chosen to send you and make the best of it. Now that you have come to our country, you won't lack for clothes or anything else a traveler in distress might need. I will show you the way to our town and tell you about our people. We are the Phaeacians, and I am the daughter of Alcinous, who holds all the power of the state."

She then called to her maids, saying, "Stay here, girls. Can you not see a man without running away? Do you think he's a robber or a murderer? Neither he nor anyone else can harm us Phaeacians, for we are dear to the gods and live apart at the end of the land that juts into the sea, with no dealings with other people. This is just a poor man who has lost his way, and we must be kind to him. Strangers and travelers in distress are under Jove's protection, and they will take what they can get and be grateful. So, girls, give the poor fellow something to eat and drink, and help him wash in the stream where it is sheltered from the wind."

At this, the maids stopped running away and began calling each other back. They made Ulysses sit down in a sheltered spot as Nausicaa had instructed, and they brought him a shirt and cloak. They also gave him a small golden flask of oil and told him to wash in the stream. But Ulysses said, "Young women, please step aside a little so I can wash the salt off my shoulders and apply some oil, for it has been far too long since my skin has felt any. I can't wash with you all standing there. I feel ashamed to strip in front of such lovely young women."

So the maids moved aside and went to tell Nausicaa, while Ulysses washed himself in the stream, scrubbing the salt from his back and broad shoulders. After thoroughly cleaning himself and getting the salt out of his hair, he anointed himself with oil and put on the clothes the girl had given him. At that moment, Minerva made him appear taller and stronger than before. She also made his hair grow thick on his head and fall in curls like hyacinth blossoms. She adorned him like a skilled craftsman, who, under Vulcan and Minerva, enriches a piece of silver by gilding it—making it truly beautiful. Ulysses then moved to a spot a little way off on the beach, looking quite young and handsome, and Nausicaa gazed at him in admiration. She then said to her maids:

"Quiet, my dears, I want to say something. I believe the gods who live in heaven have sent this man to the Phaeacians. When I first saw him, I thought he was plain, but now his appearance is like that of the gods. I would like my future husband to be just like him if he would only stay here and not want to leave. But first, give him something to eat and drink."

The maids did as they were told and set food before Ulysses, who ate and drank eagerly, for it had been a long time since he had tasted food. Meanwhile, Nausicaa thought about other matters. She folded the linen and placed it in the wagon, then yoked the mules. As she took her seat, she called out to Ulysses:

"Stranger, rise and let's go back to the town. I will introduce you to my excellent father, and I assure you that you will meet all the best people among the Phaeacians. But you must follow my instructions, as you seem sensible. As we pass the fields and farmland, follow the wagon with the maids while I lead the way. Soon we will arrive at the town, where you will see a high wall surrounding it and a good harbor on either side with a narrow entrance into the city. The ships will be pulled up by the roadside, for everyone has a place for their own ship. You will see the marketplace with a temple of Neptune in the center, paved with large stones. This is where people deal in all kinds of ship gear, like cables and sails, and here are the places where oars are made. The Phaeacians are not archers; they know nothing about bows and arrows but pride themselves on their ships, masts, and oars, traveling far across the sea.

"I'm worried about what people might say later. The townsfolk can be very judgmental. Some low fellow might say, 'Who is this handsome stranger with Nausicaa? Where did she find him? Is she going to marry him? Perhaps he is a vagabond sailor she picked up from a foreign ship, for we have no neighbors, or maybe a god has finally come down from heaven in answer to her prayers, and she plans to live with him forever. Wouldn't it be better if she found a husband elsewhere, since she won't even look at the many excellent young Phaeacians who are in love with her?' This kind of gossip would be directed at me, and I could hardly complain, for I would be scandalized if I saw another girl doing the same thing, going around with men while her parents were still alive and without being married in public.

"If you want my father to help you and provide an escort home, do as I say. You will see a lovely grove of poplars dedicated to Minerva by the roadside; it has a well and a meadow around it. My father has a field there, not far from the town, where a man's voice can easily be heard. Sit there and wait for a while until the rest of us can get into the town and reach my father's house. When you think we must have done this, come into the town and ask the way to my father Alcinous' house. You won't have any trouble finding it; any child can point it out to you, for no one else in the whole town has such a magnificent home. Once you get past the gates and through the outer court, walk across the inner court until you find my mother. She will be sitting by the fire, spinning her purple wool. It is a beautiful sight to see her leaning against one of the pillars, with her maids gathered behind her. Close to her seat is my father's, where he sits like an immortal god. Don't worry about him, but go up to my mother and lay your hands on her knees if you want to return home quickly. If you can win her over, you may hope to see your homeland again, no matter how far away it is."

With that, she urged the mules on with her whip, and they left the river. The mules pulled well, and their hooves clopped along the road. Nausicaa was careful not to go too fast for Ulysses and the maids following on foot, using her whip judiciously. As the sun began to set, they arrived at the sacred grove of Minerva, and Ulysses sat down to pray to the mighty daughter of Jove.

"Hear me," he cried, "daughter of Aegis-bearing Jove, hear me now, for you ignored my prayers when Neptune was wrecking me. Now, please have pity on me and grant that I may find friends and be welcomed by the Phaeacians."

Thus did he pray, and Minerva heard him, but she didn't reveal herself to him directly, for she was still wary of her uncle Neptune, who was angry and trying to prevent Ulysses from getting home.

BOOK 7:

Ulysses waited and prayed, while Nausicaa drove her wagon to the town. Upon reaching her father's house, she stopped at the gateway, and her brothers, handsome like the gods, gathered around her. They took the mules out of the wagon and carried the clothes into the house, while she went to her own room. An old servant named Eurymedusa from Apeira lit the fire for her. She had been brought from Apeira by sea and chosen as a prize for Alcinous because he was the king of the Phaeacians, and the people obeyed him as if he were a god. Eurymedusa had been Nausicaa's nurse and now prepared her supper in her room.

Meanwhile, Ulysses rose to head toward the town. Minerva surrounded him with a thick mist to hide him from any of the proud Phaeacians who might be rude or ask who he was. Just as he was entering the town, she approached him in the form of a little girl carrying a pitcher. She stood in front of him, and Ulysses asked:

"My dear, could you please show me the way to King Alcinous' house? I am an unfortunate traveler in distress, and I don't know anyone in your town."

"Yes, stranger," she replied, "I will show you the house you seek. Alcinous lives quite close to my father's home. I'll go ahead and lead the way, but don't speak or look at anyone as we walk. The people here dislike strangers and don't trust those from other lands. They are a sea-faring folk, sailing by the grace of Neptune in ships that glide smoothly across the sea, like birds in the air."

With that, she led the way, and Ulysses followed her. No Phaeacians could see him as he passed through the city, for

Minerva had hidden him in a thick cloud of mist out of goodwill. He admired their harbors, ships, meeting places, and the tall walls of the city, which were striking with palisades on top. When they arrived at the king's house, Minerva said:

"This is the house, stranger, that you wish to see. You'll find many great people sitting at the table, but don't be afraid. Just go straight in; the bolder a man is, the more likely he is to achieve his goals, even as a stranger. First, look for the queen. Her name is Arete, and she is from the same family as her husband Alcinous. They both trace their lineage back to Neptune, who fathered Nausithous with Periboea, a beautiful woman. Periboea was the youngest daughter of Eurymedon, who once ruled the giants but met his own doom.

"Neptune, however, lay with his daughter, and she bore Nausithous, who ruled over the Phaeacians. Nausithous had two sons, Rhexenor and Alcinous. Apollo killed the first before he could have children, leaving behind a daughter, Arete, whom Alcinous married and honors more than any other woman in the household.

"Arete is still greatly respected by her children, Alcinous, and the entire community, who regard her as a goddess. They greet her whenever she walks through the city because she is a good woman in mind and heart. She also helps the wives of her friends settle disputes. If you can win her favor, you may hope to see your friends again and return safely to your home and country."

Then Minerva departed from Scheria and crossed the sea, heading to Marathon and the wide streets of Athens, where she entered the home of Erechtheus. Meanwhile, Ulysses approached the house of Alcinous, pausing for a moment at the entrance, as the palace sparkled like the sun or moon. The walls were bronze, and the cornices were made of blue enamel. The doors were gold, hung on silver pillars rising from a bronze floor, with a silver lintel and gold door hooks.

On either side of the entrance stood golden and silver mastiffs, crafted by Vulcan to guard the palace of King Alcinous. They were immortal and would never grow old. Seats lined the walls, covered in fine woven textiles made by the women of the house. Here the chief people of the Phaeacians would sit to eat and drink, enjoying an abundance at all times. Golden figures of young men holding lighted torches stood on pedestals, illuminating the nights for those dining. There were fifty maidservants in the house; some ground rich yellow grain at the mill, others worked at the loom, and their shuttles flew back and forth like aspen leaves, weaving linen so tightly that it could hold oil. The Phaeacians were the best sailors, and their women excelled in weaving, as Minerva had taught them many useful arts, making them very clever.

Outside the outer court gate, there was a large garden of about four acres, surrounded by a wall, full of beautiful trees—pears, pomegranates, and the tastiest apples, along with luscious figs and flourishing olives. The fruits never rotted or failed throughout the year, regardless of winter or summer, because the air was so mild that a new crop ripened before the old dropped. Pear grew on pear, apple on apple, and fig on fig, as well as grapes in an excellent vineyard. In one part, grapes were made into raisins; in another, they were being gathered; some were being trodden in wine tubs, others had shed their blossoms and were beginning to bear fruit, while others were changing color. In the farthest part of the garden, beautifully arranged flower beds bloomed all year round. Two streams flowed through it: one was directed throughout the garden, and the other ran underground to the house, providing water for the townspeople. Such were the splendid gifts the gods had given to King Alcinous' house.

Ulysses stood for a moment to take it all in before he crossed the threshold and entered the palace. Inside, he found all the chief people of the Phaeacians making drink offerings to Mercury, which they always did before leaving for the night. He moved through the court, still hidden by the darkness Minerva had wrapped around him, until he reached Arete and King Alcinous. There, he knelt and laid his hands on the queen's knees, at which moment the miraculous mist lifted, and he became visible. Everyone was speechless with surprise at seeing him, but Ulysses immediately began his appeal.

"Queen Arete," he exclaimed, "daughter of the great Rhexenor, I humbly pray you in my distress, as well as your husband and your guests (may heaven grant them long life and happiness, and may they pass their possessions on to their children), to help me return to my homeland as soon as possible; for I have suffered long and been away from my friends."

Then he sat down on the hearth among the ashes, and everyone fell silent until an elder named Echeneus, a respected speaker among the Phaeacians, addressed them clearly and honestly:

"Alcinous," he said, "it's not proper for a stranger to be sitting among the ashes of your hearth; everyone is waiting to hear what you will say. Tell him to rise and take a seat on a silver-inlaid stool, and have your servants mix some wine and water so we can make a drink offering to Jove, the lord of thunder, who protects all honorable suppliants. And let the housekeeper provide him with some supper from what we have in the house."

When Alcinous heard this, he took Ulysses by the hand, raised him from the hearth, and invited him to sit in the place of Laodamas, his favorite son. A maidservant brought water in a beautiful golden ewer and poured it into a silver basin for him to wash his hands. Another maid set a clean table beside him, while an upper servant offered him bread and a variety of delicious foods from the household, and Ulysses ate and drank.

Then Alcinous said to one of the servants, "Pontonous, mix a cup of wine and pass it around so we can make drink offerings to Jove, the lord of thunder, who is the protector of all honorable suppliants."

Pontonous mixed the wine and water, then handed it around after giving each man his drink offering. Once they had made their offerings and drunk as much as they wished, Alcinous addressed the assembly:

"Elders and town councillors of the Phaeacians, listen to me. You've had your supper, so now go home to bed. Tomorrow morning I will invite even more elders and will hold a sacrificial banquet in honor of our guest; we can then discuss providing him with an escort and consider how we may send him home joyfully and safely, no matter how far away it is. We must ensure he is unharmed during his journey, but once he returns home, he will have to take the luck he was born with, for better or worse, like everyone else. It's possible, however, that the stranger is one of the immortals come down from heaven to visit us, but if that were the case, the gods are acting differently than usual, for they have always made themselves known to us during our hecatombs. They come and join our feasts as if they were one of us, and if a traveler happens to encounter one of them, they don't hide their identity, for we are as closely related to the gods as the Cyclopes and the wild giants."

Then Ulysses spoke: "Please, Alcinous, don't entertain such thoughts about me. I have nothing of the immortal about me, neither in body nor mind; I most resemble those among you who are most afflicted. If I were to share all that heaven has inflicted upon me, you would see that I am worse off than they. Nevertheless, let me dine despite my sorrow, for an empty stomach is quite insistent, demanding attention no matter how dire the situation. I am in great trouble, yet it insists that I eat and drink, urging me to forget my sorrows and focus solely on satisfying my hunger. As for you, please proceed as you plan, and at dawn set about helping me return home. I would be content to die if I could first see my property, my servants, and all the splendor of my house once more."

Ulysses spoke, and everyone agreed with him, deciding that he should have an escort since he had spoken reasonably. After making their drink offerings and drinking as much as they wished, each man returned to his own home, leaving Ulysses in the cloister with Arete and Alcinous while the servants cleared away after supper. Arete was the first to speak; she recognized the shirt, cloak, and fine clothes Ulysses wore as her own handiwork and that of her maids. She asked, "Stranger, before we go further, I have a question: who are you, where do you come from, and who gave you those clothes? Did you not say you arrived here from across the sea?"

Ulysses replied, "It would take a long time to tell you my tale, Madam, for I have faced many hardships laid upon me by the gods. However, to answer your question, there is an island far away in the sea called Ogygia, where the clever and powerful goddess Calypso, daughter of Atlas, lives. She resides there alone, far from all human and divine neighbors. I ended up at her hearth, lost and alone, because Jove struck my ship with his thunderbolts, breaking it apart in mid-ocean. All my brave comrades drowned, but I clung to the keel and drifted for nine days until, during the darkness of the tenth night, the gods brought me to the Ogygian island where Calypso resides. She took me in and treated me kindly, wanting to make me immortal so I would never grow old, but I couldn't agree to that.

"I stayed with Calypso for seven years, shedding tears over the fine clothes she gave me. At last, in the eighth year, she told me to leave, whether because Jove commanded her or because she had changed her mind. She sent me off on a raft, provisioned with plenty of bread and wine, along with sturdy clothing and a favorable wind. For seven days and nights I sailed the sea, and on the eighteenth day, I caught sight of the mountains on your coast—how glad I was to see them! Yet, trouble awaited me still. At that point, Neptune wouldn't let me go further and stirred up a great storm against me. The waves rose so high that I could no longer stay on my raft, which broke apart in the fierce gale, and I had to swim until the wind and current brought me to your shores.

"I tried to land, but the place was rocky and dangerous, so I swam on until I found a river that seemed a good spot to reach, as it had no rocks and was sheltered from the wind. I managed to get out of the water and gather my thoughts again. Night was falling, so I left the river and entered a thicket, covering myself with leaves. Eventually, I fell into a deep sleep. Despite my weariness and sadness, I slept among the leaves all night and into the next day until afternoon. When I awoke, I saw your daughter's maidservants playing on the beach, with your daughter among them, looking like a goddess. I begged for her help, and she proved to be kind, much more than I expected from someone so young. She gave me plenty of bread and wine, helped me wash in the river, and provided the clothes you see me wearing now. So, although it pains me to recount my misfortunes, I have told you the whole truth."

Alcinous responded, "Stranger, it was not right for my daughter to leave you behind and not bring you to my house with the maids, especially since she was the first to assist you."

"Please don't blame her," Ulysses said. "She told me to follow along with the maids, but I was too ashamed and afraid you might be displeased if you saw me. Everyone can be a little suspicious and irritable sometimes."

"Stranger," Alcinous replied, "I'm not one to get angry over trifles; it's always better to be reasonable. By Father Jove, Minerva, and Apollo, now that I see what kind of person you are and how much you think like me, I wish you would stay here, marry my daughter, and become my son-in-law. If you stay, I will give you a house and land, but I assure you that no one, heaven forbid, will keep you here against your will. Tomorrow, I will arrange for your escort. You can sleep during the whole voyage if you like, and my men will sail you over smooth waters to your home or wherever you wish, even if it's much farther than Euboea, which my people visited when they took yellow-haired Rhadamanthus to see Tityus, the son of Gaia. They completed the journey in one day without difficulty and returned afterwards. This will show you how much my ships excel all others and how magnificent my sailors are."

Ulysses felt glad and prayed aloud, "Father Jove, grant that Alcinous does as he has promised, for he will earn an everlasting reputation among mankind, and I will finally return to my home."

As they continued their conversation, Arete instructed her maids to prepare a bed in the room at the gatehouse, laying it with fine red rugs and spreading coverlets on top for Ulysses. The maids left with torches, and when they had made the bed, they approached Ulysses and said, "Rise, sir stranger, and come with us; your bed is ready." He was indeed glad to go and rest.

So Ulysses slept in a bed placed in a room above the echoing gateway, while Alcinous lay in the inner part of the house with the queen by his side.

BOOK 8:

When rosy-fingered Dawn appeared, both Alcinous and Ulysses rose. Alcinous led the way to the Phaeacian assembly place near the ships. Once they arrived, they sat down side by side on a polished stone seat. Minerva took the form of one of Alcinous' servants and went around the town to gather people for Ulysses' escort. She approached the citizens one by one and said, "Aldermen and town councillors of the Phaeacians, come to the assembly and listen to the stranger who has just arrived after a long journey to the house of King Alcinous; he looks like an immortal god."

Her words stirred everyone to come, and soon the assembly was filled to capacity. All were struck by Ulysses' appearance, for Minerva had enhanced his looks, making him appear taller and stronger than he really was, so he would impress the Phaeacians as a remarkable man during the various contests they would set for him. Once everyone had gathered, Alcinous spoke:

"Hear me, aldermen and town councillors of the Phaeacians, as I share my thoughts. This stranger has come to my house from somewhere, either East or West. He seeks an escort and wishes for arrangements to be made. Let's prepare one for him, as we have done for others before him; no one who has visited my house has ever complained about a lack of assistance on my part. Let's draw a ship into the sea—one that has never been on a voyage—and man her with fifty-two of our finest young sailors. Once the oars are secured to their seats, we can leave the ship and return to my house for a feast. I will provide everything you need. I instruct the young men who will crew the ship, while the rest of you aldermen and town councillors will join me in hosting our guest in the cloisters. I won't accept any excuses, and we will have Demodocus to sing for us; he is the best bard there is, no matter the subject."

Alcinous led the way, and the others followed while a servant went to fetch Demodocus. The fifty-two selected oarsmen went to the seashore as instructed. When they arrived, they drew the ship into the water, placed the mast and sails inside her, secured the oars to the thole-pins with leather thongs, and spread the white sails aloft. They moored the vessel a little way out from land, then came ashore and headed to King Alcinous' house. The outbuildings, yards, and all the precincts were filled with a great multitude of people, both young and old. Alcinous ordered the slaughter of a dozen sheep, eight fully grown pigs, and two oxen, which they skinned and prepared for a magnificent banquet.

A servant then led in the famous bard Demodocus, who had been favored by the Muse. Though she blessed him with a divine gift of song, she also took away his sight. Pontonous set a seat for him among the guests, leaning it against a bearing-post. He hung the lyre for him on a peg over his head and showed him where to feel for it. He also placed a table with food by his side and a cup of wine for him to drink whenever he wished.

The guests then began to eat and drink, and once they were satisfied, the Muse inspired Demodocus to sing about the feats of heroes, particularly focusing on the quarrel between Ulysses and Achilles, and the harsh words they exchanged at a banquet. Agamemnon was pleased to hear his chieftains bickering, as Apollo had foretold this at Pytho when he consulted the oracle. This marked the beginning of the troubles that fell upon both the Danaans and Trojans by the will of Jove.

As the bard sang, Ulysses covered his head with his purple mantle, hiding his face, ashamed to let the Phaeacians see his tears. When the bard finished singing, he wiped his eyes and uncovered his face, then took his cup and made a drink offering to the gods. But when the Phaeacians urged Demodocus to sing again, eager to hear more, Ulysses once more drew his mantle over his head and wept bitterly. No one noticed his distress except Alcinous, who sat nearby and heard the heavy sighs escaping him. He then spoke, "Aldermen and town councillors of the Phaeacians, we have had enough of the feast and the accompanying music; let us move on to athletic competitions, so our guest may tell his friends how much we excel all other nations in boxing, wrestling, jumping, and running."

With that, Alcinous led the way, and the others followed. A servant hung Demodocus' lyre on its peg for him, guided him out of the cloister, and led him along the path to the place where the chief men of the Phaeacians were going to watch the games. A large crowd followed them, with many excellent competitors vying for prizes. Among them were Acroneos, Ocyalus, Elatreus, Nauteus, Prymneus, Anchialus, Eretmeus, Ponteus, Proreus, Thoon, Anabesineus, and Amphialus, son of Polyneus. Euryalus, son of Naubolus, who was as handsome as Mars, was also there, along with Alcinous' three sons: Laodamas, Halios, and Clytoneus.

The foot races began first. The course was set, and they kicked up dust as they rushed forward all at once. Clytoneus finished first, leaving everyone behind by the length of a furrow that a pair of mules can plow in a fallow field. Next, they turned to wrestling, where Euryalus excelled. Amphialus outperformed everyone in jumping, while Elatreus was unmatched in throwing the discus. Laodamas, Alcinous's son, was the best boxer, and after everyone had enjoyed the games, he said, "Let us ask the stranger if he excels in any of these sports; he looks very strong; his thighs, calves, hands, and neck are all powerful, and though he seems not old, he has suffered greatly recently, and nothing wears a man down like the sea."

"You're right, Laodamas," Euryalus replied. "Go ask your guest yourself."

Laodamas approached the crowd and said to Ulysses, "I hope, sir, that you'll join in one of our competitions if you have skill in any of them—you must have participated in many before. There's nothing that brings someone credit for life like showing himself as a strong competitor with his hands and feet. So, give it a try and let go of your worries. Your journey home won't take long, for the ship is already ready and the crew is gathered."

Ulysses responded, "Laodamas, why do you tease me? My mind is more focused on my troubles than on contests; I've faced countless hardships, and I've come to you as a suppliant, seeking your king and people's help for my return home."

Euryalus then insulted him, saying, "So it seems you lack skill in the many sports that men enjoy. I take it you are one of those greedy traders who sail the seas as captains or merchants, thinking only of their cargo and profits. You don't appear to have the physique of an athlete."

"For shame, sir," Ulysses shot back angrily. "You are an insolent fellow—it's clear that the gods do not endow all men equally with speech, presence, and understanding. Some men may appear weak, but heaven has blessed them with a way of speaking that charms everyone who hears them; their wise moderation draws their listeners in, making them leaders in assemblies and esteemed wherever they go. Yet another may be as handsome as a god, but lacks wisdom. That describes you. No god could create a finer-looking man than you, but you are a fool. Your reckless remarks have offended me, and you are wrong to think I lack skill; in many athletic contests, I excelled in my youth. Now, however, I am worn down by labor and sorrow, having endured much in battle and on the treacherous sea. Yet, despite all this, I will compete, for your taunts have stung me deeply."

With that, he rushed forward without even removing his cloak and grabbed a discus, larger, heavier, and much more massive than those typically used by the Phaeacians in their contests. He swung it back and released it from his powerful hand, producing a humming sound as it flew through the air. The Phaeacians flinched as they watched the discus soar gracefully from his grip, landing far beyond any previous throw. Minerva, taking the form of a man, marked the spot where it fell. "Sir," she said, "even a blind man could easily find your mark—it's so far ahead of the rest. You need not worry about this contest; no Phaeacian can match such a throw as yours."

Ulysses felt pleased to have support among the onlookers, so he spoke more cheerfully. "Young men," he challenged, "come see if you can reach that throw; I will throw another discus, just as heavy or even heavier. If anyone wishes to compete with me, let him come forth, for I am very eager; I will box, wrestle, or run with any man here, except Laodamas, for I am his guest, and it's not right to compete against a friend. I do not think it wise for a guest to challenge his host's family, especially in a foreign land; that would be cutting his own feet from under him. However, I will not exclude anyone else, as I want to see who is the best man. I excel at every athletic sport known to mankind. I am an excellent archer, and in battle, I am always the first to bring down an enemy with my arrow, even when many others are aiming at him alongside me. Only Philoctetes could shoot better than I did when we Achaeans were before Troy. I surpass all who still eat bread on this earth, but I would not dare to shoot against the mighty dead, like Hercules or Eurytus, who could challenge the gods themselves. This was how Eurytus met his early death, for Apollo killed him out of anger after he challenged him as an archer. I can throw a spear farther than anyone can shoot an arrow. Running is the only area where I fear some Phaeacians might surpass me, for I am weak from my journeys at sea; my provisions have run short, and I still feel weak."

Everyone fell silent, except for King Alcinous, who began, "Sir, we have enjoyed listening to your words. I gather you are willing to showcase your abilities, feeling aggrieved by some rude comments from one of our athletes, which no knowledgeable person would utter. I hope you will understand my point, and when you return home, explain to any of your prominent friends that we are naturally skilled in all kinds of endeavors. We might not stand out in boxing or wrestling, but we are exceptionally fast runners and excellent sailors. We take great pleasure in fine meals, music, and dancing, as well as changes of linen, warm baths, and comfortable beds. So now, let the best dancers among you show your skills, so our guest can share with his friends how we excel all other nations in sailing, running, dancing, and music. Demodocus has left his lyre at my house, so someone run and fetch it for him."

At this, a servant hurried off to retrieve the lyre from the king's house, while nine selected stewards prepared the grounds for the events. They smoothed the area and marked off a wide space for the dancers. Soon the servant returned with Demodocus' lyre, and he took his place among them. The best young dancers in the town then began to dance so gracefully that Ulysses was delighted by the joyful movements of their feet.

Meanwhile, the bard began to sing about the loves of Mars and Venus, recounting how their affair began in the house of Vulcan. Mars showered Venus with gifts and dishonored King Vulcan's marriage bed. The sun, who witnessed their actions, reported this to Vulcan. Furious upon hearing the news, Vulcan went to his forge, brooding over his plans for revenge. He set up his anvil and began to craft chains that no one could loosen or break, intending to trap them in their betrayal.

Once he completed his snare, he decorated the bed with chains like cobwebs, allowing many to dangle down from the ceiling. They were so fine and subtle that even a god would have trouble spotting them. After preparing the trap, Vulcan pretended to leave for the island of Lemnos, which he loved most of all. But Mars was on high alert, and as soon as he saw Vulcan leave, he rushed to Venus's side, burning with love.

Venus had just returned from visiting her father, Jove, and was about to sit down when Mars entered, taking her hand and saying, "Let's go to Vulcan's bed; he is not home and has gone off to Lemnos among the Sintians, whose speech is barbarous."

She was more than willing, so they went to the bed to rest. Unfortunately for them, they fell right into the trap that cunning Vulcan had set, unable to get up or move a single hand or foot, realizing too late that they were ensnared. Shortly after, Vulcan returned, having turned back before reaching Lemnos when the sun told him of the affair. He was in a furious rage, standing at the entrance and calling out loudly to all the gods.

"Father Jove," he shouted, "and all you other blessed gods who live forever, come see this ridiculous and disgraceful sight! Jove's daughter Venus is always dishonoring me because I am lame. She loves Mars, who is handsome and well-built, while I am a cripple—my parents are to blame for that, not I; they should never have brought me into the world. Come, see the pair asleep on my bed. It makes me furious just to look at them. They care for each other, but I doubt they will stay much longer, for they shall remain here until her father pays me back the dowry I gave him for his beautiful but dishonest daughter."

Upon hearing this, the gods gathered at Vulcan's house. Earth-encircling Neptune, Mercury the bringer of luck, and King Apollo arrived, but all the goddesses stayed away out of shame. The gods crowded at the doorway, and they roared with laughter at the clever trap Vulcan had set. One would turn to another and say:

"Ill deeds do not prosper, and the weak confound the strong. Look how limping Vulcan, with his lameness, has caught Mars, who is the fleetest god in heaven; now Mars will be paying for his misdeeds."

King Apollo then said to Mercury, "Messenger Mercury, giver of good things, would you care how strong the chains were if you could sleep with Venus?"

"King Apollo," answered Mercury, "I would welcome the chance, even if there were three times as many chains—and you could all look on, gods and goddesses, but I would still choose to sleep with her."

The immortal gods laughed heartily at this, but Neptune remained serious, continually imploring Vulcan to free Mars. "Let him go," he cried, "and I promise that he will pay you all the damages that you deem reasonable among the immortal gods."

"Do not," replied Vulcan, "ask me to do this; the bond of a bad man is unreliable; what remedy could I use against you if Mars escaped without paying his debts along with his chains?"

"Vulcan," said Neptune, "if Mars leaves without settling his debts, I will pay you myself." Vulcan then said, "In that case, I cannot and must not refuse you."

With that, he released the bonds that held them. Once free, Mars rushed to Thrace, while laughter-loving Venus headed to Cyprus and Paphos, where her grove and fragrant altar awaited her. There, the Graces bathed her and anointed her with ambrosial oil, the kind used by the immortal gods, dressing her in garments of enchanting beauty.

Thus the bard sang, charming both Ulysses and the seafaring Phaeacians as they listened.

Then Alcinous instructed Laodamas and Halius to dance alone, as there were no competitors for them. They took a red ball crafted by Polybus, and one of them bent backward, throwing it up toward the clouds while the other jumped to catch it before it fell. After tossing the ball into the air, they began to dance, tossing it back and forth, as the young men applauded, stamping their feet in excitement. Ulysses remarked:

"King Alcinous, you said your people were the nimblest dancers in the world, and they have certainly proven so. I was amazed to see them."

The king was pleased and said to the Phaeacians, "Aldermen

and town councillors, our guest seems to possess exceptional judgment; let us show him the hospitality he deserves. There are twelve chief men among you, and including myself, there are thirteen. Contribute, each of you, a clean cloak, a shirt, and a talent of fine gold; let us give it all to him at once, so that when he has his supper, he may do so with a light heart. As for Euryalus, he must make a formal apology and a gift, for he has been rude."

The others applauded his words and sent their servants to gather the gifts. Euryalus then said, "King Alcinous, I will provide the stranger with all the satisfaction you ask. He shall receive my bronze sword, save for the silver hilt. I will also give him the scabbard made of freshly cut ivory. It will be of great worth to him."

As he spoke, he handed the sword to Ulysses and said, "Good luck to you, father stranger; if anything has been said amiss, may the winds blow it away, and may heaven grant you a safe return, for I understand you have been long away from home and have faced much hardship."

Ulysses replied, "Good luck to you too, my friend, and may the gods grant you every happiness. I hope you will not miss the sword you have given me along with your apology."

With these words, he strapped the sword around his shoulders, and as the sun began to set, the presents started to arrive, as the servants of the donors brought them to King Alcinous' house. His sons received them and placed them under their mother's care. Then Alcinous led everyone to his house and invited them to take their seats.

"Wife," he said to Queen Arete, "go fetch the best chest we have and place a clean cloak and shirt inside it. Also, set a copper pot on the fire to heat some water; our guest will want to take a warm bath. See to the careful packing of the presents from the noble Phaeacians; this will allow him to enjoy both his supper and the music that will follow. I shall also give him this exquisite golden goblet, so he will remember me for the rest of his life whenever he makes a drink offering to Jove or any of the gods."

Arete instructed her maids to set a large tripod over the fire quickly. They placed a pot full of bathwater on the fire, adding sticks to make the flames blaze, and soon the water was hot. Meanwhile, Arete fetched a magnificent chest from her own room, and inside it, she packed all the beautiful gifts of gold and clothing that the Phaeacians had brought. Finally, she added a cloak and a shirt from Alcinous, telling Ulysses:

"See to the lid yourself and secure it quickly, lest anyone rob you while you sleep on the ship."

Upon hearing this, Ulysses placed the lid on the chest and secured it with a bond that Circe had taught him. After finishing, a servant told him it was time to come for his bath. He was glad for the warm bath, as he had not been cared for since leaving Calypso's home, where she had treated him like a god. Once the servants washed and anointed him with oil, giving him a clean cloak and shirt, he left the bath and joined the guests sitting over their wine. Lovely Nausicaa stood by one of the bearing posts of the cloister and admired him as he passed. "Farewell, stranger," she said, "do not forget me when you reach home safely, for it is I who first saved your life."

Ulysses replied, "Nausicaa, daughter of great Alcinous, may Jove, the mighty husband of Juno, grant that I return home; I will bless you as my guardian angel all my days, for you are the one who saved me."

After this, he took his place beside Alcinous. Supper was served, and the wine was poured. A servant brought in the favorite bard, Demodocus, and placed him among the company, near a bearing post so he could lean against it. Ulysses then cut off a piece of roast pork, rich with fat, and handed it to a servant, saying, "Take this to Demodocus and tell him to eat it; for despite the pain his songs may cause me, I will salute him nonetheless;

bards are honored and respected everywhere, for the Muse teaches them their songs and loves them."

The servant brought the pork to Demodocus, who received it with great pleasure. They then laid their hands on the abundant food before them. Once they had eaten and drunk their fill, Ulysses said to Demodocus, "Demodocus, there is no one in the world I admire more than you. You must have studied under the Muse, Jove's daughter, and under Apollo, so accurately do you sing the return of the Achaeans with all their suffering and adventures. If you weren't there yourself, you must have heard it from someone who was. Now, however, change your song and tell us about the wooden horse that Epeus made with the help of Minerva, which Ulysses got into the fortress of Troy by trickery, carrying the men who later sacked the city. If you sing this tale well, I will proclaim to all how magnificently heaven has endowed you."

Inspired by the Muse, the bard began his tale at the point when some of the Argives set fire to their tents and sailed away while others, hidden within the horse, waited with Ulysses in the Trojan assembly. The Trojans had brought the horse into their fortress, and while they sat in council around it, they debated what to do. Some wanted to break it apart immediately; others suggested dragging it to the top of the fortress and throwing it off the cliff; while still others thought it best to leave it as an offering to the gods. Ultimately, they decided to keep the horse, sealing the city's doom by taking it in, as it contained the bravest of the Argives, waiting to bring death and destruction upon the Trojans.

The bard sang of how the Achaeans emerged from the horse and ravaged the city, and how Ulysses fought fiercely with Menelaus at the house of Deiphobus. That was where the battle raged most fiercely, but thanks to Minerva's help, he was victorious.

Ulysses was overcome by emotion as he listened, and tears streamed down his cheeks. He wept like a woman who throws herself on her fallen husband, who has bravely fought for their city and family. She screams and clings to him as he gasps for breath, but her enemies beat her from behind and drag her away into slavery, to a life of toil and sorrow, her beauty fading away. In the same way, Ulysses wept, but only Alcinous, who sat near him, noticed his tears, hearing the heavy sighs he breathed. The king immediately stood up and said:

"Aldermen and town councillors of the Phaeacians, let Demodocus stop singing, for some of us do not seem to enjoy it. Since we finished supper and Demodocus began his song, our guest has been groaning and lamenting the entire time. He is clearly in great distress, so let the bard cease, so we can all enjoy ourselves, both hosts and guest alike. This would be more appropriate, as all these festivities, the escort, and the gifts we are presenting him are entirely in his honor, and anyone with a sense of decency knows that he ought to treat a guest and a suppliant like a brother.

"Therefore, Sir, you should not hold back or be reserved regarding my next question; it is more polite to give me a straightforward answer. Please tell me your name, the one your father and mother called you, and the name by which you were known among your fellow citizens. No one, rich or poor, is without a name, as people's fathers and mothers give them names at birth. Also, tell me your country, your nation, and your city, so our ships may prepare to take you there. The Phaeacians have no pilots; their vessels lack the rudders that other nations possess. Our ships understand what we think and desire, knowing all the cities and countries in the world. They can traverse the sea, even when it is enveloped in mist and cloud, making it impossible to wreck or harm. I do remember my father saying that Neptune was angry with us for being too easy-going in providing escorts, and he claimed one day he would sink one of our ships upon returning from escorting someone and bury our city under a high mountain. This is what my father often said, but whether the god will carry out his threat or not is something only he can decide.

"Now, tell me the truth. Where have you wandered, and what countries have you visited? Describe the people you encountered —who were hostile, savage, and uncivilized, and who were hospitable and humane. Tell us why you become so unhappy when you hear about the return of the Argive Danaans from Troy. The gods arranged all this and sent them their misfortunes so that future generations would have stories to sing about. Did you lose a brave kinsman of your wife's in Troy? Perhaps a son-in-law or father-in-law, as these are the closest relations outside of one's own blood? Or was it a brave and kind-hearted comrade? A good friend is as dear to a man as his brother."

BOOK 9:

Ulysses replied, "King Alcinous, it is truly wonderful to hear a bard with such a divine voice. There is nothing more delightful than when a whole people gathers to celebrate together, with guests sitting in order to listen, tables loaded with bread and meats, and the cup-bearer pouring wine for everyone. This is indeed one of the fairest sights a man can behold. However, since you wish to hear the story of my sorrows and rekindle my own sad memories, I am unsure how to begin or how to continue and conclude my tale, for the hand of heaven has weighed heavily upon me.

"First, let me share my name so that you may know it, and perhaps one day, if I survive this period of sorrow, I may become your guest, even living so far from you all. I am Ulysses, son of Laertes, known among men for my cunning, so much so that my fame has reached the heavens. I reside in Ithaca, where a high mountain named Neritum rises, covered in forests. Close by, there are a group of islands—Dulichium, Same, and the wooded island of Zacynthus. Zacynthus lies to the west in the sea towards the sunset, while the others are positioned towards the dawn. Ithaca is a rugged island, yet it breeds brave men, and my eyes know none whom they love to look upon more than my homeland. The goddess Calypso kept me in her cave and wished to marry me, as did the cunning goddess Circe; yet neither could persuade me, for nothing is dearer to a man than his own country and parents. No matter how splendid a home he might find in a foreign land, if it is far from father or mother, he cannot cherish it.

"Now, let me recount the many perilous adventures I faced by

Jove's will on my journey home from Troy.

"When I set sail from there, the wind first carried me to Ismarus, the city of the Cicons. There, we sacked the town and slaughtered the people. We took their wives and much booty, which we divided fairly among us to ensure none had cause to complain. I urged my men to leave immediately, but they foolishly disobeyed, staying behind to drink wine and slaughter many sheep and oxen on the shore. Meanwhile, the Cicons called for help from other Cicons living inland. These reinforcements were more numerous and better skilled in war, capable of fighting from chariots or on foot as the situation required. By morning, they came upon us in great numbers, and the hand of heaven turned against us. The battle lines formed near our ships, and each side hurled bronze-tipped spears at the other.

"Throughout the morning, we held our ground despite being outnumbered, but as the sun set and evening fell, the Cicons gained the upper hand, and we lost six men from each ship; we fled with those who remained.

"From there, we sailed onward, heavy-hearted but thankful to have escaped death, even with our losses. We did not leave until we had called out three times in memory of our fallen comrades. Then Jove sent the North wind against us, raising a hurricane that shrouded land and sky in thick clouds, and night fell upon us. We let our ships run with the storm, but the wind tore our sails to tatters. Fearing shipwreck, we took them down and rowed with all our might toward land. We endured two days and nights of suffering from toil and mental anguish, but on the morning of the third day, we raised our masts again, set sail, and took our places, letting the wind and steersmen guide our ship. I would have reached home unharmed had the North wind and currents not opposed me while rounding Cape Malea, pushing me off course near the island of Cythera.

"I was driven by foul winds for nine days across the sea, but on the tenth day, we finally reached the land of the Lotus-eaters, who live on a fruit that comes from a flower. We landed to gather fresh water and took our midday meal on the shore near the ships. After eating and drinking, I sent two of my men to discover what kind of people lived there, accompanied by a third man. They set off at once and encountered the Lotus-eaters, who did them no harm but offered them the delicious lotus fruit. Those who ate it lost all desire to return home, forgetting their journey and only wishing to stay there and munch on lotus with the Lotus-eaters.

"Despite their bitter weeping, I forced them back to the ships and secured them beneath the benches. I then ordered the rest to board immediately, lest any should taste the lotus and lose their longing for home. They took their places and rowed vigorously across the grey sea.

"We sailed on, still in distress, until we arrived at the land of the lawless and savage Cyclopes. The Cyclopes neither plant nor plow; they rely on providence and live off the wild wheat, barley, and grapes that grow without cultivation. They have no laws or public assemblies; instead, they dwell in caves atop high mountains, each ruling his own family and paying little heed to their neighbors.

"Off their harbor lies a wooded and fertile island, not far from the land of the Cyclopes, but not too close either. It is filled with wild goats, which breed there in great numbers, undisturbed by human foot; sportsmen—who usually endure much hardship in forests or on mountain cliffs—do not go there. The island remains a wilderness, untilled and unsown year after year, with no living creatures except for goats. The Cyclopes have no ships or shipwrights to build vessels for them, so they cannot travel from city to city or sail across the sea to visit one another as those with ships can. If they had ships, they would colonize the island, for it is excellent and yields bountiful harvests in due season.

"There are meadows that stretch right down to the shore, well-watered and lush with grass. Grapes would thrive there, and there is level land for plowing, always heavy with harvest, for the soil is rich. A fine harbor exists where no cables or anchors are needed; all one must do is beach the vessel and wait until the wind turns fair again. At the head of the harbor is a spring of clear water from a cave, surrounded by poplar trees.

"Here we entered, but so dark was the night that some god must have guided us, for nothing was visible. A thick mist enveloped our ships; the moon was obscured by clouds, making it impossible to see the island even if we had been searching for it. We had no warning of our approach until we found ourselves on land. Once we beached the ships, we took down the sails and camped on the beach until daybreak.

"When rosy-fingered Dawn appeared, we admired the island and explored it, while Jove's daughters, the nymphs, stirred the wild goats so we could have some meat for dinner. We fetched our spears, bows, and arrows from the ships, and divided into three groups to hunt the goats. Fortune favored us; I had twelve ships with me, and each ship caught nine goats, while my own ship caught ten. Thus, throughout the day until sunset, we feasted and drank our fill, with plenty of wine left over from the Cicons, where we had taken many jars full, and this supply had not yet run out. As we feasted, we kept glancing toward the land of the Cyclopes nearby, and we could almost hear their voices and the bleating of their sheep and goats. But as night fell and darkness enveloped us, we camped down on the beach, and the next morning I called a council.

"'Stay here, my brave fellows,' I said, 'while I go with my ship to explore these people myself: I want to see if they are uncivilized savages or a hospitable and humane race.'

"I boarded the ship, instructing my men to do the same and release the hawsers; they took their places and rowed hard across the grey sea. Upon reaching the land, which was close by, we saw a great cave on a cliff near the sea, overhung with laurels.

This cave was home to many sheep and goats, and outside was a large yard enclosed by a high wall made of stones set into the ground and trees, both pine and oak. This was the dwelling of a huge creature who was away from home tending his flocks. He shunned others and lived like an outlaw. He was a terrifying being, not resembling a human at all, but more like a crag standing boldly against the sky atop a high mountain.

"I instructed my men to draw the ship ashore and remain where they were, except for the twelve best among them who would accompany me. I also took a goatskin of sweet black wine given to me by Maron, son of Euanthes, priest of Apollo, the patron god of Ismarus, who lived in the wooded precincts of the temple. When we sacked the city, we respected him and spared his life, along with his wife and child. In gratitude, he presented me with valuable gifts—seven talents of fine gold, a silver bowl, and twelve jars of exquisite wine, unblended. Only he, his wife, and one servant knew about it. When he drank, he mixed twenty parts water to one part wine, and yet the fragrance from the mixing bowl was so wonderful that it was impossible to resist drinking. I filled a large skin with this wine and took a wallet full of provisions, for I feared I might have to contend with a savage who was immensely strong and would respect neither right nor law.

We soon reached his cave, but he was out tending his flocks, so we went inside to explore. His cheese racks were full of cheeses, and he had more lambs and kids than his pens could hold. They were kept in separate flocks: first the hoggets, then the oldest of the younger lambs, and lastly the very young ones. His dairy vessels, bowls, and milk pails were swimming with whey. When my men saw all this, they begged me to let them steal some cheeses and make off with them to the ship. They would then return, drive down the lambs and kids, and sail away with them. It would have been better had we done so, but I wouldn't listen; I wanted to see the owner himself, hoping he might give me a gift. When we finally saw him, my poor men found him hard to deal with.

We lit a fire, offered some cheeses as a sacrifice, ate others, and then waited for the Cyclops to return with his sheep. When he came, he brought a massive load of firewood to light a fire for his supper, which he flung onto the cave floor with such a noise that we hid ourselves in fear at the back of the cavern. He drove in all the ewes and the she-goats he planned to milk, leaving the rams and he-goats outside in the yards. Then he rolled a massive stone to the mouth of the cave—so large that twenty-two strong four-wheeled wagons could not move it from its place. After that, he sat down, milked his ewes and goats in order, and let each have her young one. He curdled half the milk and set it aside in wicker strainers, pouring the other half into bowls to drink for his supper. Once he finished all his work, he lit the fire and spotted us, saying:

"'Strangers, who are you? Where do you sail from? Are you traders, or do you roam the seas as pirates, with your hands against every man, and every man's hand against you?'

We were terrified by his loud voice and monstrous form, but I managed to reply, "We are Achaeans returning home from Troy, but by the will of Jove and harsh weather, we have been driven far off course. We are the people of Agamemnon, son of Atreus, who has earned immense fame by sacking a great city and killing many people. We humbly pray you to show us hospitality and provide us with gifts as visitors may expect. Fear the wrath of heaven, for we are your suppliants, and Jove protects all respectable travelers. He avenges all suppliants and foreigners in distress."

To this, he responded cruelly, "Stranger, you are a fool, or else you know nothing of this land. You talk about fearing the gods or avoiding their wrath? We Cyclopes do not care about Jove or any of your blessed gods, for we are much stronger than they. I shall not spare you or your companions out of any regard for Jove unless I feel inclined to do so. Now tell me, where did you make your ship fast when you came ashore? Was it around the point, or is she lying straight off the land?"

He asked this to draw me out, but I was too clever to be caught like that, so I answered with a lie: "Neptune sent my ship onto the rocks at the far end of your country, and wrecked it. We were driven upon them from the open sea, but I and those who are with me escaped death."

The cruel creature did not reply, but suddenly grabbed two of my men at once and dashed them to the ground as if they were puppies. Their brains spilled upon the ground, and the earth was soaked with their blood. Then he tore them limb from limb and devoured them, consuming flesh, bones, marrow, and entrails without leaving anything behind. We wept and raised our hands to heaven at the sight of such horror, knowing not what else to do. But when the Cyclops had filled his massive belly and washed down his meal with a drink of milk, he lay down among his sheep and fell asleep. I was initially inclined to seize my sword and stab him, but I realized that if I did, we would all certainly perish, as we would never be able to move the stone blocking the entrance. So we stayed, sobbing and sighing, until morning came.

When rosy-fingered Dawn appeared, he lit his fire again, milked his goats and ewes as usual, and let each have her young one. After he completed his tasks, he grabbed two more of my men and began eating them for breakfast. Presently, he rolled the stone away from the door and drove his sheep outside, then replaced it with ease, as though he were simply putting the lid on a quiver full of arrows. After doing this, he shouted and called out to his sheep to drive them up the mountain. I was left to devise a way to take my revenge and secure my glory.

Ultimately, I decided on a plan. The Cyclops had a large club lying near one of the sheep pens; it was made of green olive wood and he had cut it, intending to use it as a staff once it dried. It was so huge that we could only compare it to the mast of a twentyoared merchant vessel capable of venturing into open sea. I approached this club, cut off about six feet of it, and gave this piece to the men, instructing them to fine it evenly at one end. They complied, and I sharpened it, charring the end in the fire to make it harder. I then hid it under dung, which was piled all over the cave, and told my men to draw lots to determine who would venture with me to poke it into the monster's eye while he slept. The lot fell upon the very four I would have chosen, making five of us in total.

In the evening, the creature returned from shepherding and drove all his flocks into the cave this time, not leaving any outside. He must have had some whim or a god must have prompted him to do this. Once he rolled the stone back into place, he sat down, milked his ewes and goats, and let each have her young one. After completing this work, he grabbed two more of my men and devoured them for supper. I approached him with an ivy-wood bowl of black wine in my hands and said:

"'Look here, Cyclops, you have consumed a great deal of human flesh; take this and drink some wine, that you may see what kind of liquor we had on board my ship. I brought it to you as a drink offering, hoping you would take pity on me and help me on my way home, rather than going on rampaging intolerably. You ought to be ashamed; how can you expect people to visit you if you treat them this way?'

He took the cup and drank, delighted by the taste of the wine, begging me for another bowl full. "Be kind," he said, "and give me some more, and tell me your name at once. I want to make you a present that you will be glad to have. We have wine even in this country, for our soil yields grapes and the sun ripens them, but this tastes like Nectar and Ambrosia combined."

I then filled his cup again; three times I filled it for him, and three times he drank without thought or heed. When I saw that the wine had gone to his head, I said as persuasively as I could: "Cyclops, you ask for my name, and I will tell it to you; grant me the present you promised; my name is Noman; that is what my father, mother, and friends have always called me."

The cruel creature replied, "Then I will eat all of Noman's comrades before Noman himself, saving Noman for last. This will be my gift to him."

As he spoke, he fell sprawling, face upwards on the ground. His great neck hung heavily backward, and a deep sleep overtook him. Presently he turned sick, vomiting both wine and the human flesh he had gorged upon, for he was quite drunk. I thrust the beam of wood deep into the embers to heat it and encouraged my men so they wouldn't lose heart. When the green wood was ready to blaze, I drew it from the fire glowing with heat. My men gathered around me, for heaven had filled their hearts with courage. We drove the sharp end of the beam into the monster's eye, and with all my weight, I turned it round and round as if boring a hole in a ship's plank with an auger, which two men can turn for as long as they like. Even so, we worked the red-hot beam into his eye until the boiling blood bubbled all over it as we twisted it, scalding his eyelids and eyebrows, and the roots of his eye sputtered in the fire.

As a blacksmith plunges an axe or hatchet into cold water to temper it—for this gives strength to the iron—and it hisses as he does so, even so did the Cyclops' eye hiss around the olive beam, and his terrible screams echoed through the cave. We fled in fear, but he pulled the bloodied beam from his eye and hurled it away in a fit of rage and pain, shouting to the other Cyclopes living on the bleak headlands nearby. They gathered from all directions when they heard him cry and asked what was wrong.

"'What troubles you, Polyphemus,' they asked, 'that you make such a noise, breaking the stillness of the night and preventing us from sleeping? Surely no man is carrying off your sheep or trying to kill you by trickery or force?'

But Polyphemus shouted back from inside the cave, "Noman is

killing me by trickery; no man is attacking me by force!"

"Then," they replied, "if no man is attacking you, you must be ill. When Jove makes people ill, there is no remedy for it, and you had better pray to your father Neptune."

With that, they left him, and I chuckled inwardly at the success of my clever trick. But the Cyclops, groaning and in agony, felt about until he found the stone and removed it from the entrance. He sat in the doorway, stretching his hands in front of it, hoping to catch anyone trying to escape with his sheep, believing I might be foolish enough to attempt this.

Meanwhile, I kept on pondering how I could save my own life and those of my companions. The danger was great, and I knew I had to think quickly. In the end, I devised a plan: I noticed the male sheep were well grown, carrying heavy black fleece, so I quietly bound them together in threes with the withies that the savage had used to rest on. Each man would hide under a sheep, with the two on either side covering him. I picked the finest ram for myself, caught hold of it from behind, and nestled myself beneath its belly, holding onto its fleece, face upward, and keeping my grip firm.

Thus, we waited in fear until morning came. When rosy-fingered Dawn appeared, the male sheep rushed out to feed, while the ewes remained bleating in the pens, full and heavy with milk. Their master, despite his pain, felt the backs of all the sheep as they stood upright but did not realize that the men were hiding beneath their bellies. As the last ram, heavy with its fleece and with the weight of my crafty self, passed out, Polyphemus laid hold of it, saying:

"My good ram, what makes you the last to leave my cave this morning? You are not accustomed to lag behind the ewes, always leading the flock to the meadows or bubbling springs, and returning home first at night; but now you are last. Is it because you know your master has lost his eye and are sorry for that wicked Noman and his horrid crew? But I will have revenge on him yet. If you could understand and talk, you would tell me where the wretch is hiding, and I would dash his brains out on the ground till they flew all over the cave. Then I would find some satisfaction for the harm that Noman has done me."

As he spoke, he pushed the ram outside. When we were a little way from the cave and the yards, I got free from under the ram and then freed my comrades. We drove the sheep down to the ship. The crew rejoiced at seeing us alive, but they mourned for those lost to the Cyclops. I gestured for them to hush their cries and told them to load the sheep onto the ship quickly and set sail. They hurried on board, took their places, and rowed hard.

Once we were far enough out, I couldn't help but jeer at the Cyclops.

"Cyclops," I called, "you should have thought better before eating my companions in your cave. You wretch! You devour your guests in your own home? Surely you must have known that your sin would find you out. Now Jove and the other gods have punished you."

He grew furious at my taunts, lifted a massive rock, and hurled it toward my ship with tremendous force. It landed just short of the ship, almost striking the end of the rudder. The sea shook as the rock splashed down, and the wave it created swept us back toward the shore. I quickly grabbed a long pole and pushed the ship away, urging my men to row for their lives, and they complied with urgency. We made it twice as far as before when I felt compelled to taunt the Cyclops again, despite my men's pleas to remain silent.

"Cyclops," I yelled, "if anyone asks who it was that blinded you and spoiled your beauty, tell them it was the valiant warrior Ulysses, son of Laertes, who lives in Ithaca!"

He groaned, shouting, "Alas, alas! Then the old prophecy is coming true! There was once a prophet among us, brave and of great stature, Telemus son of Eurymus, who prophesied for the Cyclopes until he grew old. He told me this day would come and that I would lose my sight at the hands of Ulysses. I have been waiting for someone of great strength and presence, yet he turns out to be a weak little man who has tricked me into blindness while I was drunk! Come here, Ulysses, that I may reward you with gifts and urge Neptune to help you on your journey—for he is my father. If he so wishes, he can heal me, which no one else, god or man, can do."

To this, I replied, "I wish I could be as sure of killing you outright and sending you down to Hades, as I am that it will take more than Neptune to heal that eye of yours."

With that, he lifted his hands to the heavens and prayed, "Hear me, great Neptune! If I am indeed your true begotten son, grant that Ulysses never reaches his home alive. Or if he must return to his friends at last, let him do so late and in great distress after losing all his men, and let him arrive in another man's ship to find trouble in his house."

Thus, he prayed, and Neptune heard his plea. He picked up an even larger rock and flung it with incredible force, falling just short of our ship but very close to the end of the rudder. The sea roared as the rock splashed down, and the waves it created pushed us onward toward the island where we had left the rest of our ships.

Upon finally reaching the island, we found our comrades lamenting our fate, anxiously awaiting our return. We beached our vessel and disembarked onto the shore, unloading the Cyclops' sheep, which we divided among us equitably to ensure no one had cause to complain. I received the ram as my extra share; I sacrificed it on the beach, burning its thigh bones to Jove, the lord of all. But he ignored my sacrifice, only thinking of how to destroy my ships and my men.

Thus, we feasted on meat and drink throughout the day until

sunset, and as darkness fell, we camped on the beach. When rosy-fingered Dawn appeared, I ordered my men aboard and to loosen the hawsers. They took their places and smote the grey sea with their oars, sailing on with heavy hearts but relieved to have escaped death despite the loss of our comrades.

BOOK 10:

We then traveled to the Aeolian island, where Aeolus, the son of Hippotas, lives. He is favored by the gods. This island seems to float on the sea, surrounded by a strong wall of iron. Aeolus has six daughters and six strong sons, and he made the sons marry the daughters. They all live happily with their parents, enjoying delicious feasts and all kinds of luxuries. The house is filled with the smell of roasting meat all day, and at night, everyone sleeps in their comfortable beds with their wives. This was where we had come.

Aeolus welcomed me for a whole month, asking me many questions about Troy, the Argive fleet, and how the Achaeans got home. I told him everything that had happened. When it was time for me to leave, I asked for his help, and he was happy to oblige. He gave me a special ox-hide to hold the fierce winds, locking them inside like a sack. You see, he was in charge of the winds and could control them. He put the sack on my ship and tied it shut with a silver thread so no wind could escape. Only the West Wind, which was good for us, was allowed to blow. But it didn't matter, because we lost our way due to our own mistakes.

We sailed for nine days and nights, and on the tenth day, we finally saw our homeland on the horizon. We got close enough to see the fields burning with stubble fires. Exhausted, I fell into a light sleep because I had been steering the ship to get home quickly. Meanwhile, my crew began to whisper among themselves, thinking I was bringing back gold and silver in the sack from Aeolus. One of them said, "Look at how this guy gets all the riches! We've traveled just as far and have nothing to show for it. Let's see what he has in that sack!"

They talked and decided to open the sack. When they did, the winds rushed out, causing a storm that swept us away from our homeland. I woke up, not knowing if I should jump into the sea or just endure it. I stayed in the ship, covering myself, while my men cried out as the winds took us back to Aeolus's island.

When we arrived, we went ashore to get water and ate by the ships. After dinner, I took a messenger and one of my men to Aeolus's house. When we arrived, he was having a feast with his family, and we sat down at the entrance. They were shocked to see us and asked, "Ulysses, what brings you back? What god has treated you badly? We tried to help you get home!"

I replied sadly, "My men have undone me. They and sleep have ruined everything. Please help me fix this mess!"

I spoke as best as I could, but they didn't say much. Then Aeolus spoke up angrily, "You are the worst! Get out of my island! I will not help someone whom the gods hate!" With that, he sent me away, and I left feeling very sad.

We sailed on, tired from rowing with no wind to help us. For six days and nights, we worked hard, and on the seventh day, we reached the rocky place called Telepylus, the city of the Laestrygonians. Here, herdsmen greet each other as they work with their sheep and goats.

When we got to the harbor, we found it was surrounded by steep cliffs, with only a narrow entrance. My captains brought all their ships inside and tied them close together since it was calm. I kept my ship outside, tying it to a rock at the point. I climbed up a tall rock to look around but saw no signs of people, just smoke rising from the ground. So, I sent two men to find out what kind of people lived there.

When my men got ashore, they followed a flat road that the locals used to carry firewood from the mountains. Soon, they met a young woman who was the daughter of a Laestrygonian named Antiphates. She was getting water from a fountain. My men asked her about the king and the people of the land, and she told them to go to her father's house. But when they got there, they were shocked to find that his wife was a giantess!

She called for her husband, and he started attacking my men. He grabbed one of them and began to eat him right away! The other two ran back to the ships as fast as they could, but Antiphates yelled for help, and soon many strong Laestrygonians came out. They threw huge rocks at us like they were nothing, and I heard the awful sound of our ships crashing together and my men screaming as the Laestrygonians speared them like fish to take them home to eat.

While they were attacking my crew, I cut the rope of my own ship and shouted for my men to row for their lives. We made it out into the open water, thankful to have escaped, but we had lost everyone else.

We sailed sadly away, grateful to be alive but mourning our friends, until we reached the island of Aeaea, where Circe lives. She is a powerful goddess and sister to the magician Aeetes, both children of the sun. We brought our ship into a safe harbor without saying a word, guided there by a god. We landed and rested for two days and nights, completely worn out.

On the third day, I took my spear and sword and went to look for signs of people or hear voices. I climbed to a high lookout and saw smoke rising from Circe's house in the middle of a thick forest. I debated whether to investigate further but decided it was better to go back, feed the men, and send some of them instead of going myself.

Just as I was returning to the ship, a god took pity on me and sent a large stag right into my path. It was coming down to drink water, and as it passed, I shot it with my spear. It fell, and I prepared it for dinner. Then I made a strong rope from grass and tied the stag's legs together, hanging it around my neck as I walked back to the ship, supporting it with my spear since it was too heavy to carry.

When I got to the ship, I called my men and said, "Look, friends! We won't die early after all, and we won't starve since we have something to eat!" They uncovered their heads on the shore and admired the stag because it was truly magnificent. After feasting their eyes on it, they washed their hands and began to cook it for dinner.

So, we spent the whole day eating and drinking until sunset, but when it got dark, we camped on the shore. When morning came, I called a meeting and said, "Friends, we are in a tough spot; listen to me. We don't know where the sun rises or sets, so we can't tell east from west. I see no way out of this, but we must try to find one. We are definitely on an island because I climbed high and saw the sea all around us to the horizon. It is low, but in the middle, I saw smoke rising from a thick forest."

The men's hearts sank when they heard me, remembering how the Laestrygonian Antiphates and the fierce giant Polyphemus had treated them. They cried bitterly, but crying wouldn't help, so I split them into two groups and chose a captain for each. I gave one group to Eurylochus and took charge of the other myself. We drew lots to see who would go first, and Eurylochus got the unlucky draw. He set out with twenty-two men, and we all wept for them as they left.

When they arrived at Circe's house, they found it made of cut stones and easy to see from far away, right in the middle of the forest. There were wild wolves and lions wandering around —poor animals who had been enchanted by Circe and made to obey her. The animals didn't attack my men; instead, they wagged their tails and rubbed against them like friendly dogs do when their owner comes home. But the men were scared to see such strange creatures. Eventually, they reached the gates of Circe's house and heard her beautiful singing as she worked at her loom, creating a soft, colorful web that only a goddess could weave.

Polites, one of my most trusted men, said, "There's someone inside working at a loom and singing beautifully! Let's call her and see if she's a woman or a goddess."

They called out to her, and she came down, opened the door, and invited them in. They followed her without thinking twice, except for Eurylochus, who was suspicious and stayed outside. Once inside her home, Circe made them sit down and mixed them a drink with cheese, honey, flour, and wine, but she had poisoned it to make them forget their homes. After they drank, she waved her wand, and they turned into pigs, trapped in her pigsty. They looked like pigs, but they still remembered everything that had happened.

As they squealed in their pigsty, Circe tossed them acorns to eat. Meanwhile, Eurylochus hurried back to tell me about what had happened to our friends. He was so shaken that he could hardly speak; tears filled his eyes, and he sobbed until we got him to share the story.

"We went through the forest as you told us," he said, "and found a beautiful house made of cut stones in a clearing. Inside, we saw a woman, or maybe she was a goddess, working at her loom and singing sweetly. The others called to her and went in, but I stayed behind because I thought something was wrong. After that, I never saw them again, even though I waited a long time."

I grabbed my bronze sword and slung it over my shoulder. I told Eurylochus to show me the way back, but he held onto me tightly, pleading, "Please don't make me go with you! Let me stay here. You won't bring any of them back, and you might not come back yourself! Let's try to escape with the few of us that are left!"

"Stay here and eat and drink by the ship if you want," I replied. "But I must go; I need to."

With that, I left the ship and went up into the land. As I walked through the enchanted grove and neared Circe's house, I met Mercury, who had a golden wand. He looked like a handsome young man with a bit of facial hair. He took my hand and said, "My poor friend, where are you going alone over this mountain? Your men are trapped in Circe's pigsties like wild boars. Do you really think you can save them? I'm afraid you won't be able to escape and will end up stuck there too. But don't worry; I'll help you.

"Take this special herb with you to protect yourself from her magic. She will try to make you drink a potion and use a drug in her food, but you will resist because of this herb. When she strikes you with her wand, draw your sword and rush at her as if you are going to kill her. She will be scared and will ask you to sleep with her. Don't refuse her right away, because you want her to free your friends and to keep yourself safe. But you must make her promise not to plot any more harm against you. If you don't, she will unman you and make you useless."

He showed me the herb, which had a black root and a white flower. The gods call it Moly, and mortals can't uproot it, but the gods can.

Mercury then returned to Olympus, and I continued to Circe's house, feeling worried as I walked. When I got to the gates, I called for Circe. She heard me and came down, opened the door, and asked me to come in. I followed her, troubled in my mind. She sat me on a beautifully decorated seat and mixed a drink for me in a golden goblet. But she had poisoned it, wanting to do me harm. After I drank and didn't feel enchanted, she struck me with her wand and said, "Get back to the pigsty and join the others!"

But I charged at her with my sword drawn, ready to attack. She screamed and fell to her knees, holding onto me. "Who are you? Where do you come from? How can my magic not work on you? No man has ever resisted my spells before! You must be the brave Ulysses that Mercury said would come here someday!"

"Circe," I replied, "how can you expect me to trust you after you turned all my men into pigs? Now that you've caught me, you want to do me harm by asking me to sleep with you. I will not agree unless you promise not to harm me anymore."

She quickly swore the oath, and when she finished, I agreed to sleep with her.

Meanwhile, her four servants, who were like maidens of the woods and waters, began to work. One laid out a fine purple cloth on a seat and put a carpet underneath. Another brought silver tables and set them with golden baskets. A third mixed sweet wine with water in a silver bowl and put golden cups on the tables. The fourth brought water to boil in a large cauldron over a fire. When the water was ready, she mixed it with cold water just how I liked it, then set me in the bath and washed me, easing the tiredness from my body. After she had finished washing and anointing me with oil, she dressed me in a fine cloak and shirt and led me to a beautifully decorated seat with a footstool under my feet.

One maid brought water in a golden pitcher and poured it into a silver basin for me to wash my hands. Another set a clean table beside me with bread and many delicious things. Circe then urged me to eat, but I wouldn't touch the food; I just sat there, gloomy and suspicious.

Seeing me sad and not eating, Circe came to me and asked, "Ulysses, why are you sitting there like you're in a daze, refusing to eat or drink? Are you still suspicious? You shouldn't be; I've sworn that I won't hurt you."

I replied, "Circe, no sensible person can eat or drink in your house until you free my friends and let me see them. If you want me to eat and drink, you must bring my men to me so I can see them with my own eyes."

After I spoke, she went through the court with her wand and

opened the pigsty doors. My men came out, looking like pigs and stood there staring at her. Circe walked among them, anointing each with a second potion, and the bristles from the first spell fell away. They became men again, younger and better-looking than before. They recognized me, grabbed my hands, and wept for joy, filling the house with their cheers. Circe felt sorry for them too and said, "Ulysses, noble son of Laertes, go back to the sea where you left your ship. First, pull it onto the land, then hide all your gear and belongings in a cave, and come back here with your men."

I agreed and returned to the shore, finding the men at the ship, crying and wailing. When they saw me, they leaped around me joyfully like calves dancing around their mothers after a long day of grazing. They were as happy as if they had just returned home to Ithaca, where they were born. "Sir," they said, "we're so glad to see you! Tell us what happened to our friends."

I comforted them, saying, "We need to pull the ship onto the land and hide our belongings in a cave. Then come with me to Circe's house, where you'll find our friends eating and drinking with plenty of food."

The men wanted to come with me right away, but Eurylochus tried to stop them, saying, "Oh no, what will happen to us? Don't rush to your doom by going to Circe's house, where she'll turn us all into pigs or wolves or lions, and we'll have to guard her home. Remember how the Cyclops treated us when our friends went into his cave, and Ulysses was with them? It was his foolishness that got those men killed."

Hearing this made me consider whether I should draw my sword and cut off Eurylochus's head, even though he was a relative. But the men pleaded for him, saying, "Sir, if you can, let him stay here to watch the ship. Take the rest of us to Circe's house."

So, we all went inland, and Eurylochus ended up coming along too, scared by the reprimand I had given him.

Meanwhile, Circe had been taking care of the men who stayed behind. She washed them, anointed them with olive oil, and gave them warm cloaks and shirts. When we arrived, we found them having a nice dinner in her house. As soon as they saw each other and recognized one another, they cried tears of joy, and their voices filled the palace. Circe came up to me and said, "Ulysses, noble son of Laertes, tell your men to stop crying. I know how much you've all suffered at sea and how poorly you've been treated by cruel people on the mainland, but that is all in the past now. Stay here and enjoy food and drink until you are as strong and healthy as you were when you left Ithaca. You've been through so much that you've lost your cheerfulness."

We agreed with her, and we stayed with Circe for a whole year, feasting on endless meat and wine. But when the year was over, my men called me aside and said, "Sir, it's time to think about going home. We want to see our house and homeland again if we can."

I agreed with them. So we spent the whole day feasting until the sun set. When it got dark, the men settled down to sleep in the covered porches. I, however, after getting into bed with Circe, begged her at her knees to keep her promise about helping me get home. I said, "Circe, please help me and my men. They keep bothering me about getting back home whenever you're not around."

The goddess replied, "Ulysses, noble son of Laertes, you won't have to stay here any longer if you don't want to. But there is another journey you must take before you can sail home. You need to go to the house of Hades and speak to the ghost of the blind prophet Teiresias, who still has his wits about him. Proserpine has left him his understanding, but the other ghosts wander about lost."

I was shocked to hear this. I sat up in bed and cried, wishing I could just end my life and never see the sun again. But after a while, when I stopped crying and tossing around, I said, "Who will guide me on this journey? The house of Hades is a place no ship can reach."

"You won't need a guide," she answered. "Raise your mast, set your white sails, and just sit still. The North Wind will take you there. When your ship crosses the Oceanus, you will arrive at Proserpine's land, which has tall poplar and willow trees. There, beach your ship on the Oceanus shore and head straight to the dark home of Hades. It's near where the rivers Pyriphlegethon and Cocytus flow into Acheron, and there will be a rock where the two roaring rivers meet.

"When you reach that spot, dig a trench about a cubit long, wide, and deep, and pour a drink offering for the dead. First, mix honey with milk, then wine, and finally water, sprinkling white barley meal on top. You should offer many prayers to the weak ghosts and promise that when you return to Ithaca, you will sacrifice a barren heifer, the best you have, and pile the pyre with good things. Most importantly, promise that Teiresias will get a black sheep all to himself, the finest from your flock.

"After you've prayed, offer a ram and a black ewe, bending their heads towards Erebus, but turn away from them as if you are going to the river. This will bring many dead ghosts to you. Tell your men to skin the two sheep you just killed and offer them as a burnt sacrifice with prayers to Hades and Proserpine. Then draw your sword and sit there to keep any other ghosts from coming near the spilled blood until Teiresias answers your questions. He will tell you about your journey and how to sail home."

It was daybreak by the time she finished speaking, so she dressed me in my shirt and cloak. She put on a lovely light fabric over her shoulders, tied it with a golden belt, and covered her head with a mantle. I then walked around the house, speaking kindly to each man: "You can't stay sleeping here any longer; we must go, for Circe has told me what we need to do." They obeyed me.

But even so, I didn't get them away without trouble. We had a young man named Elpenor with us, who wasn't very brave or smart. He had gotten drunk and was lying on the roof, trying to sleep it off in the cool air. When he heard the noise of the men getting ready, he jumped up, forgot how to get down, and fell off the roof, breaking his neck. His spirit went down to the house of Hades.

When I gathered the men together, I said, "You think we are about to head home, but Circe has told me we must go to the house of Hades and Proserpine to consult the ghost of the prophet Teiresias."

The men were heartbroken to hear this. They fell to the ground, groaning and tearing their hair, but crying wouldn't change anything. When we reached the shore, we were weeping and lamenting our fate. Circe brought us a ram and a ewe, which we tied near the ship. She moved through us without us noticing because no one can see a god unless the god wants to be seen.

BOOK 11:

Then, when we reached the shore, we pulled our ship into the water, set up her mast and sails, and loaded the sheep on board. We took our places, weeping and feeling very sad. Circe, the clever goddess, sent us a fair wind that blew steadily behind us, keeping our sails filled. We did what we needed to do with the ship's gear and let her go as the wind and helmsman directed. All day long, the sails were full as we sailed over the sea. When the sun set and darkness fell, we entered the deep waters of the Oceanus River, where the land and city of the Cimmerians lay. They lived in mist and darkness that the sun's rays never pierced, neither at sunrise nor sunset, so these poor souls lived in a never-ending night.

Once we reached that place, we beached the ship, took the sheep out, and walked along the waters of Oceanus until we found the spot Circe had described. Here, Perimedes and Eurylochus held the sheep while I drew my sword and dug a trench about a cubit long and wide. I made a drink offering to all the dead, starting with honey and milk, then wine, and finally water, sprinkling white barley meal over everything. I prayed earnestly to the weak ghosts and promised that when I returned to Ithaca, I would sacrifice a barren heifer, the best I had, and fill the pyre with good things. I also promised that Teiresias would receive a black sheep all to himself, the finest from my flock.

After I prayed to the dead, I cut the throats of the two sheep and let their blood run into the trench. Soon, the ghosts began to gather from Erebus—brides, young men, tired old men, maids who had been hurt in love, and brave warriors who had died in battle, their armor still stained with blood. They came from every direction, surrounding the trench with a strange, eerie sound that made me pale with fear. I told the men to hurry and flay the carcasses of the sheep to make burnt offerings, while I kept my sword drawn to prevent the ghosts from coming near the blood until Teiresias had answered my questions.

The first ghost to arrive was Elpenor, my comrade, who had not yet been buried. We had left his body unburied in Circe's house because we had too much to do. I felt very sorry for him and cried when I saw him. "Elpenor," I said, "how did you end up here in this darkness? You got here on foot faster than I did with my ship."

"Sir," he groaned, "it was bad luck and my own foolish drunkenness. I was lying asleep on the roof of Circe's house, and I forgot to come down the stairs. I fell off the roof and broke my neck, so my soul came to the house of Hades. I beg you, for the sake of those you have left behind, even though they are not here, for your wife, your father who raised you, and for Telemachus, your only hope, do what I ask. I know that when you leave this place, you will return to the Aeaean island. Don't leave me unburied behind. Burn me with whatever armor I have, build a mound for me on the shore, so that in the future people will know what a poor, unlucky fellow I was, and plant my rowing oar over my grave." I promised him, "My poor friend, I will do everything you've asked."

We sat and talked sadly, I on one side of the trench with my sword over the blood, and Elpenor's ghost on the other side. Then the ghost of my mother, Anticlea, came. I had left her alive when I set out for Troy, and seeing her moved me to tears, but even in my sorrow, I wouldn't let her come near the blood until I had asked my questions of Teiresias.

Next came the ghost of the Theban prophet Teiresias, holding a golden scepter. He recognized me and said, "Ulysses, noble son of Laertes, why have you left the light of day to visit the dead in this sad place? Step back from the trench and put away your sword so

I can drink the blood and answer your questions truthfully."

I stepped back and sheathed my sword. After he drank the blood, he began to prophesy. "You want to know about your return home, but heaven will make this difficult for you. I doubt you will escape the wrath of Neptune, who still holds a grudge against you for blinding his son. Still, after much suffering, you might get home if you can control yourself and your crew when you reach Thrinacian Island, where the sun's sheep and cattle graze. If you leave them unharmed and focus only on getting home, you may eventually reach Ithaca. But if you harm them, I warn you of the destruction of your ship and your men. Even if you escape, you will return in bad shape, having lost all your men, in another ship, and you will find trouble in your house, which will be overrun by powerful people who are consuming your wealth under the pretense of courting your wife.

"When you get home, you will take your revenge on these suitors. After you kill them, either by force or trickery in your own house, you must take a well-made oar and carry it until you reach a place where people have never seen the sea and don't even know how to use salt in their food. They won't know anything about ships or oars, which are like the wings of a ship. I will give you a sign that you cannot miss: a traveler will meet you and say that you must have a winnowing shovel on your shoulder. You will then plant the oar in the ground and sacrifice a ram, a bull, and a boar to Neptune. Then go home and offer sacrifices to all the gods of heaven, one by one. As for yourself, you will die from the sea, but your death will come gently when you are old and at peace, and your people will bless you. Everything I have said will come true."

I replied, "Let it be as heaven wishes, but please tell me, why does my mother's ghost sit by the blood without speaking? She doesn't recognize me, even though I am her son. How can I make her know me?"

"I can tell you how to do that," he replied. "Any ghost that tastes the blood will talk to you like a living person, but if you don't let them drink, they will leave."

With that, Teiresias returned to the house of Hades, having shared his prophecies. I waited until my mother approached and tasted the blood. As soon as she did, she recognized me and said fondly, "My son, how did you end up in this dark place while still alive? It is hard for the living to see this realm, for between us lies the great and terrible waters of Oceanus, which no one can cross on foot. You must have a good ship to take you. Have you been trying to find your way home from Troy and not yet returned to Ithaca or seen your wife in your own house?"

"Mother," I replied, "I came here to consult the ghost of the Theban prophet Teiresias. I haven't been to Achaean land nor set foot in my homeland. I've had nothing but misfortunes since the day I left with Agamemnon for Ilius to fight the Trojans. But tell me, how did you die? Did you suffer a long illness, or did heaven grant you a gentle death? Also, tell me about my father and the son I left behind. Is my property still safe with them, or has someone else taken it, thinking I will not return? What is my wife planning to do? Does she live with my son and protect my estate, or has she remarried?"

My mother replied, "Your wife still stays in your house, but she is very sad and spends her days and nights in tears. No one has taken your property, and Telemachus still holds your lands. He must entertain many guests, considering his position as a leader. Your father remains in the countryside and doesn't go into town. He has no comfortable bed or bedding; in the winter, he sleeps on the floor by the fire with the workers and wears rags. In summer, when it gets warm, he sleeps in the vineyard on a bed of vine leaves thrown on the ground. He is grieving because you haven't come home and suffers more as he grows older. As for my death, it wasn't swift or painless; I was not taken by an illness like those that usually wear people out. It was my longing to know what you were doing and my love for you that ultimately caused my death."

Then I tried to find a way to embrace my poor mother's ghost. Three times I sprang towards her, trying to hold her in my arms, but each time she slipped away from my grasp like a dream or a phantom. Hurt and confused, I said, "Mother, why do you not stay still when I want to embrace you? If we could hold each other, we might find some comfort in sharing our sorrows, even here in Hades. Is Proserpine trying to add to my grief by mocking me with only a shadow?"

"My son," she replied, "most unfortunate of all mankind, it is not Proserpine deceiving you. All spirits behave like this once they are dead. The sinews no longer hold the flesh and bones together; they perish in the fierce flames after life has left the body, and the soul drifts away like a dream. Now, go back to the light of day as soon as you can, and remember all these things to share with your wife later."

We continued to converse, and soon Proserpine sent up the ghosts of the wives and daughters of the most famous men. They gathered around the blood, and I considered how to question them individually. In the end, I decided it would be best to draw my sharp sword and keep them from all drinking the blood at once. So they came one after another, and each one told me her lineage as I questioned her.

The first I saw was Tyro, daughter of Salmoneus and wife of Cretheus, son of Aeolus. She fell in love with the beautiful river Enipeus. One day, while walking by the river, Neptune, disguised as her lover, lay with her at the river's mouth. A huge wave rose like a mountain to cover them both, and he loosened her virgin girdle, putting her into a deep sleep. When he had finished, he took her hand and said, "Tyro, be happy; the embraces of the gods are not in vain, and in a year, you will have beautiful twins. Take good care of them. I am Neptune; now go home and don't tell anyone."

Then he dived under the sea, and she later gave birth to Pelias and Neleus, who served Jove well. Pelias became a great sheep breeder in Iolcus, while Neleus lived in Pylos. The rest of her children were with Cretheus: Aeson, Pheres, and Amythaon, a mighty warrior and charioteer.

Next, I saw Antiope, daughter of Asopus, who could boast of having slept with Jove himself. She bore him two sons, Amphion and Zethus, who founded Thebes and built its seven gates. Strong as they were, they couldn't hold Thebes until they had built a wall around it.

Then I saw Alcmena, the wife of Amphitryon, who also bore Jove the indomitable Hercules; and Megara, daughter of King Creon, who married the powerful son of Amphitryon.

I also saw Epicaste, mother of King Oedipus, who married her own son without knowing it. He married her after killing his father, but the gods revealed the whole truth, so he remained king of Thebes, filled with sorrow for the gods' spite. Epicaste hanged herself in grief, and the avenging spirits haunted him for the loss of his mother.

Next, I saw Chloris, whom Neleus married for her beauty, having given great gifts for her. She was the youngest daughter of Amphion, king of Orchomenus, and was queen in Pylos. She bore Nestor, Chromius, and Periclymenus, as well as the beautiful Pero, who was sought after by many suitors. But Neleus would only give her to the man who could raid the cattle of Iphicles. This was a hard task, and the only one willing to do it was an excellent seer. However, heaven was against him, and the cattle keepers caught him and imprisoned him. After a year had passed, Iphicles released him after he had explained all the prophecies.

Then I saw Leda, wife of Tyndarus, who bore him two famous sons, Castor the horseman and Pollux the mighty boxer. Both heroes lie under the earth but are still alive; thanks to a special favor from Jove, they die and come back to life every other day for all time, and they are honored as gods.

After her, I saw Iphimedeia, wife of Aloeus, who boasted of Neptune's embrace. She bore two sons, Otus and Ephialtes, who were short-lived but the finest-looking children ever born, except for Orion. At nine years old, they stood nine fathoms tall and measured nine cubits around the chest. They threatened to wage war against the gods in Olympus and tried to stack Mount Ossa on top of Mount Olympus and Mount Pelion on top of Ossa to reach heaven, and they would have succeeded if they had grown up, but Apollo killed them before they could even grow hair on their cheeks.

Then I saw Phaedra, Procris, and fair Ariadne, daughter of the magician Minos. Theseus was carrying her off from Crete to Athens, but before he could enjoy her, Diana killed her on the island of Dia because of what Bacchus had said against her.

I also saw Maera and Clymene, as well as the hateful Eriphyle, who sold her husband for gold. But if I were to name every single wife and daughter of heroes I saw, it would take me all night. Now it's time for me to go to bed, either on the ship with my crew or here. As for my escort, heaven and you will take care of it."

With that, he finished speaking, and the guests were left captivated and silent throughout the covered cloister. Then Arete said to them:

"What do you think of this man, O Phaeacians? Is he not tall and handsome, and clever? True, he is my guest, but you all share in the honor. Do not rush to send him away, nor be stingy with the gifts you give to someone in such great need, for heaven has blessed all of you with abundance."

Then spoke the aged hero Echeneus, one of the oldest among them. "My friends," he said, "what our esteemed queen has just said is both wise and sensible. Let us listen to her; but the decision, whether in word or deed, ultimately rests with King

Alcinous."

"It shall be done," exclaimed Alcinous, "as surely as I live and reign over the Phaeacians. Our guest is eager to return home, but we must persuade him to stay until tomorrow. By then, I will gather the gifts I plan to give him. As for his escort, that will be for all of you, and especially for me as the chief among you."

Ulysses replied, "King Alcinous, if you were to ask me to stay here for a whole twelve months and then send me on my way, loaded with your noble gifts, I would gladly accept. It would greatly benefit me, as I would return to my people with more to offer and be better respected by all who see me when I get back to Ithaca."

"Ulysses," Alcinous said, "none of us who sees you believes you are a charlatan or a fraud. Many people wander around telling stories that seem true, making it hard to see through them, but your language shows your good character. You've told the tale of your misfortunes and those of the Argives as if you were a practiced bard. But tell me, did you see any of the mighty heroes who went to Troy with you and perished there? The evenings are still long, and it is not yet bedtime—continue your divine story, for I could listen until morning as long as you keep sharing your adventures."

"Alcinous," Ulysses answered, "there is a time for speaking and a time for sleep; but since you desire it, I will share with you the sad tale of my comrades who did not fall fighting the Trojans but perished on their return through the treachery of a wicked woman.

When Proserpine had sent away the female ghosts, the ghost of Agamemnon, son of Atreus, came to me, surrounded by those who had perished with him in Aegisthus's house. As soon as he tasted the blood, he recognized me and wept bitterly, stretching out his arms to embrace me; but he had no strength or substance anymore, and I too wept for him. "How did you die, King

Agamemnon?" I asked. "Did Neptune raise his winds and waves against you at sea, or did your enemies kill you on land when you were raiding cattle or sheep, or fighting to defend their wives and cities?"

"Ulysses," he replied, "noble son of Laertes, I was not lost at sea in a storm nor slain by my enemies on land. It was Aegisthus and my wicked wife who caused my death. He invited me to his house, feasted me, and then butchered me like a fat beast in a slaughterhouse, while my comrades were killed around me like sheep or pigs for a wedding feast. You may have seen many men die in battle, but you have never witnessed anything as truly pitiable as how we fell in that cloister, with the mixing bowls and loaded tables all around, the ground soaked with our blood. I heard Priam's daughter Cassandra scream as Clytemnestra killed her beside me. I lay dying on the ground with a sword in my body, reaching out to kill the murderous woman, but she slipped away and wouldn't even close my lips or eyes as I died. Nothing in this world is as cruel and shameless as a woman who has committed such a crime. Fancy, murdering her own husband! I thought I would be welcomed home by my children and servants, but her horrible actions have brought disgrace upon herself and all women who will come after, even upon the good ones."

I said, "Truly, Jove has hated the house of Atreus from the beginning when it comes to their women's advice. Look how many of us fell for Helen, and now it seems Clytemnestra plotted against you during your absence."

"Therefore," Agamemnon continued, "be careful not to be too friendly even with your own wife. Don't tell her everything you know; share only part of it and keep the rest to yourself. Not that your wife, Ulysses, is likely to kill you—Penelope is a wonderful woman with a good nature. We left her a young bride nursing an infant when we went to Troy. That child must be a man now, and he and his father will have a joyful reunion, whereas my wicked wife didn't even let me see my son before she killed me. Furthermore, listen closely: do not tell anyone when you are bringing your ship to Ithaca; sneak in quietly, for you cannot trust women. But now tell me, do you have any news of my son Orestes? Is he in Orchomenus, Pylos, or Sparta with Menelaus? I presume he is still alive."

I replied, "Agamemnon, why do you ask me? I don't know if your son is alive or dead, and it's not right to speak about what you don't know."

As we sat weeping and talking sadly, the ghost of Achilles approached us with Patroclus, Antilochus, and Ajax, the mightiest and handsomest of all the Danaans after the son of Peleus. The great descendant of Aeacus recognized me and spoke sadly, saying, "Ulysses, noble son of Laertes, what daring deed brings you to the house of Hades among us spirits who can do no more labor?"

I answered, "Achilles, son of Peleus, foremost champion of the Achaeans, I came to consult Teiresias to see if he could advise me on my return home to Ithaca, for I have never been able to set foot in my own country and have been in trouble all the time. As for you, Achilles, no one has ever been as fortunate as you, nor will anyone be. You were loved by all of us Argives while you were alive, and now you are a great prince among the dead. So don't let it trouble you too much that you are dead."

"Do not speak well of death," he replied. "I would rather be a paid servant in a poor man's house and live above ground than be king of kings among the dead. But tell me about my son; has he gone to war and become a great warrior, or not? Also, what of my father Peleus? Does he still rule among the Myrmidons, or has he lost respect throughout Hellas and Phthia now that he is old and frail? If I could stand by his side in the light of day, with the same strength I had when I killed our bravest foes on the plains of Troy, I would defend him fiercely against anyone who tried to do him harm."

"I have heard nothing of Peleus," I answered, "but I can tell you about your son Neoptolemus. I took him in my ship from Scyros with the Achaeans. In our councils before Troy, he was always the first to speak, and his judgment was true. Nestor and I were the only ones who could surpass him. In battle, he never stayed with his men but rushed ahead, always the bravest. Many did he kill; I cannot name them all, but I will say he killed the valiant hero Eurypylus, son of Telephus, who was the most handsome man I ever saw, except for Memnon. Many Ceteians fell around him due to a woman's bribes. Moreover, when the bravest of the Argives went inside the horse that Epeus built, and it was left to me to decide when to open the door or close it, although the other leaders were frightened, Neoptolemus did not flinch or wipe a tear. He urged me to break out of the horse, ready for battle with his sword and spear. Yet after we sacked Priam's city, he took his fair share of the spoils and went aboard without a wound, neither from a spear nor in close combat, for the rage of war is unpredictable."

When I finished speaking, Achilles strode off across a meadow of asphodel, pleased with my words about his son's bravery.

The ghosts of other dead men surrounded me, each telling their own sad stories, but Ajax, son of Telamon, stood apart—still angry with me for winning the armor of Achilles in our dispute. Thetis had offered it as a prize, but the Trojan prisoners and Minerva were the judges. If only I had never won that contest, for it cost us Ajax, who was the strongest of all the Danaans after Achilles, both in stature and strength.

When I saw him, I tried to make peace, saying, "Ajax, will you not forgive me even in death? Must you still hold onto your anger about that cursed armor? We mourned you as much as we mourned Achilles himself, and the blame lies not with you but with Jove's spite against the Danaans, which led to your destruction. Come here, let go of your pride, and listen to what I can tell you."

He didn't respond but turned away to Erebus and the other ghosts. I would have continued speaking to him despite his anger, but I wanted to see more of the dead.

Then I saw Minos, son of Jove, holding his golden scepter and sitting in judgment over the dead. The ghosts gathered around him, sitting and standing in the spacious house of Hades to hear his judgments.

After him, I saw huge Orion in a meadow of asphodel, driving the ghosts of the wild beasts he had killed on the mountains. He held a great bronze club that could never break.

I also saw Tityus, son of Gaia, stretched out over nine acres of ground. Two vultures pecked at his liver, and he tried to fend them off with his hands but couldn't; he had violated Leto, Jove's mistress, as she passed through Panopeus on her way to Pytho.

I witnessed the dreadful fate of Tantalus, standing in a lake up to his chin. He was dying of thirst, but could never drink, for whenever he stooped, the water vanished, leaving only dry ground—parched by heaven's wrath. Tall trees above him shed their fruit—pears, pomegranates, apples, sweet figs, and juicy olives—but whenever he reached out, the branches would pull away, back to the clouds.

Then I saw Sisyphus, engaged in his endless task of rolling a huge stone uphill. He pushed with all his strength, but just as he was about to roll it over the top, it would roll back down, and he would have to start all over, sweating as he struggled.

After him, I saw the mighty Hercules, but only his phantom, for he feasts with the immortal gods now, married to lovely Hebe, daughter of Jove and Juno. The ghosts surrounded him, crying out like frightened birds. He looked fierce, his bow in hand and an arrow on the string, ready to aim. Around his chest was a wondrous golden belt adorned with bears, wild boars, and lions, and scenes of war, battle, and death. The man who made that belt could never replicate it. Hercules recognized me immediately and spoke sadly, saying, "My poor Ulysses, noble son of Laertes, are you also leading the same wretched life I did when I was alive? I was the son of Jove, but endured endless suffering, forced into servitude by a man far beneath me—one who gave me many tasks. He even sent me here to fetch the hellhound, thinking it would be the hardest task for me, but I managed to bring it back with the help of Mercury and Minerva."

With that, Hercules went back down into Hades, but I stayed where I was, hoping to see more of the great dead. I wanted to see Theseus and Pirithous, glorious children of the gods, but so many thousands of spirits surrounded me, crying out in despair, that I feared Proserpine might send up the head of that terrifying Gorgon. So, I hurried back to my ship and ordered my men to board immediately and untie the mooring lines. They got on and took their places, and the ship began to drift down the river Oceanus. We rowed at first, but soon a fair wind sprang up.

BOOK 12:

After we were clear of the river Oceanus and out in the open sea, we continued until we reached the Aeaean island, where dawn and sunrise are like anywhere else. We then pulled our ship onto the sand and got out onto the shore, where we went to sleep and waited for daybreak.

When rosy-fingered Dawn appeared, I sent some men to Circe's house to fetch the body of Elpenor. We cut firewood from a nearby grove and, after wept over him and lamented his loss, we performed his funeral rites. Once we burned his body and armor to ashes, we raised a mound, set a stone over it, and placed his rowing oar on top.

While we were doing this, Circe, knowing we had returned from the house of Hades, dressed herself and hurried to us, accompanied by her maidservants who brought bread, meat, and wine. She stood among us and said, "You have done a brave thing by going down alive to the house of Hades; you will have experienced death twice while others only once. Now, stay here for the rest of the day, feast to your heart's content, and set sail at daybreak tomorrow. Meanwhile, I will tell Ulysses about your journey and explain everything to him to prevent any misadventures, whether by land or sea."

We agreed to follow her advice and feasted throughout the day until the sun set. When it was dark, the men lay down to sleep by the ship's stern. Circe took me by the hand and led me to sit away from the others while she reclined by my side and asked about our adventures.

"So far so good," she said when I finished my story, "but now pay attention to what I am about to tell you; heaven itself will remind you of it. First, you will encounter the Sirens, who enchant anyone who comes near. If anyone unwittingly gets too close and hears their singing, he will never return home to his wife and children. They sit in a green meadow and sing sweetly, luring men to their doom. There is a great pile of dead men's bones around them, with flesh still rotting off. Therefore, sail past the Sirens and stop your men's ears with wax so that none of them can hear. But if you wish to listen yourself, have your men bind you standing upright on the mast and lash the ends of the ropes to the mast itself. If you beg them to set you free, they must bind you tighter.

"Once your crew has passed the Sirens, I cannot give you clear instructions on which of two paths to take; I will present both options, and you must choose. On one side, there are steep rocks where the fierce waves of Amphitrite crash. The blessed gods call these rocks the Wanderers. No bird can pass them, not even the doves that bring ambrosia to Father Jove. The rocks always catch one, forcing Jove to send another to replace it. No ship that has ever approached these rocks has escaped; the waves and whirlwinds are filled with wreckage and dead bodies. The only ship to have made it through was the famous Argo on her way from the house of Aetes, and even she would have perished if Juno had not guided her past for the love she bore to Jason.

"Of these two rocks, one reaches to the heavens, its peak lost in a dark cloud that never clears, even in summer. No man could climb it; it is too steep and smooth as if polished. There is a large cave in the middle, facing west towards Erebus; you must steer your ship this way, but the cave is so high that no archer could shoot into it. Inside, Scylla sits and yelps, her voice like that of a young hound, but she is a dreadful monster. She has twelve shapeless feet and six long necks, with a frightening head at the end of each neck, three rows of teeth in each, ready to devour anyone who comes close. She waits in her dark lair, sticking out her heads and looking for dolphins or larger prey from the many that swim in the sea. No ship has ever passed without losing men, as she strikes out with all her heads at once and snatches a man in each mouth.

"You will find the other rock lower, but they are so close together that there is barely a bowshot between them. A large fig tree grows on it, and beneath it lies the swirling whirlpool of Charybdis. Three times a day she spits out her waters, and three times she sucks them back down; you must not be there when she sucks, for if you are, not even Neptune could save you. You must hug the side of Scylla and drive your ship past as quickly as possible, for it is better to lose six men than your entire crew."

"Is there no way," I asked, "to escape Charybdis while keeping Scylla from harming my men?"

"Impulsive one," the goddess replied, "you always want to fight, even against the immortals. Scylla is not mortal; she is savage, ruthless, and invincible. There's no way to protect your men from her. The best chance is to get past her as fast as you can; if you linger near her rock while you're preparing for battle, she may catch you with a second strike and take another half-dozen of your men. So hurry past her and call out loudly to Crataiis, Scylla's mother, to help you, and she will keep Scylla from making a second attack."

"You will then come to the Thrinacian island, where you will see many herds of cattle and flocks of sheep belonging to the sun-god—seven herds of cattle and seven flocks of sheep, with fifty in each flock. They do not breed nor decrease in number, and they are tended by the goddesses Phaethusa and Lampetie, daughters of the sun-god Hyperion and Neaera. Their mother sent them to Thrinacian island to look after their father's herds. If you leave these flocks unharmed and focus only on getting home, you may eventually reach Ithaca after much hardship; but if you harm them, I warn you of the destruction of both your ship and your crew. Even if you escape, you will return late and in poor condition, having lost all your men."

With that, she finished speaking, and dawn, crowned in gold, began to rise in the sky as she returned inland. I then went aboard and told my men to untie the ship. They got on quickly, took their places, and began to row through the gray sea. Soon, the great and cunning goddess Circe favored us with a fair wind blowing directly behind us, keeping our sails well filled. We did whatever needed to be done with the ship's gear and let her sail according to the wind and the helmsman's direction.

Feeling troubled, I addressed my men, "My friends, it's not right that only one or two of us should know the prophecies Circe has shared. I will tell you everything so that whether we live or die, we do so with our eyes wide open. First, she warned us to steer clear of the Sirens, who sit and sing beautifully in a meadow of flowers. But she said I could listen myself as long as no one else did. So, bind me to the mast, standing upright, with ropes so strong that I cannot break free, and lash the ends to the mast itself. If I beg you to let me go, bind me even tighter."

I had barely finished telling the men everything when we reached the island of the two Sirens, for the wind had been very favorable. Suddenly, the wind fell dead calm; there was not a breath of air nor a ripple on the water. The men furled the sails and stowed them, then took to their oars, churning the water into foam as they rowed. Meanwhile, I took a large wheel of wax and cut it into small pieces with my sword. I kneaded the wax in my strong hands until it became soft, warmed by the sun's rays. I then plugged the ears of all my men with the wax and had them bind me, hands and feet, to the mast as I stood upright. They continued to row.

As we got within earshot of the shore, and the ship was moving quickly, the Sirens saw us approaching and began to sing.

"'Come here,' they sang, 'renowned Ulysses, honor of the Achaean name, and listen to our sweet voices. No one has ever sailed past us without stopping to hear the enchanting beauty of our song—and those who listen leave not only charmed but wiser. We know all the troubles the gods brought upon the Argives and Trojans before Troy, and we can tell you everything that will happen across the world.'

Their beautiful song made me long to hear more, so I signaled to my men, frowning, to set me free. But they quickened their strokes, and Eurylochus and Perimedes bound me with even tighter knots until we had passed beyond the Sirens' voices. Then my men removed the wax from their ears and untied me.

Once we were past the island, I spotted a huge wave rising and heard a loud roar. The men, terrified, loosened their grip on the oars, and the whole sea echoed with the rushing waters. The ship halted because the men had stopped rowing. I went around, encouraging each of them not to lose heart.

"'My friends,' I said, 'this is not our first danger; it's not as dire as when the Cyclops trapped us in his cave. My courage and wisdom saved us then, and we will live to remember this too. So let us do as I say—trust in Jove and row with all your strength. Coxswain, these are your orders: pay attention, for the ship is in your hands. Turn her away from these dangerous rapids and hug the rock, or we'll be lost before we know it, and you will cause our deaths.'

They followed my advice, but I didn't mention the dreadful monster Scylla, knowing my men would refuse to row if I did and huddle together in fear. The only command I disobeyed from Circe was to put on my armor. I took two strong spears and stood at the bow, expecting to see the monster first, but I couldn't spot her anywhere, despite scanning the gloomy rock.

Then we entered the straits, gripped with fear. On one side was Scylla, and on the other, the terrifying Charybdis, sucking down the salt water. As she vomited it up, it looked like water boiling over a fire, with spray reaching the top of the rocks on either side. When she started sucking again, we saw the water swirling around, making a deafening noise as it crashed against the rocks. The bottom of the whirlpool was dark with sand and mud, and the men were terrified. As we braced for our end, Scylla suddenly struck, snatching my six best men. I was watching both the ship and my men when I saw their hands and feet struggling in the air as Scylla carried them off. I heard them cry out my name one last time. Like a fisherman who sits on a jutting rock, casting bait to catch fish, I saw Scylla take my men to her rock and devour them while they screamed and reached out to me in their agony. This was the most horrific sight I witnessed throughout my travels.

After passing the rocks of Scylla and terrible Charybdis, we reached the noble island of the sun-god, where the fine cattle and sheep of Hyperion grazed. While still at sea, I could hear the cattle lowing and the sheep bleating. Remembering the warning from the blind prophet Teiresias and Circe's advice to avoid the island, I felt troubled and said to my men, "My friends, I know you are hard-pressed, but listen while I share the prophecy Teiresias gave me and how Circe warned us to avoid the blessed sun-god's island. This is where our greatest danger lies. Steer the ship away from the island."

The men were disheartened by this, and Eurylochus replied insolently, "Ulysses, you are cruel. You are strong and tireless, as if made of iron. Now, even though your men are exhausted and hungry, you will not let them land and cook a proper meal, but instead tell them to set sail and suffer through the night. It is at night that the winds blow the hardest and cause the most trouble; how can we escape if a sudden storm comes from the southwest or west, as often happens when the gods are against us? Let us obey the night and prepare our supper near the ship; tomorrow morning we will board again and set out to sea."

Eurylochus spoke, and the men agreed with him. I realized the gods intended us harm and said, "You force me to give in, as you are many against one. But each of you must take a solemn oath that if you find a herd of cattle or a flock of sheep, you will not kill a single one, but will be satisfied with the food Circe has provided."

They all swore as I asked, and once they completed their oath, we anchored the ship near a stream of fresh water, and the men went ashore to prepare their meals. After they had eaten and drunk enough, they began to talk about the comrades Scylla had taken and eaten, which led them to weep until they fell asleep.

In the third watch of the night, as the stars shifted, Jove sent a great gale that turned into a hurricane, covering land and sea in thick clouds, plunging us into darkness. When rosy-fingered Dawn appeared, we brought the ship to land and pulled her into a cave where the sea-nymphs hold their gatherings and dances. I called my men together for a council.

"'My friends,' I said, 'we have food and drink on the ship. Let us promise not to touch the cattle, or we shall suffer; for these cattle and sheep belong to the mighty sun, who sees and hears everything.' They promised they would obey.

For a whole month, the wind blew steadily from the south, with no other wind. As long as the supplies lasted, the men did not touch the cattle. But when the food ran out, they were forced to catch birds and take whatever they could find, for they were starving. One day, I went inland to pray for help to get away. I went far enough to be out of sight of my men and found a sheltered spot from the wind. I washed my hands and prayed to all the gods until I fell into a sweet sleep.

Meanwhile, Eurylochus was giving the men bad advice. "Listen to me," he said, "my poor friends. All deaths are bad, but none is worse than starvation. Why not drive in the best of the cattle and offer them to the immortal gods? If we make it back to Ithaca, we can build a fine temple to the sun-god and decorate it beautifully. If he is determined to sink our ship in revenge, I'd rather face the sea once for all than starve to death on this desolate island."

Eurylochus spoke, and the men agreed with him. The beautiful cattle were grazing not far from the ship, so they rounded up the best ones, saying their prayers as they gathered them, using young oak shoots in place of barley-meal since there was none left. After praying, they killed the cattle and prepared the meat. They cut out the thigh bones, wrapped them in fat, and placed pieces of raw meat on top. With no wine for drink offerings during cooking, they poured a little water on it as the meat grilled. When the thigh bones were burned and they had tasted the innards, they cut the rest into smaller pieces and put them on spits.

By this time, my deep sleep had faded, and I returned to the ship and the shore. As I approached, I caught the scent of roasting meat, which made me groan and pray to the immortal gods. "Father Jove," I exclaimed, "and all you gods who live in eternal bliss, you have done me a cruel wrong by letting me sleep; look what my men have done in my absence!"

Meanwhile, Lampetie went straight to the sun and informed him that we had killed his cattle. Furious, he said to the gods, "Father Jove, and all you gods in everlasting bliss, I must have revenge on the crew of Ulysses' ship. They had the audacity to kill my beloved cattle, which I cherished while traveling in heaven. If they do not pay me back for my cattle, I will go down to Hades and shine among the dead."

"'Sun,' said Jove, 'keep shining on us gods and on all mankind over the fruitful earth. I will strike their ship into tiny pieces with a bolt of white lightning as soon as they set sail.'

I learned all this from Calypso, who said she heard it from Mercury.

As soon as I reached my ship and the shore, I scolded each of the men individually, but there was nothing we could do since the cows were already dead. The gods began showing strange signs among us; the hides of the cattle twitched, the joints on the spits began to moo like cows, and the meat, whether cooked or raw, made sounds just like cows do.

For six days, my men kept rounding up the best cows and feasting on them. On the seventh day, when Jove, the son of Saturn, sent a strong wind, we went on board, raised our masts, spread our sails, and set out to sea. Once we were far from the island, with only sky and sea in sight, the son of Saturn sent a black cloud over our ship, and the sea turned dark beneath it. We couldn't make much progress because, in an instant, a terrifying squall from the west hit us. It snapped the forestays of the mast, causing it to fall back, while all the ship's gear tumbled about the bottom of the vessel. The mast fell on the helmsman at the ship's stern, crushing his skull, and he fell overboard as if diving, lifeless.

Then Jove struck with his thunderbolts, and the ship spun around, filled with fire and brimstone from the lightning. The men were thrown into the sea, swimming around the ship like seabirds, but the god took away all hope of them returning home.

I clung to the ship until the waves broke her apart, leaving the keel floating alone. The mast was knocked off in the direction of the keel, but there was still a sturdy backstay made of ox-thong hanging from it. With that, I lashed the mast and keel together and got astride of them, carried wherever the winds took me.

The fierce gale from the west had spent its force, and the wind shifted back to the south, which worried me because I feared being pulled back to the terrible whirlpool of Charybdis. And indeed, that's what happened. I was swept along by the waves all night, and by sunrise, I reached the rock of Scylla and the whirlpool. She was sucking down the salt water, and I was pulled up toward a fig tree. I grabbed hold of it and hung on like a bat. I couldn't find a solid place to stand because the roots were far away, and the branches overshadowing the whirlpool were too high and too wide for me to reach. So, I hung there, waiting for my mast and raft to be discharged from the whirlpool again. It felt like an eternity.

A jury member is never happier to get home for supper after being stuck in court than I was to see my raft finally begin to float out of the whirlpool. At last, I let go with my hands and feet, falling heavily into the sea next to my raft. I climbed onto it and began to row with my hands. As for Scylla, the father of gods and men kept her from seeing me again, or I would have certainly been lost.

I drifted for nine days until on the tenth night, the gods washed me ashore on the island of Ogygia, where the powerful goddess Calypso lives. She took me in and treated me kindly, but I don't need to say more about that, since I told you and your noble wife all about it yesterday. I dislike repeating myself."

BOOK 13:

Thus he spoke, and everyone listened in silence, captivated by his story, until Alcinous began to speak.

"Ulysses," he said, "now that you have reached my home, I have no doubt you will make it back without further trouble, no matter how much you have suffered in the past. However, to you others who come here night after night to enjoy my fine wine and listen to my bard, I must insist on this: our guest has already packed up the clothes, gold, and other valuables you have given him; let us now present him each with a large tripod and a cauldron. We can share the cost among ourselves, as it's unreasonable to expect a few individuals to bear the burden of such a generous gift."

Everyone agreed, and then they all went home to sleep in their own houses. When rosy-fingered Dawn appeared, they hurried down to the ship with their cauldrons. Alcinous boarded the ship and ensured everything was secured under the benches so nothing could break loose and harm the rowers. Then they went back to Alcinous's house for dinner, where he sacrificed a bull to honor Jove, the lord of all. They grilled the steaks and had a wonderful meal. Afterward, the inspired bard, Demodocus, who was loved by all, sang for them. But Ulysses kept turning his eyes toward the sun, eager for it to set, for he longed to be on his way. Like a farmer who has been plowing a field all day and looks forward to supper, glad when night falls, Ulysses felt the same relief as the sun finally went down. He then addressed the Phaeacians, especially King Alcinous:

"Sir, and all of you, farewell. Make your drink offerings and send me on my way with joy, for you have fulfilled my heart's desire by giving me an escort and making me splendid gifts. May I find my dear wife safe among friends, and may you whom I leave behind find happiness with your wives and children. May heaven bless you all, and may no harm come to your people."

His words were well received, and everyone agreed he should have his escort since he spoke wisely. Alcinous then instructed his servant, "Pontonous, mix some wine and distribute it to everyone, so we can offer a prayer to father Jove and send our guest on his way."

Pontonous mixed the wine and served it to each person. The others made drink offerings to the blessed gods in heaven, but Ulysses stood and handed the double cup to Queen Arete.

"Farewell, Queen," he said. "From now until age and death, the common fate of mankind, lay their hands upon you, I take my leave. May you find happiness here with your children, your people, and King Alcinous."

As he spoke, he crossed the threshold. Alcinous sent a man to guide him to his ship and to the shore. Arete also sent maidservants with him—one with a clean shirt and cloak, another to carry his strong box, and a third with food and wine. When they reached the water, the crew took the things on board, including all the food and drink. They spread a rug and a linen sheet on deck for Ulysses to sleep soundly in the stern of the ship. Then he went aboard and lay down without a word, while the crew took their places and untied the hawser from the pier. As they began to row out to sea, Ulysses fell into a deep, sweet, almost deathlike sleep.

The ship sped forward like a chariot racing over a course when the horses feel the whip. The prow rose like the neck of a stallion, and a great wave of dark blue water surged behind her. She held her course steadily, moving faster than even a falcon, the swiftest of birds. Thus, she cut through the water, carrying a man as clever as the gods, who was now peacefully asleep, forgetting all his hardships in battle and on the weary sea.

As the bright star that signals dawn began to show, the ship approached land. In Ithaca, there is a harbor of the old merman Phorcys, which lies between two points that protect it from the raging storms of wind and sea. Once inside, a ship can lie safely without needing to be moored. At the head of this harbor stands a large olive tree, and nearby is a beautiful cave sacred to the Naiads. Inside it, there are mixing bowls, stone wine jars, and beehives. The nymphs also use great stone looms to weave their sea-purple robes—truly remarkable to see—and there is always water within. The cave has two entrances: one faces north and allows mortals to enter, while the other, from the south, is mysterious and impassable to mortals; it is the path taken by the gods.

The crew brought the ship into this harbor, for they knew the place well. She had so much momentum that she ran half her length onto the shore. After landing, they lifted Ulysses, still asleep, with his rug and linen sheet from the ship and laid him down on the sand. They then took out the gifts the Phaeacians had prepared for him, influenced by Minerva, and placed them by the root of the olive tree, away from the road, to prevent any passerby from stealing them before Ulysses woke up. Then they hurried home.

But Neptune did not forget his threats against Ulysses. He consulted Jove, saying, "Father Jove, I will no longer be respected among the gods if mortals like the Phaeacians, who are my own kin, show such little regard for me. I said I would let Ulysses get home after he had suffered enough. I did not say he should never return, knowing you had already promised he would. Now they have brought him back in a ship, asleep, and loaded him with more magnificent gifts of bronze, gold, and clothing than he could have brought back from Troy if he had shared in the spoils without trouble."

Jove answered, "What are you talking about, O Lord of the Earthquake? The gods do respect you. It would be shameful to insult someone as old and honored as you. If any mortals are being insolent and treating you disrespectfully, it is up to you to deal with them as you see fit."

"I would have done so immediately," replied Neptune, "if I were not trying to avoid doing anything that might upset you. Now, I would like to wreck the Phaeacian ship on its way back from escorting Ulysses. This will prevent them from escorting anyone in the future, and I would also like to bury their city under a huge mountain."

"My good friend," Jove said, "I recommend that just as the people of the city are watching the ship return, you turn it into a rock near the land that looks like a ship. This will astonish everyone, and then you can bury their city under the mountain."

When Neptune heard this, he went to Scheria, the home of the Phaeacians, and waited until the ship, moving swiftly, was close in. Then he approached it, turned it into stone, and pushed it down into the ground with his hand. After that, he went away.

The Phaeacians began to talk among themselves, one turning to his neighbor, saying, "What could have caused the ship to root in the sea just as she was about to come into port? We could see her clearly just a moment ago."

They spoke among themselves, not understanding what had happened. Alcinous said, "I remember my father's old prophecy. He said that Neptune would be angry with us for safely bringing everyone across the sea and would one day wreck a Phaeacian ship on its return and bury our city under a high mountain. This is what my father always said, and now it is coming true. So let us do as I say: first, we must stop giving escorts to visitors, and second, let us sacrifice twelve fine bulls to Neptune, asking him to have mercy on us and not bury our city under the mountain."

When the people heard this, they were frightened and prepared the bulls for sacrifice.

Thus, the chiefs and rulers of the Phaeacians prayed to King Neptune at his altar, while Ulysses woke up on his own soil. He had been away so long that he did not recognize it, and Jove's daughter Minerva had made it foggy so that no one would know he had returned. She wanted to ensure he could learn everything without his wife or fellow citizens recognizing him until he took his revenge on the wicked suitors. Everything appeared different to him—the long straight paths, the harbors, the cliffs, and the trees—all looked changed as he stood up and gazed at his homeland. He smote his thighs with his hands and cried out in despair.

"Alas," he exclaimed, "among what people have I fallen? Are they savage and uncivilized, or hospitable and kind? Where shall I store all this treasure, and which way shall I go? I wish I had stayed with the Phaeacians, or found another great chief who would treat me well and provide an escort. Now, I don't know where to put my treasures, and I cannot leave them here for fear someone will take them. The Phaeacians have not treated me fairly, leaving me in the wrong place; they promised to take me back to Ithaca, and they have not done so. May Jove, the protector of guests, punish them, for he watches over all and punishes those who do wrong. Still, I suppose I must count my goods and see if the crew has taken any."

He counted his treasures—coppers, cauldrons, gold, and clothing—but nothing was missing. Still, he mourned for not being in his own country and wandered along the shore of the noisy sea, lamenting his fate. Then Minerva approached him, disguised as a young shepherd with a noble appearance, a fine cloak draped over her shoulders, sandals on her feet, and a javelin in hand. Ulysses was glad to see her and walked up to her.

"My friend," he said, "you are the first person I've met in this country. I greet you and ask for your goodwill. Please protect my goods and me, for I embrace your knees and pray to you as if you were a god. Tell me, and tell me truly, what land is this? Who are its people? Am I on an island, or is this the coast of a continent?"

Minerva replied, "Stranger, you must be quite simple or from very far away if you don't know what country this is. It's a well-known place, recognized by everyone from East to West. It's rugged and not great for driving, but it's still a good island. It grows plenty of corn and wine, thanks to the rain and dew; it raises cattle and goats; all kinds of timber thrive here, and there are water sources that never run dry. So, sir, Ithaca is known even as far away as Troy, which I understand is a long way from this Achaean land."

Ulysses felt happy to find himself, as Minerva said, in his own country. He began to reply, but he did not tell the truth and instead spun a clever tale from the cunning in his heart.

"I heard of Ithaca," he said, "while I was in Crete, and now it seems I have reached it with all these treasures. I left just as much behind for my children, but I'm fleeing because I killed Orsilochus, the son of Idomeneus, the fastest runner in Crete. I killed him because he tried to rob me of the spoils I had taken from Troy, which I earned through much trouble and danger both in battle and at sea. He accused me of not serving his father loyally at Troy, claiming I had set myself up as an independent ruler, so I ambushed him by the roadside and speared him as he was returning to town from the countryside. It was a dark night, and no one saw us; therefore, it wasn't known that I had killed him. Afterward, I went to a ship and begged the Phoenician owners to take me aboard and set me down in Pylos or Elis, where the Epeans rule, giving them enough spoils to satisfy them. They meant no harm, but the wind blew them off course, and we sailed until we arrived here by night. We managed to get into the harbor, and no one mentioned supper, even though we wanted it badly; instead, we all went ashore and lay down just as we were. I was very tired and fell asleep immediately, so they took my goods out of the ship and placed them beside me on the sand. Then they sailed away to Sidonia, leaving me here in great distress."

That was his story, but Minerva smiled and stroked him gently with her hand. Then she took the form of a beautiful, stately, and wise woman and said, "You must indeed be a crafty liar, for who could outsmart you in deceit, even if they were a god? Daredevil that you are, full of guile and tireless in your trickery, can't you drop your lies, now that you are back in your own country? But let's not dwell on this; we can both deceive when we need to—you are the best counselor and speaker among men, while I have no equal among the gods when it comes to diplomacy and cunning. Don't you know Jove's daughter Minerva—me, who have always been with you, watching over you in your troubles, and who made the Phaeacians so fond of you? Now, I have come here to discuss things with you and help you hide the treasure I had the Phaeacians give you. I want to inform you of the troubles that await you in your own house; you must face them, but tell no one, neither man nor woman, that you have come home again. Endure everything and put up with every man's insolence without a word."

Ulysses replied, "A goddess may know much, but you change your appearance so often that it's hard for a man to recognize you when he meets you. However, I do know this very well: you were kind to me while we Achaeans were fighting before Troy, but from the day we boarded ship after sacking the city of Priam, when heaven scattered us, I saw no more of you. I cannot recall you coming to my ship to help me in my troubles; I had to wander sick and sorry until the gods saved me and I reached the Phaeacians, where you encouraged me and brought me into the town. Now, I beg you, in your father's name, tell me the truth. I do not believe I am truly back in Ithaca. I feel like I am in some other land, and you are mocking and deceiving me. Tell me honestly—have I really returned to my own country?"

"You always get these thoughts in your head," Minerva replied, "and that's why I cannot abandon you in your troubles. You are so clever and crafty. Anyone else returning from such a long journey would go straight home to see their wife and children, but you don't seem to care about asking after them or hearing news until you've assessed the situation here, while your wife is at home, grieving for you and suffering from the lack of you day and night. As for my not visiting you, I was never worried about you, for I was sure you would return safely, even though you would lose all your men. I didn't want to anger my uncle Neptune, who never forgave you for blinding his son. Now, let me show you the lay of the land, and then you might believe me. This is the harbor of the old merman Phorcys, and here is the olive tree at its head; near it is the cave sacred to the Naiads; this is the grand cave where you have offered many sacrifices to the nymphs, and here is the wooded mountain Neritum."

As she spoke, the goddess cleared the mist, revealing the land. Ulysses rejoiced at finding himself again in his own country and kissed the bounteous soil. He lifted his hands and prayed to the nymphs, saying, "Naiad nymphs, daughters of Jove, I feared I would never see you again. Now I greet you with all my love, and I will bring you offerings as in the old days, if Jove's daughter grants me life and brings my son to manhood."

"Take heart and don't worry about that," Minerva responded. "Let's get started on stowing your things in the cave where they will be safe. We should see how best to manage it."

With that, she went into the cave to find the safest hiding places while Ulysses gathered the treasures of gold, bronze, and fine clothing the Phaeacians had given him. They stored everything carefully, and Minerva set a stone against the cave's door. Then they sat down by the root of the great olive tree and discussed how to deal with the wicked suitors.

"Ulysses," said Minerva, "noble son of Laertes, think about how you can take care of these unruly people who have been living in your house for three years, courting your wife and giving her wedding gifts while she mourns your absence, giving hope and sending encouraging messages to every one of them, while meaning the very opposite."

Ulysses replied, "Indeed, goddess, it seems I would have met the same tragic fate in my own house as Agamemnon if you had not given me such timely information. Advise me on how to best take my revenge. Stand by me and fill my heart with courage as you did on the day we seized Troy's crown. Help me now as you did then, and I will take on three hundred men if you, goddess, are with me."

"Count on that," she said. "I won't lose sight of you once we begin, and I believe those who are consuming your resources will soon find their blood on the pavement. I will start by disguising you so no one will recognize you; I'll cover your body with wrinkles, remove your yellow hair, and clothe you in garments that will repulse everyone who sees you, including your wife and son. Then you should go to the swineherd who cares for your pigs; he has always been loyal to you and devoted to Penelope and your son. You'll find him tending his pigs near the rock called Raven, by the spring Arethusa, where they feed on beech mast and fresh water. Stay with him and find out how things are going, while I go to Sparta to see your son, who is with Menelaus. He has gone there to learn whether you are still alive."

"But why," Ulysses asked, "did you not tell him? You knew everything. Did you want him to suffer hardships while others devour his estate?"

Minerva answered, "Don't worry about him. I sent him to earn a good reputation for having gone. He is not in any trouble but is quite comfortably staying with Menelaus, enjoying abundance. The suitors have set sail and are waiting to kill him before he can return home. I don't think they will succeed; rather, some of those who are now consuming your estate will find their own graves first."

As she spoke, Minerva touched him with her wand, giving him wrinkles, taking away his yellow hair, and withering his flesh. She dimmed his fine eyes, changed his clothes to rags, and threw an old filthy wrap around him; she also gave him an unprocessed deer skin for outerwear, along with a staff and a tattered, holey wallet to carry over his shoulder.

After laying their plans, the two parted ways, and the goddess went straight to Lacedaemon to fetch Telemachus.

BOOK 14:

Ulysses now left the harbor and took the rough path through the wooded area and over the mountain crest until he arrived at the spot where Minerva said he would find the swineherd, his most diligent servant. He found him sitting in front of his hut, which was located by the yards he had built on a visible site. The swineherd had made them spacious and attractive, allowing the pigs to roam freely around. He built them during his master's absence using stones he gathered without telling Penelope or Laertes, and he fenced them with thorn bushes. He also ran a strong fence of oak posts outside the yard, set close together, and constructed twelve sty pens nearby for the sows. There were fifty breeding sows in each sty, while the boars, fewer in number, slept outside since the suitors continually consumed them, and the swineherd had to provide them the best he had. In total, he had three hundred sixty boar pigs, and his four fierce hounds slept with them. At that moment, the swineherd was cutting a pair of sandals from a sturdy oxhide. Three of his men were herding the pigs in various places, while he sent the fourth to town with a boar he had to deliver to the suitors for their feast.

When the hounds saw Ulysses, they started barking furiously and lunged at him. However, Ulysses was clever enough to sit down and drop the stick he was holding. Still, he would have been attacked had not the swineherd dropped his oxhide, rushed through the yard gate, and driven the dogs away with shouts and stones. He then said to Ulysses, "Old man, the dogs might have made short work of you, and then I would have faced trouble. The gods have already given me enough worries without that, for I have lost my best master and am in continual grief for him. I must tend pigs for others to eat while he, if he still lives, is starving in a distant land. Come inside, and after you've had your fill of bread and wine, tell me where you're from and all about your troubles."

The swineherd then led Ulysses into the hut and invited him to sit down. He spread a thick bed of rushes on the floor and laid a shaggy chamois skin on top for Ulysses to rest on. Ulysses felt grateful for the warm welcome and said, "May Jove and the other gods grant you your heart's desire for your kindness in receiving me."

Eumaeus, the swineherd, replied, "Stranger, even if a poorer man comes here, it wouldn't be right for me to insult him, for all strangers and beggars come from Jove. You must take what you can get and be thankful, for servants live in fear when they have young masters. This is my misfortune now; heaven has delayed the return of my master, who would have always treated me well, giving me a house, land, a beautiful wife, and all else a generous master provides a hardworking servant. If my master had grown old here, he would have done great things for me, but he is gone. I wish Helen's whole lineage were utterly destroyed, for she has caused the deaths of many good men. It was this issue that took my master to Ilium, the land of noble steeds, to fight the Trojans in King Agamemnon's cause."

As he spoke, he fastened his girdle and went to the pens where the young pigs were kept. He selected two, brought them back, sacrificed them, singed them, cut them up, and skewered them. When the meat was cooked, he served it hot and still on the spit before Ulysses, who sprinkled it with white barley meal. The swineherd then poured wine into an ivy-wood bowl and, taking a seat opposite Ulysses, told him to start eating.

"Dig in, stranger," he said, "on a dish of servant's pork. The prime pigs go to the suitors, who eat them without shame; the blessed gods do not like such shamelessness and respect those who act justly. Even fierce raiders who attack other lands and are granted spoils by Jove feel guilt when they return home; yet some god seems to have told these suitors that Ulysses is dead and gone. Therefore, they will not return to their homes and make marriage proposals in the usual manner but waste his estate with no fear or limits. Not a day or night passes without them sacrificing one or two victims, and they take the best of his wine, for he was exceedingly rich. No other man in Ithaca or on the mainland had as much; he had as much as twenty men combined. I'll tell you what he had: there are twelve herds of cattle on the mainland, as many flocks of sheep, and twelve droves of pigs. His own men and hired hands feed twelve extensive herds of goats. Here in Ithaca, he even runs large flocks of goats at the far end of the island, watched over by excellent herders. Each one of them sends the best goat from the flock to the suitors every day. I, myself, am in charge of the pigs you see here, and I have to keep picking out the best I have to send to them."

That was his story, but Ulysses continued to eat and drink ravenously without a word, brooding over his revenge. After he had eaten his fill, the swineherd took the bowl from which he usually drank, filled it with wine, and handed it to Ulysses, who accepted it gratefully and said, "My friend, who was this master of yours, who bought you and paid for you, so rich and powerful as you tell me? You say he perished in King Agamemnon's cause; tell me who he was in case I might have met him. Jove and the other gods know, but I might be able to give you news of him, for I have traveled widely."

Eumaeus answered, "Old man, no traveler who comes here with news will get Ulysses' wife and son to believe him. Nevertheless, beggars needing a place to stay keep coming here, full of lies and not a word of truth. Everyone who arrives in Ithaca goes to my mistress and tells her falsehoods, and she takes them in, makes much of them, and asks them all kinds of questions, crying like a woman will when she has lost her husband. And you too, old man, for a shirt and cloak, could certainly spin a pretty tale.

But the wolves and birds of prey have long since torn Ulysses to pieces, or fish have eaten him, and his bones lie buried deep in sand on some foreign shore; he is dead, and it's a terrible thing for all his friends, especially for me. No matter where I go, I will never find a master as good as he was, not even if I return home to my parents, where I was born and raised. I do not much care about my parents now, though I would dearly like to see them again; it's the loss of Ulysses that troubles me most. I cannot speak of him without reverence, though he is no longer here, for he was very kind to me and took such care of me that wherever he is, I will always honor his memory."

"My friend," replied Ulysses, "you are very positive and hard to convince about your master's return; nevertheless, I will not merely say, but swear, that he is coming. Do not give me anything for my news until he has actually arrived. You may then give me a shirt and cloak if you wish. I am in great need, but I will not accept anything until then, for I hate a man who allows his poverty to tempt him into lying, as I hate hellfire. I swear by King Jove, by the rites of hospitality, and by the hearth of Ulysses to which I have now come, that everything will happen just as I have said. Ulysses will return this same year; at the end of this moon and the beginning of the next, he will come to take vengeance on all those who are mistreating his wife and son."

To this, you answered, O swineherd Eumaeus, "Old man, you will neither get paid for bringing good news, nor will Ulysses ever return. Drink your wine in peace and let's talk about something else. Do not keep reminding me of all this; it always pains me when anyone speaks of my honored master. As for your oath, we'll let it go, but I only wish he would come back, as do Penelope, his old father Laertes, and his son Telemachus. I am terribly worried about this boy of his; he is growing fast into manhood and promises to be as good-looking and capable as his father, but someone, either a god or a man, has unsettled his mind, so he has gone off to Pylos to seek news of his father. The suitors are lying in wait for him as he returns, hoping to leave the house of Arceisius without a name in Ithaca. But let's not dwell on him; let fate take him, whether to be captured or to escape if the son of Saturn watches over him. Now, old man, tell me your own story; tell me also, for I want to know, who you are and where you come from. Tell me about your town and your parents, what kind of ship you came in, how your crew brought you to Ithaca, and from what country they claimed to come, for you cannot have come by land."

Ulysses answered, "I will tell you all about it. If there were enough food and wine, and we could stay here in the hut with nothing to do but eat and drink while the others work, I could easily talk for twelve months without finishing the tale of the sorrows with which heaven has chosen to visit me."

I am originally from Crete, where my father was a well-to-do man with many legitimate sons. I was born to a slave he had purchased as a concubine. However, my father Castor, son of Hylax, who was highly regarded among the Cretans for his wealth and bravery, treated me as an equal to my brothers. When he passed away, his sons divided his estate by casting lots. They gave me a small holding and little else. Yet, thanks to my bravery, I managed to marry into a wealthy family, as I was not one to boast or shy away from battle. It's all in the past now; still, the hardships I faced show my worth. Mars and Minerva made me a warrior; when I selected my men for an ambush, I never thought of death and was always the first to charge, spearing whoever I could catch. That was my nature in battle, but I never cared for farming or the humble life of those who raise children. My passions were ships, fighting, javelins, and arrows—things that most men fear. Everyone has their own inclinations, and that was mine. Before the Achaeans sailed to Troy, I commanded men and ships on foreign missions nine times and amassed considerable wealth, having the first pick of the spoils, with much more allotted to me later.

My home prospered, and I became a great man among the

Cretans. However, when Jove urged that disastrous expedition that claimed many lives, the people insisted I and Idomeneus lead their ships to Troy, and we had no choice but to comply. We fought there for nine long years, but in the tenth, we sacked Priam's city and sailed home, as the gods scattered us. It was then that Jove plotted my downfall. I spent just one month happily with my children, wife, and possessions before I decided to make an expedition to Egypt. I prepared a splendid fleet and manned it with nine ships, gathering a crowd to fill them. For six days, my men feasted, and I provided many victims for sacrifices to the gods and for themselves. On the seventh day, we boarded the ships and set sail from Crete with a favorable North wind, though we were traveling down a river. Everything went smoothly; there was no illness aboard, and we let the winds and steersmen guide our ships. On the fifth day, we reached the river Aegyptus. I stationed my ships there, telling my men to guard them while I sent scouts to reconnoiter from high ground.

But the men disobeyed my orders, taking matters into their own hands and pillaging the Egyptian land, killing men, and capturing their wives and children. Soon, the alarm reached the city, and at dawn, the plain filled with horsemen, foot soldiers, and the glint of armor. Jove struck fear into my men, and they lost their resolve, finding themselves surrounded. The Egyptians killed many of us and captured the rest to force into labor. At that moment, I wished I had died instead, for much sorrow awaited me. I took off my helmet and shield, dropped my spear, and approached the king's chariot, clasping his knees and kissing them. He spared my life, ordered me into his chariot, and took me weeping to his home. Many aimed their spears at me, trying to kill me in their rage, but the king protected me, fearing the wrath of Jove, the protector of strangers.

I stayed there for seven years, collecting a fortune from the Egyptians, who all gave me something. When nearly eight years had passed, a certain cunning Phoenician, who had already done many villainous acts, persuaded me to go with him to Phoenicia, where his home and wealth lay. I stayed there for twelve months, but after that time, when the seasons changed again, he put me on board a ship bound for Libya, pretending I was to take a cargo with him, but intending to sell me as a slave for his profit. I suspected his intentions but boarded the ship, feeling I had no choice.

The ship sailed before a fresh North wind until we reached the sea between Crete and Libya. However, Jove planned our destruction. Once we were well away from Crete and could see nothing but sea and sky, he cast a black cloud over our ship, and the sea grew dark beneath it. Then Jove unleashed his thunderbolts, and the ship spun wildly, filled with fire and brimstone from the lightning strike. The men fell into the sea, flailing about like gulls, but the god denied them any chance of returning home. I was filled with despair. Yet Jove sent the ship's mast within my reach, which saved my life; I clung to it and drifted in the storm. I drifted for nine days, and on the tenth night, a great wave brought me to the coast of Thesprotia. There, Pheidon, king of the Thesprotians, welcomed me hospitably, charging me nothing, for his son found me nearly dead from cold and fatigue. He helped me to his father's house and gave me clothes.

While there, I learned news of Ulysses, as the king told me he had hosted him and shown him much hospitality on his journey home. The king even showed me the treasure of gold and wrought iron that Ulysses had gathered, enough to support his family for ten generations. The king said Ulysses had gone to Dodona to learn Jove's will from the god's sacred oak tree, to discover whether he should return to Ithaca openly or in secret. The king swore in my presence, making drink offerings in his home, that the ship was waiting by the shore and the crew was ready to take Ulysses back. However, he sent me away before Ulysses returned, as a Thesprotian ship was leaving for the grain-growing island of Dulichium, and he instructed the crew to take me safely to King Acastus.

These men plotted against me, intending to reduce me to the depths of misery. Once the ship was a ways from land, they decided to sell me into slavery. They stripped me of the shirt and cloak I was wearing and gave me the tattered rags you see now. By nightfall, they reached the cultivated lands of Ithaca, binding me with a strong rope aboard the ship while they went ashore for supper. But the gods soon released my bonds, and I pulled my rags over my head and slid down the rudder into the sea. I swam until I was well clear of them and came ashore near a dense wood, where I lay hidden. They searched for me, but eventually gave up and returned to their ship. The gods had hidden me, taking me to the door of a good man, for it seems I am not to die just yet."

You, O swineherd Eumaeus, replied, "Poor unhappy stranger, I find your story of misfortunes fascinating, but that part about Ulysses seems unconvincing; you won't persuade me to believe it. Why would a man like you go about telling lies? I know all about my master's return. The gods all despise him; otherwise, he would have been taken before Troy or died surrounded by friends after his fighting days. Then the Achaeans would have built a mound over his ashes, and his son would have inherited his renown. But now, the storm winds have spirited him away, and we know not where.

"As for me, I live out here with the pigs, and I only go to town when Penelope sends for me when news of Ulysses arrives. Then everyone gathers to ask questions, both those who grieve for the king's absence and those who rejoice, because they can consume his property without paying. I have stopped asking others since I was tricked by an Aetolian who had killed a man and traveled far until he reached my place. I was kind to him, and he claimed to have seen Ulysses with Idomeneus among the Cretans, repairing his ships that had been damaged in a storm. He said Ulysses would return the following summer or autumn with his men, bringing back much wealth. And now you, unfortunate old man, since fate has brought you to my door, do not try to flatter me with vain hopes. I will treat you kindly, not because of any such reason, but only out of respect for Jove, the god of hospitality, as I fear him and pity you."

Ulysses replied, "I see you are skeptical; I've given you my oath, and yet you refuse to believe me. Let us make a bargain, and call all the gods in heaven to witness it. If your master comes home, give me a cloak and shirt of good wear, and send me to Dulichium where I want to go; but if he does not return as I say he will, then have your men throw me from that precipice, as a warning to travelers not to spread lies."

Eumaeus replied, "I would look quite foolish if I were to kill you after welcoming you into my hut and showing you hospitality. If I did that, I'd have to pray earnestly for forgiveness. But it's supper time, and I hope my men will come in soon so we can cook something tasty."

As they talked, the swineherds arrived with the pigs, which were squealing loudly as they were driven into their styes. Eumaeus called to his men, "Bring in the best pig you have so I can sacrifice it for this stranger. We've worked hard raising these pigs while others reap the rewards."

He began chopping firewood while the others brought in a fine, fat five-year-old boar and set it at the altar. Eumaeus was a principled man and didn't forget the gods. The first thing he did was cut off some bristles from the pig's face and toss them into the fire, praying to all the gods for Ulysses' return. Then, using a hefty oak club he had kept back, he stunned the pig while the others slaughtered and singed it. Afterward, they cut it up, and Eumaeus began by placing raw pieces from each joint onto some of the fat, sprinkling it with barley meal, and laying it on the embers. The rest of the meat was cut into small pieces, put on spits, and roasted until it was done. Once off the spits, the meat was piled onto a dresser. Eumaeus, being fair, stood up to distribute the portions, making seven in total. One portion was set aside for Mercury, son of Maia, and the nymphs, while the others were given to the men one by one. He honored Ulysses with slices cut from the loin, and Ulysses appreciated it. "I hope, Eumaeus," he said, "that Jove will look favorably upon you as I do, for your kindness to an outcast like me."

Eumaeus replied, "Eat, my friend, and enjoy your supper, such as it is. The gods decide what we receive, granting some things while withholding others, as they see fit."

As he spoke, he cut off the first piece and offered it as a sacrifice to the immortal gods. Then he made a drink-offering, placed the cup in Ulysses' hands, and sat down to his portion. Mesaulius, whom Eumaeus had brought from the Taphians and paid for during his master's absence, brought the bread. They laid their hands on the good food before them, and when they had eaten and drunk enough, Mesaulius took away the leftover bread. After a hearty supper, they all went to bed.

Night fell, stormy and dark, without a moon. It poured relentlessly, and the wind blew strong from the West, a wet direction. Ulysses thought about whether Eumaeus, in his excellent care, would take off his cloak and give it to him or have one of his men do so. "Listen to me," he said, "Eumaeus and the rest of you; after I pray, I will share something. Wine makes me talk this way; it can even make wise men sing, chuckle, dance, and say things they should keep quiet about. But since I've started, I'll continue. I wish I were as young and strong as I was when we set an ambush before Troy. Menelaus and Ulysses led, but I was also in command, as they insisted. We crouched down under our armor by the city wall, covered by reeds and thick brushwood around the swamp. The North wind blew cold, and fine snow fell like frost, coating our shields. The others had cloaks and shirts, sleeping comfortably with their shields about them, but I had foolishly left my cloak behind, thinking I wouldn't be too cold, and went off in nothing but my shirt and shield.

When the night was two-thirds over and the stars had moved, I nudged Ulysses, who was nearby, with my elbow, and he quickly gave me his attention.

"'Ulysses,' I said, 'this cold will be the death of me, for I have no cloak. Some god tricked me into leaving with only my shirt, and I don't know what to do.'

"Ulysses, clever as he was brave, devised a plan.

"'Keep still,' he whispered, 'or the others will hear you.' Then he propped himself on his elbow.

"'My friends,' he said, 'I had a dream from heaven. We are far from the ships; I wish someone would go tell Agamemnon to send us more men.'

"On this, Thoas, son of Andraemon, threw off his cloak and ran to the ships, and I took the cloak and lay down comfortably until morning. I wish I were still young and strong as I was then; if so, one of you swineherds would give me a cloak out of goodwill and respect for a brave soldier. But now, people look down on me because my clothes are ragged."

Eumaeus replied, "You've told an excellent story, and so far, nothing you've said has been unsatisfactory. Therefore, for the present, you will want for neither clothing nor anything else a distressed stranger might reasonably expect. But tomorrow morning, you must put your old rags back on, for we don't have many spare cloaks or shirts here. Each man has only one. When Ulysses' son comes home, he will give you a cloak and shirt and send you wherever you wish to go."

With that, he got up and made a bed for Ulysses, laying down some goatskins and sheepskins on the ground in front of the fire. Ulysses lay down there, and Eumaeus covered him with a heavy cloak he kept for exceptionally bad weather.

Thus did Ulysses sleep, with the young men beside him. The

swineherd, however, did not want to sleep away from his pigs, so he prepared to go outside. Ulysses was glad to see he was attentive to his property during his master's absence. He slung his sword over his strong shoulders, donned a thick cloak to fend off the wind, took the skin of a well-fed goat, and grabbed a javelin in case of an attack from men or dogs. Equipped thus, he went to rest where the pigs were camping under an overhanging rock that shielded them from the North wind.

BOOK 15:

Minerva went to the beautiful city of Lacedaemon to tell Ulysses' son that he needed to return home immediately. She found him and Pisistratus sleeping in the forecourt of Menelaus's house. While Pisistratus was fast asleep, Telemachus couldn't rest that night, worrying about his unfortunate father. Minerva approached him and said:

"Telemachus, you shouldn't stay away from home any longer or leave your property in the hands of dangerous people. They will consume everything you own, and your journey will have been in vain. Ask Menelaus to send you home quickly if you wish to find your excellent mother still there when you return. Her father and brothers are already urging her to marry Eurymachus, who has given her more than any of the others and is increasing his wedding gifts. I hope nothing valuable has been taken from your house, but you know how women can be—they often want to do the best they can for the man who marries them and forget the children of their first husbands when they're gone. So go home and put everything in the care of your most respectable servant until heaven sends you a wife of your own.

Let me also warn you of another matter: the chief men among the suitors are lying in wait for you in the Strait between Ithaca and Samos, intending to kill you before you reach home. I don't think they will succeed; it's more likely that some of those consuming your property will find their own graves. Sail night and day and keep your ship well away from the islands; the god who protects you will send a fair wind. Once you reach Ithaca, send your ship and crew to the town, but go straight to the swineherd who looks after your pigs; he is loyal to you. Stay with him for the night and send him to tell Penelope that you have returned safely from Pylos."

After delivering her message, she returned to Olympus. Telemachus nudged Pisistratus with his heel to wake him, saying, "Wake up, Pisistratus! Yoke the horses to the chariot; we must head home."

Pisistratus replied, "No matter how eager we are, we cannot drive in the dark. Morning will be here soon; let's wait for Menelaus to bring his gifts and load them into the chariot, and let him bid us farewell in the usual way. A guest should always remember the kindness of his host."

As he spoke, dawn began to break. Menelaus, having risen and leaving Helen in bed, came toward them. Telemachus hurried to put on his shirt, threw a great cloak over his shoulders, and went out to meet him. "Menelaus," he said, "please let me return to my own country, for I long to go home."

Menelaus answered, "Telemachus, if you are set on leaving, I won't keep you. I don't like to see a host too fond of his guest or too rude. Moderation is best in all things. It's just as wrong to prevent a man from leaving when he wants to go as it is to tell him to leave if he wishes to stay. Therefore, wait until I can load your beautiful gifts into your chariot and until you see them for yourself. I'll tell the women to prepare a proper dinner for you from what we have in the house. It's more appropriate and cheaper for you to eat before embarking on such a long journey. Moreover, if you wish to tour Hellas or the Peloponnese, I will yoke my horses and escort you through all our principal cities. No one will send us away empty-handed; everyone will offer us something—a bronze tripod, a couple of mules, or a gold cup."

"Menelaus," replied Telemachus, "I want to go home immediately, for I left my property unprotected, and I fear that while looking for my father I may come to ruin or find something valuable has been stolen during my absence."

When Menelaus heard this, he ordered his wife and servants to prepare a sufficient dinner from what they had. At that moment, Eteoneus joined him, having just risen, and Menelaus told him to light the fire and cook some meat, which he promptly did. Menelaus then went to his fragrant storeroom, not alone, but with Helen and Megapenthes. When he reached the place where the treasures of his house were kept, he selected a double cup and told his son Megapenthes to bring a silver mixing bowl. Meanwhile, Helen went to her chest, where she kept the lovely dresses she had made with her own hands, and took out the largest and most beautifully embroidered one, which glittered like a star and lay at the bottom of the chest.

Then they all returned to Telemachus, and Menelaus said, "Telemachus, may Jove, the mighty husband of Juno, bring you home safely, as you desire. I will present you with the finest and most precious piece of silverware in all my house. This mixing bowl is made of pure silver, except for the rim, which is inlaid with gold; it is the work of Vulcan. Phaedimus, king of the Sidonians, gifted it to me during a visit on my way home. I would like to give it to you."

With those words, he placed the double cup in Telemachus' hands while Megapenthes brought the beautiful mixing bowl and set it before him. Lovely Helen stood nearby with the robe ready in her hand.

"I too, my son," she said, "have something for you as a keepsake from me, Helen; it's for your bride to wear on her wedding day. Until then, ask your dear mother to keep it for you. May you return rejoicing to your country and home."

Saying this, she handed the robe to him, and he received it gladly. Then Pisistratus loaded the presents into the chariot, admiring them as he did so. Soon after, Menelaus took Telemachus and Pisistratus into the house, where they sat down to a meal. A maidservant brought them water in a beautiful golden ewer and poured it into a silver basin for them to wash their hands, setting a clean table beside them. An upper servant brought them bread and offered many delicious things from what was available in the house. Eteoneus carved the meat and served each their portions while Megapenthes poured out the wine. They laid their hands on the good food before them, and after eating and drinking enough, Telemachus and Pisistratus yoked the horses and took their places in the chariot. They drove out through the inner gateway and under the echoing gatehouse of the outer court, with Menelaus following, holding a golden goblet of wine so they could make a drink-offering before departing. He stood in front of the horses and pledged them, saying, "Farewell to both of you; make sure to tell Nestor how kindly I treated you, for he was as good to me as any father could be while we Achaeans were fighting before Troy."

"We will be sure to tell him everything as soon as we see him," answered Telemachus. "I wish I were as certain of finding Ulysses back when I return to Ithaca, so I might tell him of your great kindness and the beautiful gifts I am taking with me."

As he spoke, a bird flew on his right—an eagle with a great white goose in its talons that it had snatched from a farmyard—and all the men and women were chasing after it, shouting. The eagle flew close to them and passed in front of the horses. Seeing this, they were glad, and their hearts were comforted. Pisistratus then asked, "Tell me, Menelaus, has heaven sent this omen for us or for you?"

Menelaus considered what would be the most fitting response, but Helen was quicker and said, "I will interpret this omen as heaven has put it in my heart, and I have no doubt it will come to pass. The eagle came from its mountain home and will return, just as Ulysses, after traveling far and suffering much, will come back to take his revenge—if he isn't already back and plotting against the suitors."

"May Jove grant it," replied Telemachus. "If it proves true, I will make vows to you as if you were a god, even when I'm home."

As he spoke, he lashed his horses, and they started off at full speed through the town toward the open country. They swayed their yokes on their necks and traveled all day long until the sun set and darkness covered the land. They reached Pherae, home of Diocles, son of Ortilochus, son of Alpheus. There, they passed the night and were treated hospitably. When rosy-fingered Dawn appeared, they yoked their horses and took their places in the chariot. They drove out through the inner gateway and under the echoing gatehouse of the outer court. Pisistratus whipped the horses, and they galloped forward eagerly. Before long, they reached Pylos, and Telemachus said:

"Pisistratus, I hope you will promise to do what I am about to ask. Our fathers were old friends before us; besides, we are both the same age, and this journey has brought us even closer. Please don't take me past my ship; just let me stay there. If I go to your father's house, he will try to keep me there out of kindness, and I must go home at once."

Pisistratus considered how best to comply with his request and ultimately decided to turn his horses toward the ship, putting Menelaus's beautiful gifts of gold and clothing in the vessel's stern. He said, "Go on board at once and tell your men to do the same before I reach home to inform my father. I know how stubborn he is, and I'm certain he won't let you leave; he'll come down here to fetch you and won't go back without you. But he will be very angry."

With that, he drove his fine steeds back to the city of the Pylians and soon reached his home. Telemachus called his men together and gave his orders. "Now, my men," he said, "get everything ready on board the ship, and let us set out for home."

Thus he spoke, and they boarded the ship just as he said. While Telemachus was busy praying and sacrificing to Minerva at the ship's stern, a man from a distant land approached him. This man was a seer fleeing from Argos after killing a man. He was descended from Melampus, who had lived in Pylos, the land of sheep; he was rich and owned a grand house but was exiled by the powerful king Neleus. Neleus seized his possessions and imprisoned him for a year in the house of King Phylacus, causing him great distress, both because of the daughter of Neleus and due to the sorrow that the dreaded Erinys had brought upon him. Eventually, he escaped with his life, drove the cattle from Phylace to Pylos, avenged his wrongs, and gave Neleus's daughter to his brother. After that, he left the country for Argos, where it was foretold that he would rule over many people. There, he married, established himself, and had two renowned sons, Antiphates and Mantius. Antiphates fathered Oicleus, who in turn was the father of Amphiaraus, beloved by both Jove and Apollo, but he did not live to old age, as he was killed in Thebes due to a woman's gifts. His sons were Alcmaeon and Amphilochus. Mantius, the other son of Melampus, was the father of Polypheides and Cleitus. Aurora, throned in gold, carried off Cleitus for his beauty, so he could dwell among the immortals, while Apollo made Polypheides the greatest seer in the world after Amphiaraus's death. He quarreled with his father and went to live in Hyperesia, where he continued to prophesy.

Now, it was Theoclymenus, the son of this seer, who came up to Telemachus while he was making drink-offerings and praying in his ship. "Friend," he said, "now that I find you sacrificing here, I beseech you by your sacrifices and the god to whom you make them, I pray you also by your own head and those of your followers, tell me the truth—who are you, and whence do you come? Tell me about your town and parents."

Telemachus replied, "I will answer you truthfully. I am from Ithaca, and my father is Ulysses, as surely as he ever lived. But he has come to a miserable end. That is why I have taken this ship and gathered my crew—to see if I can hear any news of him, for he has been away for a long time."

"I too," answered Theoclymenus, "am an exile, for I have killed a man of my own race. He has many brothers and kinsmen in Argos who hold great power among the Argives. I am fleeing to escape death at their hands and am thus doomed to wander the earth. I am your suppliant; take me on board your ship, so they do not kill me, for I know they are pursuing me."

"I will not refuse you," replied Telemachus, "if you wish to join us. Come, and in Ithaca we will treat you hospitably with what we have."

With that, he took Theoclymenus' spear and laid it down on the deck of the ship. Theoclymenus boarded and sat at the stern, bidding him sit beside him. Then the crew let go the hawsers. Telemachus instructed them to grab the ropes, and they hurried to do so. They set the mast in its socket on the cross plank, raised it, and secured it with the forestays, then hoisted their white sails with sheets of twisted oxhide. Minerva sent them a fair wind, blowing fresh and strong, propelling the ship swiftly on its course. They passed by Crouni and Chalcis.

Soon, the sun set, and darkness enveloped the land. The vessel made a quick journey to Pheae and then on to Elis, where the Epeans ruled. Telemachus directed her toward the flying islands, wondering within himself whether he would escape death or be captured.

Meanwhile, Ulysses and the swineherd were enjoying their supper in the hut, with the men dining alongside them. Once they had eaten and drunk, Ulysses began testing the swineherd to see if he would continue to treat him kindly and either invite him to stay or send him to the city. He said:

"Eumaeus, and all of you, tomorrow I want to leave and start begging around the town, so as not to trouble you or your men any longer. Please give me your advice and provide a good guide to show me the way. I will go around the city begging for food and drink, and I'd like to visit Ulysses' house to bring news of her husband to Queen Penelope. I could also go among the suitors and see if any of them will offer me a meal from their abundance. I would soon make a handy servant—putting fresh wood on the fire, chopping fuel, carving, cooking, pouring wine, and performing all the duties that poor men must do for those above them."

The swineherd was very disturbed when he heard this. "Heaven help me," he exclaimed, "what ever could have put such a notion into your head? If you approach the suitors, you will surely come to harm, for their pride and insolence reach the heavens. They would never consider taking a man like you for a servant. Their servants are all young men, well-dressed, wearing fine cloaks and shirts, with handsome faces and neatly styled hair. Their tables are always clean and laden with food, wine, and bread. So stay here; you are not in anyone's way, and I don't mind you being here. None of the others do either, and when Telemachus returns, he will give you a shirt and cloak and send you wherever you wish to go."

Ulysses replied, "I hope you may be as dear to the gods as you are to me for saving me from wandering and getting into trouble. There is nothing worse than always being on the road; yet when men have fallen low, they endure much for their miserable bellies. Since you urge me to stay here and wait for Telemachus, tell me about Ulysses' mother and father, whom he left on the brink of old age when he set out for Troy. Are they still living, or have they gone to the house of Hades?"

"I will tell you all about them," replied Eumaeus. "Laertes is still alive and prays for a peaceful end in his own house, for he is deeply troubled by the absence of his son and by the death of his wife, which grieved him greatly and aged him more than anything else could. She met an unhappy end through grief for her son; may no friend or neighbor who has treated me kindly come to such an end! While she was still living, though always grieving, I enjoyed seeing her and asking how she did, for she raised me alongside her daughter Ctimene, the youngest of her children. We were boy and girl together, and she treated me no differently from her own. However, as we grew up, they sent Ctimene to Same with a splendid dowry. As for me, my mistress gave me a good shirt and cloak and sandals for my feet, sending me off to the countryside, but she remained just as fond of me. This is all behind me now. Yet heaven has prospered my work in the position I now hold. I have enough to eat and drink and can provide for any respectable stranger who visits; but there's no getting a kind word or deed from my mistress, as the house has fallen into the hands of wicked people. Servants sometimes like to see their mistress and have a chat with her; they appreciate being offered something to eat and drink and a bit to take back with them into the countryside. This is what keeps servants in a good humor."

Ulysses replied, "Then you must have been very young when taken so far from your home and parents. Tell me, and tell me the truth: was the city where your father and mother lived sacked and pillaged, or did some enemies capture you while you were alone tending sheep or cattle, and ship you off here, selling you for whatever your master gave them?"

"Stranger," Eumaeus replied, "as for your question: sit still, make yourself comfortable, drink your wine, and listen to me. The nights are long now; there is plenty of time for sleeping and talking together. You shouldn't go to bed until bedtime; too much sleep is as bad as too little. If any of the others wish to go to bed, they can leave and do so; they can then take my master's pigs out after breakfast in the morning. We too will sit here, eating and drinking in the hut, sharing stories about our misfortunes; for when a man has suffered much and been buffeted about, he takes pleasure in recalling memories of past sorrows. Regarding your question, my tale is as follows:

"You may have heard of an island called Syra that lies above

Ortygia, where the land begins to turn and look in another direction. It isn't very thickly populated, but the soil is good, with plenty of pasture for cattle and sheep, and it abounds with wine and wheat. There is no shortage there, nor are the people plagued by sickness; when they grow old, Apollo comes with Diana and kills them with his painless arrows. It contains two communities, and the whole country is divided between them. My father, Ctesius son of Ormenus, a man comparable to the gods, reigned over both."

Now, some cunning traders from Phoenicia arrived at this place, for the Phoenicians are skilled mariners. They brought a ship loaded with all sorts of goods. Among them was a tall and beautiful Phoenician woman, an excellent servant in my father's house. One day, while she was washing near their ship, these scoundrels caught her, seduced her, and used charms that no woman could resist, no matter how virtuous she might be. The man who seduced her asked her where she was from, and she revealed her father's name. "I come from Sidon," she said, "and I am the daughter of Arybas, a wealthy man. One day, while returning to town from the countryside, some Taphian pirates seized me and brought me here over the sea, where they sold me to the man who owns this house, and he paid them well for me."

The man who had seduced her then asked, "Would you like to return to see your parents and your homeland? They are both alive and are said to be well off."

"I would gladly go," she answered, "if you swear a solemn oath that you will not harm me on the way."

They all swore as she asked, and when they finished their oath, she said, "Hush, and if any of your men meets me in the street or at the well, do not let him speak to me, for fear someone might inform my master. He would suspect something and imprison me, and would have all of you killed. Keep your counsel, buy your goods quickly, and let me know when you finish loading. I will gather as much gold as I can, and I can also help with my fare. I am the nurse to the son of the good man of the house, a little boy just learning to walk. I will carry him off in your ship, and you will get a great deal of money for him if you take him and sell him in foreign lands."

With that, she returned to the house. The Phoenicians stayed for a whole year, loading their ship with valuable merchandise. When they finally had enough, they sent to tell the woman. Their messenger, a crafty fellow, came to my father's house bearing a gold necklace with amber beads. While my mother and the servants admired it and bargained over it, he quietly signaled to the woman and returned to the ship. She took my hand and led me out of the house. In the fore part of the house, she saw the tables set with cups that guests had used when feasting with my father; these guests had now gone to a public assembly. She snatched up three cups and hid them in her dress while I followed her, knowing no better.

As the sun set and darkness covered the land, we hurried on until we reached the harbor where the Phoenician ship lay. Once aboard, they sailed away with us, and Jove sent a fair wind. We sailed both day and night for six days, but on the seventh day, Diana struck the woman, and she fell heavily into the ship's hold, as if she were a sea gull landing on the water. They threw her overboard for the seals and fish, and I was left sorrowful and alone. Soon after, the winds and waves brought the ship to Ithaca, where Laertes exchanged various goods for me. Thus, I came to set eyes upon this country.

Ulysses replied, "Eumaeus, I have listened to your tale of misfortunes with great interest and sympathy. Yet, Jove has given you both good and evil, for despite everything, you have a good master who ensures you have enough to eat and drink, while I continue to wander, begging from city to city."

As they spoke, the night drew to a close, leaving little time for sleep before daybreak. Meanwhile, Telemachus and his crew were nearing land, so they loosened the sails, took down the mast, and rowed the ship into the harbor. They cast out their mooring stones and secured the hawsers, then disembarked on the seashore to mix their wine and prepare dinner. Once they had eaten and drunk enough, Telemachus said, "Take the ship to the town, but leave me here; I want to check on the herdsmen on one of my farms. In the evening, after I've seen all I need, I will come down to the city, and tomorrow morning, as a reward for your trouble, I will give you all a good dinner with meat and wine."

Then Theoclymenus asked, "What will become of me? To whose house among your chief men am I to go? Shall I go directly to your house and to your mother?"

"At any other time," replied Telemachus, "I would have asked you to go to my house, where you would find no lack of hospitality; but at the moment, you wouldn't be comfortable there. I will be away, and my mother seldom shows herself, preferring to weave in an upper chamber away from the suitors. But I can tell you where you can go: to Eurymachus, son of Polybus, who is highly esteemed in Ithaca. He is the best and most persistent suitor of all those trying to win my mother's hand. Jove alone knows whether they will meet a bad end before the marriage takes place."

As he spoke, a bird flew by on his right—a hawk, Apollo's messenger. It held a dove in its talons, tearing off its feathers as it flew, and they fell to the ground midway between Telemachus and the ship. Theoclymenus then caught Telemachus by the hand and said, "Telemachus, that bird did not fly on your right without being sent by some god. I recognized it as an omen; it means you will remain powerful, and there will be no house in Ithaca more royal than your own."

"I wish it may prove so," replied Telemachus. "If it does, I will show you so much goodwill and give you such presents that all who see you will congratulate you."

Then he said to his friend Piraeus, "Piraeus, son of Clytius, you have always been the most willing to serve me of all those who have accompanied me to Pylos. I wish you would take this stranger to your house and entertain him hospitably until I can return for him."

Piraeus answered, "Telemachus, you may stay away as long as you wish, but I will look after him for you, and he will find no lack of hospitality."

With that, he went on board, urging the others to do the same and loosen the hawsers, so they took their places in the ship. Telemachus donned his sandals and grabbed a long, sturdy spear with a bronze tip from the ship's deck. They loosened the hawsers, pushed the ship from the shore, and headed toward the city as instructed, while Telemachus walked as fast as he could until he reached the homestead where his numerous herds of swine were feeding, where dwelled the excellent swineherd, so devoted a servant to his master.

BOOK 16:

Meanwhile, Ulysses and the swineherd had lit a fire in the hut and were preparing breakfast at daybreak, having sent the men out with the pigs. When Telemachus arrived, the dogs did not bark but welcomed him with affection. Ulysses, hearing the sound of footsteps and noticing the dogs' behavior, said to Eumaeus:

"Eumaeus, I hear footsteps; it must be one of your men or someone you know, since the dogs are fawning and not barking."

Hardly had he spoken when his son stood at the door. Eumaeus jumped to his feet, and the bowls he had been mixing wine in fell from his hands as he rushed toward his master. He kissed Telemachus on the head and both of his beautiful eyes, weeping for joy. A father could not be more delighted at the return of an only son, the child of his old age, after ten years of hardship in a foreign land. He embraced him and kissed him all over as if he had returned from the dead, speaking tenderly:

"So, you have returned, Telemachus, light of my eyes! When I heard you had gone to Pylos, I feared I would never see you again. Come in, dear child, and sit down so I can have a good look at you now that you are home. It's not often you visit us herdsmen; you usually stick close to the town to keep an eye on the suitors."

"That's true, old friend," Telemachus replied, "but I have come now to see you and to find out whether my mother is still at home or if someone else has married her, leaving Ulysses' bed bare and covered in cobwebs."

"She is still at the house," Eumaeus replied, "grieving and heartbroken, weeping both night and day without pause."

As he spoke, he took Telemachus' spear, crossed the stone threshold, and entered the hut. Ulysses rose to give him a place to sit, but Telemachus stopped him, saying, "Sit down, stranger. I can easily find another seat; there's one here that can be laid for me."

Ulysses returned to his place, and Eumaeus spread some green brushwood on the floor, placing a sheepskin on top for Telemachus to sit upon. The swineherd then brought them platters of cold meat from the previous day's feast and filled the bread baskets as quickly as he could. He mixed wine in bowls of ivy wood and took his seat facing Ulysses. They then laid their hands on the food before them, and when they had eaten and drunk enough, Telemachus asked Eumaeus, "Old friend, where does this stranger come from? How did his crew bring him to Ithaca, and who were they? He surely did not arrive here by land."

Eumaeus replied, "My son, I will tell you the truth. He claims to be a Cretan and a great traveler. Right now, he is fleeing from a Thesprotian ship and has taken refuge here, so I will hand him over to you. Do with him as you please, but remember that he is your suppliant."

"I am very troubled by what you have told me," Telemachus said. "How can I take this stranger into my house? I am still young and not strong enough to defend myself if anyone attacks me. My mother is unsure whether to remain in the house out of respect for public opinion and the memory of her husband, or to marry the best man among the suitors who makes the best offer. But since this stranger has come to your station, I will provide him with a cloak and a good shirt, a sword, and sandals, and send him wherever he wishes to go. If you prefer, you can keep him here at the station, and I will send him clothes and food so he is not a burden to you and your men. However, I will not let him go near the suitors, for they are very arrogant and would certainly mistreat him in a way that would greatly upset me; no matter how brave a man may be, he cannot stand against numbers, for they will overpower him."

Ulysses interjected, "Sir, it is only right that I should speak. I am quite disturbed by what you say regarding the suitors' arrogant behavior toward a man such as yourself. Tell me, do you endure such treatment quietly, or has some god turned your people against you? Are there not brothers you can appeal to for support, no matter how great your quarrel? If I were as young as you and in my current state of mind—if I were Ulysses' son or even Ulysses himself—I would prefer to have someone cut off my head rather than see such disgraceful behavior in my own house, witnessing strangers being mistreated, and men dragging the servants around the house in shameful ways, drinking wine recklessly, and wasting bread all for a purpose that shall never be fulfilled."

Telemachus replied, "I will tell you the truth. There is no enmity between me and my people, nor can I complain about brothers, to whom a man may look for support regardless of how great the quarrel may be. Jove has made us all only sons. Laertes was the only son of Arceisius, and Ulysses was the only son of Laertes. I am the only son of Ulysses, whom he left behind when he went away, so I have never been of any help to him. Hence, my house is in the hands of countless marauders; the chiefs from all the neighboring islands—Dulichium, Same, Zacynthus—and the principal men of Ithaca itself are consuming my estate under the pretense of courting my mother, who will neither declare that she will not marry nor bring matters to a conclusion. They are destroying my estate, and soon, I fear, they will destroy me as well. The outcome is in the hands of heaven. But you, old friend Eumaeus, go and tell Penelope that I am safe and have returned from Pylos. Tell her alone and return here without letting anyone else know, for many are plotting against me."

"I understand and will heed you," replied Eumaeus. "You do not need to instruct me further; just tell me whether I should also let poor Laertes know of your return. He used to oversee the work on his farm despite his sorrow for Ulysses. He would eat and drink with his servants, but since you set out for Pylos, they say he has not eaten or drunk properly and does not tend to his farm, but sits weeping and wasting away."

"That is unfortunate," said Telemachus. "I pity him, but we must let him be for now. If people could have everything their own way, I would wish for the return of my father. But go and deliver your message quickly, and do not stray from your path to inform Laertes. Tell my mother to send one of her women with the news immediately, and let him hear it from her."

Thus, he urged the swineherd, and Eumaeus took his sandals, bound them to his feet, and set off for the town. Minerva watched him leave the station, then approached in the form of a fair, stately woman. She stood by the entry and revealed herself to Ulysses, but Telemachus could not see her, for the gods do not allow themselves to be seen by everyone. Ulysses recognized her, as did the dogs, who did not bark but cowered, whining to the other side of the yards. She nodded and motioned to Ulysses with her eyebrows. He then left the hut and stood before her outside the main wall of the yard.

"Ulysses, noble son of Laertes," she said, "it is now time for you to reveal yourself to your son. Do not keep him in the dark any longer, but prepare to destroy the suitors and then head for the town. I will join you soon, for I am eager for the fray."

As she spoke, she touched him with her golden wand. First, she wrapped him in a fine clean shirt and cloak, then made him appear younger and more impressive; she restored his color, filled out his cheeks, and darkened his beard. After that, she left, and Ulysses returned to the hut. His son was astonished to see him and turned away, fearing he was looking upon a god.

"Stranger," he said, "how suddenly you have changed from what you were a moment ago. Your dress is different, and your color has changed. Are you one of the gods who live in heaven? If so, be gracious to me until I can make you due sacrifices and offerings of gold. Have mercy on me."

Ulysses replied, "I am no god; why would you think I am? I am your father, the one for whom you grieve and suffer so much at the hands of lawless men."

As he spoke, Ulysses kissed his son, and a tear fell from his cheek to the ground, for he had held back his tears until that moment. But Telemachus still could not believe that it was truly his father and said:

"You are not my father but some god, flattering me with empty hopes that I may grieve even more later. No mortal could change himself from old to young at a moment's notice like this unless a god were involved. Just moments ago, you looked old and ragged, and now you resemble a god come down from heaven."

Ulysses replied, "Telemachus, you ought not to be so astonished at my presence. There will be no other Ulysses arriving here. Here I am, after long wandering and many hardships, back in my own country after twenty years. What you see is the work of the great goddess Minerva, who does with me whatever she wishes, for she has the power to change my appearance. At one moment I appear as a beggar, and the next I am a young man dressed in fine clothes; it is easy for the gods who dwell in heaven to make anyone look either rich or poor."

After he spoke, he sat down, and Telemachus embraced his father and wept. They were both so moved that they cried out like eagles or vultures whose half-fledged young have been taken by farmers. Their mourning would have continued until sunset if Telemachus had not suddenly said, "In what ship, dear father, did your crew bring you to Ithaca? What nation did they say they belonged to? Surely you did not come by land."

"I will tell you the truth, my son," replied Ulysses. "It was the Phaeacians who brought me here. They are great sailors and are accustomed to escort anyone who reaches their shores. They took me across the sea while I slept and landed me in Ithaca after giving me many gifts of bronze, gold, and clothing. These treasures, thanks to heaven's mercy, are hidden in a cave. I have come here on Minerva's advice so that we can plan to deal with our enemies. First, tell me about the suitors—their number and who they are—so I can consider whether we can fight them ourselves or need to find help."

Telemachus answered, "Father, I have always heard of your great renown in battle and council, but the task you propose is monumental. I am intimidated just thinking about it. Two men cannot stand against many, especially against brave ones. There are not merely ten suitors, or even twice ten, but many times that. Here is their number: fifty-two chosen youths from Dulichium, along with six servants; twenty-four from Same; twenty young Achaeans from Zacynthus; and twelve from Ithaca, all well-born. They are accompanied by a servant, Medon, a bard, and two men who can carve at the table. If we face such numbers, you may find great cause to regret your return and your quest for revenge. Consider whether you can think of someone willing to help us."

"Listen to me," replied Ulysses, "and consider whether Minerva and her father Jove might be enough, or whether I need to find additional support."

"Those you mentioned," said Telemachus, "are indeed good allies. Even though they dwell among the clouds, they have power over gods and men."

"These two," continued Ulysses, "will not stay out of the fight when the suitors and we engage in battle in my house. Now, therefore, return home early tomorrow morning and resume your usual routine among the suitors. Later, the swineherd will bring me to the city disguised as a beggar. If you see them mistreating me, harden your heart against my suffering; even if they drag me out of the house or throw things at me, do nothing but try gently to persuade them to behave; they will not listen, for their day of reckoning is coming. Furthermore, I charge you to heed this: when Minerva puts it in my mind, I will nod my head to you. Upon seeing this, you must gather all the arms in the house and hide them in the strong storeroom. When the suitors ask you why you are moving them, say that you are doing so to protect them from the smoke, for they have become soiled since Ulysses left. Tell them you are worried Jove might incite them to quarrel over their wine, which could lead to harm and disgrace. But leave a sword and spear each for you and me, and a couple of oxhide shields so we can grab them at any moment; then Jove and Minerva will surely calm these people.

Also, if you are indeed my son, and my blood flows in your veins, do not let anyone know that Ulysses is in the house—neither Laertes nor the swineherd, nor any of the servants, nor even Penelope herself. Let you and I deal with the women, and let's also test the loyalty of some of the male servants to see who is on our side and who opposes us."

"Father," replied Telemachus, "you will come to know me in time, and when you do, you will find I can keep your counsel. However, I do not think your plan will turn out well for either of us. Think it over. It will take us a long time to go around the farms and test the men, and in the meantime, the suitors will continue to waste your estate without remorse. By all means, test the women to see who is disloyal and who is innocent, but I am not in favor of going around testing the men. We can address that later, if you truly have some sign from Jove that he will support you."

Thus did they converse. Meanwhile, the ship that had brought Telemachus and his crew from Pylos reached the town of Ithaca. Upon entering the harbor, they drew the ship ashore; their servants took their armor from them, and they left all the gifts at the house of Clytius. They then sent a servant to inform Penelope that Telemachus had gone into the country but sent the ship to the town to prevent her from worrying. This servant and Eumaeus met while both were on the same errand to tell Penelope. When they arrived at the house, the servant stood up and told the queen in the presence of the waiting women, "Your son, madam, has returned from Pylos," while Eumaeus privately informed Penelope of everything Telemachus had instructed him to tell her. After delivering his message, he left the house and returned to his pigs.

The suitors were surprised and angry at this turn of events, so they gathered outside the great wall surrounding the outer court and held a council near the main entrance. Eurymachus, son of Polybus, was the first to speak.

"My friends," he said, "Telemachus's voyage is a serious matter; we had expected it would amount to nothing. Now, however, let us draw a ship into the water and gather a crew to send after the others and call them back as quickly as possible."

He had barely finished speaking when Amphinomus turned and saw the ship in the harbor, with the crew lowering her sails and putting away their oars. He laughed and said to the others, "We need not send any message, for they are here. Some god must have informed them, or perhaps they saw the ship pass by and couldn't catch up."

With that, they rose and went to the water's edge. The crew then drew the ship ashore; their servants took their armor from them, and they went in a group to the place of assembly, but they did not allow anyone, old or young, to sit with them. Antinous, son of Eupeithes, spoke first.

"Good heavens," he said, "see how the gods have saved this man from destruction. We kept scouts stationed on the headlands all day long, and when the sun set, we stayed aboard the ship all night hoping to capture and kill him. Yet some god has brought him home despite our efforts. We must consider how to put an end to him. He must not escape us; our endeavor cannot succeed while he is alive, for he is very cunning, and public sentiment is not entirely on our side. We must act quickly before he can summon the Achaeans to assembly; he will waste no time doing so, furious with us for our failed attempt. The people will not take kindly to it when they learn of our plot, and we must ensure that they do not harm us or drive us from our own land into exile. We must catch him, either on his farm away from the city or on the way back here. Then we can divide his estate among ourselves, and let his mother and the man who marries her take the house. If this does not suit you, and you wish for Telemachus to live and hold his father's property, then we must not gather here and consume his goods in this way, but instead make our offers to Penelope, each from his own home, and she can marry the man who offers the most and whose lot it is to win her."

They all remained silent until Amphinomus stood to speak. He was the son of Nisus, who was the son of King Aretias, and he was the foremost among all the suitors from the fertile and well-grassed island of Dulichium. His manner was more agreeable to Penelope than any other suitor's, for he had a kind disposition. "My friends," he said, speaking plainly and honestly, "I am not in favor of killing Telemachus. It is a grave sin to kill one of noble blood. Let us first seek guidance from the gods; if the oracles of Jove advise it, I will help to kill him myself and will encourage everyone else to do so. But if they dissuade us, I urge you to refrain from violence."

His words pleased the others, so they rose at once and went to the house of Ulysses, where they took their usual seats.

Then Penelope decided she would confront the suitors. She was aware of their plot against Telemachus, as the servant Medon had overheard their plans and informed her. Thus, she made her way to the court, accompanied by her maidens. When she arrived among the suitors, she stood by one of the posts supporting the roof of the cloister, holding a veil before her face, and rebuked Antinous, saying:

"Antinous, insolent schemer, people say you are the best speaker and advisor among the young men in Ithaca, but that is not true. Why are you plotting to kill Telemachus, ignoring the rights of suppliants, who are under the protection of Jove himself? It is not right for you to conspire against one another. Do you not remember how your father fled to this house in fear of the people who were enraged against him for raiding the Thesprotians, who were at peace with us? They wanted to tear him apart and take everything he had, but Ulysses prevented them, even when they were furious. Yet now, you devour his property without paying for it, and you break my heart by courting his wife and plotting against his son. Cease this wickedness and urge the others to do the same."

Eurymachus, son of Polybus, replied, "Take heart, Queen Penelope, daughter of Icarius, and do not worry yourself about these matters. The man who would harm your son Telemachus is not yet born, nor will he ever be, as long as I live to see the light of day. I declare that my spear shall be stained with his blood; Ulysses often held me on his knees, offered me wine, and gave me meat. Therefore, Telemachus is like a dear friend to me, and he has nothing to fear from us suitors. But if death is meant for him from the gods, he cannot escape it." Though he spoke to reassure her, he was truly plotting against Telemachus.

Penelope then went back upstairs, mourning for her husband until Minerva caused sleep to come over her. In the evening, Eumaeus returned to Ulysses and Telemachus, who had just sacrificed a young pig and were preparing supper together. Minerva then approached Ulysses, transformed him back into an old man with a wave of her wand, and dressed him in his old clothes again, fearing that the swineherd might recognize him and spill the secret to Penelope.

Telemachus was the first to speak. "So you have returned, Eumaeus," he said. "What news from the town? Have the suitors come back, or are they still waiting over there, preparing to take me on my way home?"

"I did not think to ask about that," replied Eumaeus, "while I was in town. I intended to deliver my message and return quickly. I met a man sent by those who traveled with you to Pylos, and he was the first to inform your mother. However, I can tell you what I saw with my own eyes: I had just reached the hill of Mercury above the town when I saw a ship coming into the harbor, filled with men. They carried many shields and spears, and I thought it was the suitors, but I cannot be certain."

Hearing this, Telemachus smiled at his father, but Eumaeus did not see him.

When they had completed their tasks and the meal was ready, they sat down to eat, each man receiving a full portion, satisfying all. After they had eaten and drunk enough, they laid down to rest and enjoyed the blessings of sleep.

BOOK 17:

When rosy-fingered Dawn appeared, Telemachus put on his sandals and took a strong spear that suited his grip, as he planned to go into the city. "Old friend," he said to the swineherd, "I will now go to town to see my mother. She will not stop grieving until she sees me. As for this unfortunate stranger, take him to the city and let him beg from anyone willing to give him a drink and a piece of bread. I have enough of my own troubles and cannot take on anyone else's burden. If this angers him, so be it; I prefer to speak my mind."

Ulysses replied, "Sir, I do not wish to stay here. A beggar can fare better in town than in the countryside, where anyone can offer him something. I am too old to wait here at the beck and call of a master. Let this man do as you suggested, and take me to town as soon as I've warmed myself by the fire and the day has warmed up a bit. My clothes are terribly thin, and I will freeze in this frosty morning, especially since you say the city is some distance away."

Telemachus then strode off through the yards, brooding over his revenge against the suitors. Upon reaching home, he leaned his spear against a post in the cloister, crossed the stone floor, and went inside.

Nurse Euryclea noticed him long before anyone else. She was putting fleeces on the seats when she ran up to him, bursting into tears. The other maids soon joined her, showering him with kisses. Penelope emerged from her room, looking like Diana or Venus, and wept as she embraced her son. She kissed his forehead and both of his beautiful eyes. "Light of my eyes," she cried fondly, "you have come home! I thought I would never see you again. You went off to Pylos without telling me or seeking my consent. But come, tell me what you saw."

"Do not scold me, mother," replied Telemachus, "nor upset me, considering how narrowly I escaped. Wash your face, change your dress, go upstairs with your maids, and vow ample hecatombs to all the gods if Jove will grant us our revenge on the suitors. I must now go to the assembly to invite a stranger who has returned with me from Pylos. I sent him on with my crew, and I told Piraeus to look after him until I could come for him myself."

Penelope obeyed her son's words. She washed her face, changed her dress, and vowed full hecatombs to all the gods for revenge on the suitors.

Telemachus then exited the cloisters with his spear in hand, not alone, for his two swift dogs accompanied him. Minerva endowed him with a divine presence so striking that all marveled as he passed by. The suitors gathered around him, greeting him with friendly words, but harboring malice in their hearts. He avoided them and went to sit with Mentor, Antiphus, and Halitherses, old friends of his father's house. They pressed him to recount all that had happened. Then Piraeus approached with Theoclymenus, whom he had escorted through the town to the assembly. Telemachus immediately joined them.

"Telemachus," Piraeus said, "I wish you would send some of your women to my house to collect the gifts Menelaus gave you."

"We do not know, Piraeus," Telemachus replied, "what might happen. If the suitors kill me in my own house and divide my property among them, I would prefer you to have the presents than let those men possess them. But if I manage to kill them, I will be grateful if you return my gifts."

With these words, he took Theoclymenus to his own house. Upon arrival, they laid their cloaks on the benches and seats, then entered the baths to wash themselves. After the maids had washed and anointed them and given them cloaks and shirts, they took their places at the table. A maid brought them water in a beautiful golden ewer and poured it into a silver basin for them to wash their hands. She set a clean table beside them, while an upper servant brought them bread and offered many good things from the house. Penelope sat opposite them, reclining on a couch by a post of the cloister, spinning. Once they had enough to eat and drink, Penelope said:

"Telemachus, I will go upstairs and lie down on that sorrowful couch, which I have not stopped wetting with my tears since Ulysses set out for Troy with the sons of Atreus. You, however, did not make it clear to me before the suitors returned whether you found out anything about your father's return."

"I will tell you the truth," replied her son. "We went to Pylos and met Nestor, who treated me as if I were his own son returned after a long absence; so did his sons. But he said he had heard nothing from anyone about Ulysses, whether he was alive or dead. He sent me to Menelaus with a chariot and horses. There, I saw Helen, for whose sake so many, both Argives and Trojans, were doomed to suffer. Menelaus asked what brought me to Lacedaemon, and I told him the whole truth. He responded, 'So, then, these cowards wish to usurp a brave man's bed? A doe might as well lay her newborn fawn in the lair of a lion and then go off to feed in the woods. When the lion returns, he will make short work of both. So will Ulysses with these suitors. By Jove, Minerva, and Apollo, if Ulysses is still the man he was when he wrestled with Philomeleides in Lesbos, throwing him so that all the Greeks cheered him—if he is still such, and were to approach these suitors, they would have a short shrift and a sorry wedding. However, I will not deceive you; I will tell you what the old man of the sea told me. He said he saw Ulysses on an island, sorrowing in the house of the nymph Calypso, who keeps him prisoner. He cannot reach his home, for he has no ships or sailors to take him over the sea.' This is what Menelaus told me, and after hearing his story, I returned home. The gods then granted me a fair wind and brought me back safely."

These words moved Penelope's heart. Then Theoclymenus said to her:

"Madam, wife of Ulysses, Telemachus does not understand these things; listen to me, for I can divine them surely and will hide nothing from you. May Jove, the king of heaven, be my witness, along with the rites of hospitality and the hearth of Ulysses to which I now come, that Ulysses is even now in Ithaca, either going about the country or staying in one place, inquiring into all these evil deeds and preparing for a reckoning with the suitors. I saw an omen when I was on the ship that meant this, and I told Telemachus about it."

"May it be so," answered Penelope. "If your words come true, you shall have such gifts and good will from me that all who see you will congratulate you."

Thus they conversed. Meanwhile, the suitors were throwing discs and aiming spears at a mark on the level ground in front of the house, behaving with all their old insolence. When it was time for dinner and the flock of sheep and goats came into town from the countryside with their shepherds, Medon, their favorite servant, who waited on them at the table, said, "Now, my young masters, you have had enough sport, so come inside that we may prepare dinner. Dinner is a good thing at dinner time."

They left their games at his command. Inside the house, they laid their cloaks on the benches and seats and sacrificed some sheep, goats, pigs, and a heifer, all fat and well-grown, preparing for their meal. Meanwhile, Ulysses and the swineherd were preparing to head into town. The swineherd said, "Stranger, I suppose you still want to go to town today, as my master instructed; for my part, I would have preferred that you stayed here as a station hand. But I must obey my master, or he will scold me later, and a scolding from one's master is serious business. Let us be off, for it is now broad daylight; night will soon come again, and then it will be colder."

"I know, and I understand," replied Ulysses. "You need not say more. Let us go, but if you have a stick ready to cut, let me have it to walk with, for you say the road is very rough."

As he spoke, he threw his shabby old tattered wallet over his shoulders and Eumaeus provided him with a suitable stick. They then set out, leaving the station in charge of the dogs and herdsmen who remained behind. The swineherd led the way, and his master followed, looking like a worn-out old tramp, leaning on his staff, dressed in rags. Once they crossed the rough steep ground and neared the city, they arrived at the fountain from which the citizens drew their water. This fountain had been constructed by Ithacus, Neritus, and Polyctor. A grove of water-loving poplars surrounded it, and clear, cold water flowed down from a high rock. Above the fountain, there was an altar to the nymphs, where all wayfarers used to make sacrifices. Here Melanthius, son of Dolius, met them while driving down some goats, the best of his flock, for the suitors' dinner, accompanied by two shepherds. Upon seeing Eumaeus and Ulysses, he insulted them with outrageous and unseemly language, which angered Ulysses greatly.

"There you go," Melanthius shouted, "and what a fine pair you are! See how heaven brings together birds of a feather. Tell me, master swineherd, where are you taking this poor, miserable creature? It makes anyone sick to see such a person at a table. A fellow like this has never won a prize in his life and will just rub against every man's doorpost, begging—not for swords or cauldrons like a man, but just for a few scraps not worth asking for. If you would give him to me to help on my station, he could clean out the folds or bring some sweet feed to the kids, and he could fatten up on whey as much as he liked; but he has fallen into bad ways and does no work, just begging for food all over town to satisfy his insatiable belly. Therefore, I say—and I mean it—if he goes near Ulysses' house, he'll get his head broken by the stools they'll throw at him until he's tossed out."

As he passed, he kicked Ulysses in the hip out of sheer malice, but Ulysses stood firm, refusing to move from the path. For a moment he considered whether to fly at Melanthius and kill him with his staff or throw him to the ground and beat him senseless. However, he chose to endure the insult and keep his composure. Eumaeus looked directly at Melanthius and rebuked him, lifting his hands and praying to the heavens as he did so.

"Fountain nymphs," he cried, "children of Jove, if ever Ulysses burned thigh bones covered with fat—whether of lambs or kids—grant my prayer that heaven may send him home. He would soon put an end to the swaggering threats of men like you, who roam about insulting people while your flocks go to ruin from bad shepherding."

Then Melanthius the goatherd replied, "You ill-conditioned cur, what are you talking about? Someday I will put you on board ship and sell you to a foreign land, pocketing whatever money you bring. I wish I could be sure that Apollo would strike Telemachus dead today, or that the suitors would kill him, as I am certain Ulysses will never come home again."

With that, he hurried ahead to reach his master's house. Once there, he took his seat among the suitors opposite Eurymachus, who favored him over the others. The servants brought him a portion of meat, and a serving maid set bread before him to eat. Presently, Ulysses and the swineherd arrived at the house, drawn in by the sound of music as Phemius began to sing for the suitors. Ulysses took hold of Eumaeus' hand and said:

"Eumaeus, this house of Ulysses is indeed a fine place. No matter how far you go, you will find few like it. One building follows after another. The outer court has a wall with battlements all around; the doors are double-folding and well crafted. It would be hard to take it by force. I perceive that many people are feasting inside, for I smell roast meat and hear music, which the gods have made to accompany their banquet."

"You are correct, as you often are," Eumaeus replied, "but let us consider our best course. Will you go inside first and join the suitors, leaving me here behind you, or will you wait here while I go in first? But do not delay long; someone may see you loitering about outside and throw something at you. Please consider this."

Ulysses responded, "I understand and heed your words. Go in first and leave me here. I am used to being beaten and having things thrown at me. I have been buffeted so much in war and by sea that I am case-hardened, and this too will be just another hardship. But a man cannot hide the cravings of a hungry belly; this is an enemy that troubles all men. Because of this, ships are fitted out to sail the seas and make war on others."

As they talked, a dog that had been sleeping raised his head and perked up his ears. This was Argos, whom Ulysses had raised before going to Troy, but he had never worked. In the past, the young men took him out hunting wild goats, deer, or hares. But now that his master was gone, he lay neglected on piles of mule and cow dung outside the stables, waiting for someone to come and clear it away for fertilizing the fields. He was covered in fleas. When he saw Ulysses standing there, he drooped his ears and wagged his tail but could not reach his master. When Ulysses spotted the dog, he quickly wiped away a tear without Eumaeus seeing and said:

"Eumaeus, what a noble hound that is over yonder on the dung heap! His build is splendid; is he as fine as he looks, or is he just one of those dogs that beg around a table and are kept only for show?"

"This dog," Eumaeus answered, "belonged to the man who has died far from here. If he were still what he was when Ulysses left for Troy, he would soon show you what he could do. There was not a wild beast in the forest that could escape him once he was on its scent. But now he has fallen on hard times, for his master is dead, and the women take no care of him. Servants rarely do their work when their master is not there to oversee them, for Jove takes half the goodness out of a man when he becomes a slave."

As he spoke, he went inside the buildings to where the suitors were, but Argos died as soon as he recognized his master.

Telemachus saw Eumaeus before anyone else and beckoned him to come and sit beside him. Eumaeus looked around and found a seat near where the carver was serving portions to the suitors. He picked it up, brought it to Telemachus' table, and sat down opposite him. A servant brought him his portion and gave him bread from the basket.

Just then, Ulysses entered, looking like a poor, miserable old beggar, leaning on his staff and dressed in rags. He sat on the ash-wood threshold just inside the doors leading from the outer to the inner court, against a cypress-wood post, which the carpenter had skillfully planed and made to join with rule and line. Telemachus took a whole loaf from the bread basket, along with as much meat as he could hold in both hands, and said to Eumaeus, "Take this to the stranger and tell him to go around the suitors to beg from them; a beggar should not be ashamed to ask."

Eumaeus approached him and said, "Stranger, Telemachus sends you this and says you are to go around the suitors begging, for beggars should not be ashamed."

Ulysses replied, "May King Jove grant all happiness to Telemachus and fulfill the desire of his heart."

With both hands, he took what Telemachus had sent him and laid it in his filthy old wallet at his feet. He continued eating while the bard sang, finishing his dinner just as the song ended.

The suitors applauded the bard, and then Minerva prompted Ulysses to beg pieces of bread from each of them so he might gauge the character of the suitors and tell the good from the bad; regardless of what happened, she was not going to spare any of them. Ulysses, therefore, began his round, moving from left to right, stretching out his hands to beg as if he were a real beggar. Some felt pity for him and were curious about his story, asking one another who he was and where he came from. Melanthius the goatherd said, "Suitors of my noble mistress, I can tell you something about him, for I have seen him before. The swineherd brought him here, but I know nothing about the man himself or where he comes from."

Hearing this, Antinous began to insult the swineherd. "You precious fool," he shouted, "why have you brought this man to town? Don't we have enough beggars pestering us while we eat? Do you think it's small thing that such people gather here to waste your master's property? Must you bring this man as well?"

Eumaeus replied, "Antinous, your birth is noble, but your words are vile. It was not my doing that he came here. Who would invite a stranger from a foreign land unless they could provide public service, like a seer, healer of hurts, carpenter, or bard to entertain us with singing? Such men are welcome everywhere, but no one wants a beggar who only brings trouble. You are always harder on Ulysses' servants than the other suitors are, especially on me, but I do not care as long as Telemachus and Penelope are alive and safe here."

Telemachus said, "Hush, do not answer him; Antinous has the sharpest tongue among the suitors and makes the others worse."

Turning to Antinous, he said, "Antinous, you care for my interests as if I were your son. Why do you want to see this stranger turned out of the house? Heaven forbid; take something and give it to him yourself; I do not begrudge it; I ask you to do it. Do not worry about my mother or any of the other servants in the house; I know you will not do as I ask, for you care more for your own appetite than for giving to others."

"What do you mean, Telemachus," Antinous retorted, "by this boastful talk? If all the suitors were to give him as much as I will, he wouldn't return for another three months."

As he spoke, he drew the stool on which he rested his dainty feet from under the table, pretending to throw it at Ulysses, but the other suitors all gave him something and filled his wallet with bread and meat. He was about to return to the threshold and eat what the suitors had given him, but first he approached Antinous and said:

"Sir, give me something; you are not the poorest man here; you seem to be a chief among them all; therefore you should be the better giver, and I will tell far and wide of your generosity. I too was once a rich man and had a fine house; in those days I gave to many a wanderer like myself, regardless of who he was or what he wanted. I had many servants and all the things people have who live well and are considered wealthy, but it pleased Jove to take it all away. He sent me with a band of roving thieves to Egypt; it was a long voyage, and it led to my ruin. I stationed my ships in the river Aegyptus, and told my men to stay by them and guard them while I sent out scouts to reconnoiter from every point of advantage."

"But the men disobeyed my orders, took matters into their own hands, and ravaged the land of the Egyptians, killing the men and taking their wives and children captive. The alarm quickly spread to the city, and at daybreak, when they heard the war cry, the people rushed out until the plain was filled with foot soldiers and horsemen, all gleaming with armor. Then Jove spread panic among my men, and they could no longer face the enemy, realizing they were surrounded. The Egyptians killed many of us and took the rest captive to force them into labor. As for me, they gave me to a friend who encountered them, to take to Cyprus—a man named Dmetor, son of Iasus, a powerful figure in Cyprus. From there, I have come here in a state of great misery."

Antinous then said, "What god has sent such a pest to plague us at our dinner? Get out into the open part of the court, or I will give you Egypt and Cyprus again for your insolence; you've begged from everyone else, and they've given you generously, for they have plenty. It's easy to be generous with other people's property."

Ulysses began to move away, saying, "Your appearance, my fine sir, is better than your breeding; if you were in your own house, you wouldn't spare a poor man a pinch of salt. Even though you're in another man's house, surrounded by abundance, you cannot find it in yourself to give even a piece of bread."

This angered Antinous, and he scowled, saying, "You will pay for this before you leave the court." With that, he threw a footstool at Ulysses, hitting him on the right shoulder blade. Ulysses stood firm as a rock; the blow did not stagger him, but he shook his head in silence, brooding on his revenge. He then returned to the threshold and sat down, placing his well-filled wallet at his feet.

"Listen to me," he cried, "you suitors of Queen Penelope, that I may speak my mind. A man feels neither ache nor pain if he gets hit while fighting for his money or for his cattle; and even so, Antinous has struck me while serving my miserable belly, which always gets people into trouble. Still, if the poor have gods and avenging deities, I pray they ensure Antinous meets a bad end before his wedding."

"Sit quietly and eat your food in silence, or leave," shouted Antinous. "If you say more, I'll have you dragged through the courts, and my servants will flay you alive."

The other suitors were displeased and one of the younger men said, "Antinous, you did wrong to strike that poor wretch. It will be worse for you if he turns out to be some god—and we know that gods roam about in all sorts of disguises, traveling the world to see who does wrong and who acts justly."

Thus spoke the suitors, but Antinous paid them no mind. Meanwhile, Telemachus was furious about the blow given to his father. Though no tear fell from him, he shook his head in silence, consumed by thoughts of revenge.

When Penelope heard that the beggar had been struck in the banqueting cloister, she spoke before her maids, "I wish Apollo would strike you, Antinous," and her waiting woman Eurynome answered, "If our prayers were answered, not one of the suitors would see the sun rise again." Then Penelope said, "Nurse, I hate every single one of them, for they mean nothing but mischief, but I hate Antinous like the darkness of death itself. A poor unfortunate tramp has come begging about the house out of sheer want. Everyone else has given him something for his wallet, but Antinous has struck him on the right shoulder blade with a footstool."

Thus did she talk with her maids as she sat in her room, while Ulysses was getting his dinner. Then she called for the swineherd and said, "Eumaeus, go tell the stranger to come here; I want to see him and ask him some questions. He seems to have traveled much and may have heard or seen something about my unhappy husband."

To this, you answered, O swineherd Eumaeus, "If these Achaeans, Madam, would only keep quiet, you would be charmed by the history of his adventures. I had him with me for three days and three nights in my hut, which was the first place he reached after escaping from his ship, and he has yet to finish the story of his misfortunes. If he were the most talented minstrel in the world, whose every word held listeners enthralled, I could not have been more charmed as I sat in my hut and listened to him. He says there is an old friendship between his house and Ulysses' and that he comes from Crete, where the descendants of Minos live, after being driven about by every kind of misfortune. He also claims to have heard that Ulysses is alive and nearby among the Thesprotians, bringing great wealth home with him."

"Call him here, then," said Penelope, "that I may hear his story. As for the suitors, let them amuse themselves indoors or out as they wish, for they have nothing to fret about. Their grain and wine remain unwasted in their houses, with only servants to consume them, while they linger in our home day after day, sacrificing our oxen, sheep, and fat goats for their banquets, without a thought to the amount of wine they drink. No estate can endure such recklessness, for we now have no Ulysses to protect us. If he were to return, he and his son would soon have their revenge."

As she spoke, Telemachus sneezed so loudly that the whole house resounded. Penelope laughed when she heard this and said to Eumaeus, "Go and call the stranger; did you not hear how my son sneezed just as I was speaking? This can only mean that all the suitors are going to be killed, and that not one of them will escape. Furthermore, I say this, and lay my words to your heart: if I am satisfied that the stranger is telling the truth, I shall give him a shirt and cloak of good wear."

When Eumaeus heard this, he went straight to Ulysses and said, "Father stranger, my mistress Penelope, mother of Telemachus, has sent for you. She is in great grief but wishes to hear anything you can tell her about her husband, and if she believes you are speaking the truth, she will give you a shirt and cloak, which are what you most need. As for bread, you can beg around the town for enough to fill your belly, letting those who will give what they wish."

"I will tell Penelope," Ulysses replied, "nothing but what is strictly true. I know all about her husband and have shared in his sufferings, but I fear passing through this crowd of cruel suitors, for their pride and insolence reach the heavens. Just now, as I walked about the house without doing harm, a man struck me in a way that hurt very much, yet neither Telemachus nor anyone else defended me. Tell Penelope, therefore, to be patient and wait until sundown. Let her give me a seat close to the fire, for my clothes are worn very thin—you know they are, for you have seen them ever since I first asked for your help—then she can question me about the return of her husband."

The swineherd returned after hearing this, and Penelope said as she saw him cross the threshold, "Why do you not bring him here, Eumaeus? Is he afraid someone will mistreat him, or is he too shy to come inside? Beggars should not be ashamed."

To this, you answered, O swineherd Eumaeus, "The stranger is quite reasonable. He is avoiding the suitors and is only doing what anyone would do. He asks you to wait until sundown, and it will be much better, madam, for you to have him all to yourself, when you can listen to him and talk to him as you wish."

"The man is no fool," Penelope replied, "it would likely be as he says, for there are no more abominable people in the world than these men."

When she finished speaking, Eumaeus returned to the suitors, having explained everything. He then approached Telemachus and said quietly, so that no one could overhear, "My dear sir, I will now go back to the pigs to see to your property and my own business. You will look after what is happening here, but above all, be careful to keep out of danger, for many bear you ill will. May Jove bring them to a bad end before they cause us mischief."

"Very well," replied Telemachus, "go home after you have had your dinner, and in the morning come here with the victims we are to sacrifice for the day. Leave the rest to heaven and me."

With that, Eumaeus took his seat again, and after finishing his dinner, he left the courts and the cloister with the men at the table and went back to his pigs. As for the suitors, they began to amuse themselves with singing and dancing, for it was getting toward evening.

BOOK 18:

Now there came a common tramp known for begging all over the city of Ithaca, notorious as a glutton and drunkard. He had no strength, but he was a hulking fellow to look at. His real name, given by his mother, was Arnaeus, but the young men called him Irus because he ran errands for anyone who asked. As soon as he arrived, he began to insult Ulysses, trying to drive him out of his own house.

"Be off, old man," he shouted, "from the doorway, or you'll be dragged out neck and heels. Can't you see they all want me to throw you out by force? I don't want to do it, but get up and leave, or we'll come to blows."

Ulysses frowned and replied, "My friend, I mean you no harm. People give you much, but I am not jealous. There's room enough in this doorway for both of us, and you need not begrudge me what isn't yours to give. You seem just another tramp like me, but perhaps the gods will grant us better luck later. However, do not talk too much about fighting, or you'll incense me, and even as an old man, I'll cover your mouth and chest with blood. I'll have more peace tomorrow if I do, for you won't come to the house of Ulysses anymore."

Irus was furious and retorted, "You filthy glutton, you shuffle along like an old fishmonger. I have a good mind to grab you and knock your teeth out of your head like boar's tusks. Get ready, and let these people watch. You'll never be able to fight someone younger than you."

They exchanged insults on the smooth pavement in front of the doorway, and when Antinous saw what was happening, he laughed heartily, saying to the others, "This is the finest sport you've ever seen; heaven has never sent anything like it into this house. The stranger and Irus are quarreling and about to fight—let's set them on to do it at once."

The suitors gathered around, laughing at the two ragged tramps. "Listen to me," said Antinous, "there are goats' paunches down at the fire, filled with blood and fat, set aside for supper; whoever wins and proves himself the better man shall have his pick of the lot. He will be free of our table, and we won't allow any other beggar in the house."

Everyone agreed, but Ulysses, to throw them off the scent, said, "Sirs, an old man like myself, worn out with suffering, cannot hold his own against a young one; but my relentless belly urges me on, though I know it can only end in me getting a beating. You must swear, however, that none of you will foully strike me to favor Irus and secure his victory."

They swore as he asked, and when they completed their oath, Telemachus spoke up, "Stranger, if you want to settle with this fellow, you need not fear anyone here. Whoever strikes you will have to fight more than one. I am the host, and the other chiefs, Antinous and Eurymachus, both men of understanding, agree with me."

Everyone assented, and Ulysses girded his old rags about his loins, baring his sturdy thighs, broad chest, and mighty arms; Minerva came to him, making his limbs even stronger. The suitors were astonished, and one turned to his neighbor, saying, "The stranger has shown such strength from his rags that Irus will soon be no match for him."

Irus began to feel uneasy as he heard them, but the servants forced him into the open part of the court, trembling all over with fright. Antinous scolded him, saying, "You swaggering bully, you shouldn't have been born at all if you're afraid of such an old, broken-down creature as this tramp. I say, and it shall surely be, if he beats you and proves himself the better man, I'll send you on board a ship to the mainland and deliver you to king Echetus, who kills everyone that comes near him. He'll cut off your nose and ears and feed your entrails to the dogs."

This frightened Irus even more, but they brought him into the center of the court, and the two men raised their hands to fight. Ulysses thought about whether to strike him hard enough to end him right there, or to give a lighter blow that would just knock him down; in the end, he decided on the lighter blow, fearing the Achaeans would begin to suspect who he was. They began to fight, and Irus hit Ulysses on the right shoulder, but Ulysses landed a blow on Irus's neck under his ear, breaking the bones of his skull. Blood gushed from his mouth as he fell groaning in the dust, gnashing his teeth and kicking the ground, while the suitors threw up their hands, nearly dying of laughter. Ulysses grabbed Irus by the foot and dragged him into the outer court, propping him against the wall and putting a staff in his hands. "Sit here," he said, "and keep the dogs and pigs away. You're a pitiful creature, and if you try to make yourself king of the beggars again, you'll fare much worse."

Then he threw his old, tattered wallet over his shoulder and went back to sit down on the threshold. The suitors entered the cloisters, laughing and praising him. "May Jove and all the other gods grant you whatever you wish for having put an end to this insatiable tramp's importunity. We'll take him to the mainland shortly, to king Echetus, who kills everyone that comes near him."

Ulysses hailed this as a good omen, and Antinous set a great goat's paunch before him, filled with blood and fat. Amphinomus took two loaves from the basket and brought them to him, toasting him as he did so in a golden goblet of wine. "Good luck to you," he said, "father stranger. You are badly off now, but I hope you'll have better times soon."

Ulysses replied, "Amphinomus, you seem to be a man of good

understanding, and rightly so, considering whose son you are. I have heard your father well spoken of; he is Nisus of Dulichium, a brave and wealthy man. They tell me you are his son, and you seem to be a considerable person; listen, therefore, and take heed to what I say. Man is the vainest of all creatures on earth. While heaven grants him health and strength, he believes he will never face harm, and even when the blessed gods bring sorrow upon him, he bears it as best he can, for God grants men their daily fortune day by day. I know this well, for I was a rich man once, committing much wrong in my stubborn pride, trusting in the support of my father and brothers; therefore, let a man always fear God in all things and take the good that heaven sends without vanity. Consider the disgrace of what these suitors are doing; see how they are wasting the estate and dishonoring the wife of one who will surely return one day, and not long from now. Nay, he will be here soon; may heaven send you home quietly first, so you may not meet him on the day of his return, for once he is here, there will be no parting without bloodshed."

With these words, he made a drink-offering, and when he had drunk, he returned the gold cup to Amphinomus, who walked away, serious and bowing his head, for he foresaw evil. But even so, he did not escape destruction, for Minerva had doomed him to fall by the hand of Telemachus. He took his seat again at the place from which he had come.

Then Minerva inspired Penelope to show herself to the suitors, that she might make them even more enamored of her and win further honor from her son and husband. She feigned a mocking laugh and said, "Eurynome, I have changed my mind and want to show myself to the suitors, though I detest them. I should also like to give my son a hint that he should have nothing more to do with them. They speak fairly enough but they mean mischief."

"My dear child," replied Eurynome, "all that you have said is true; go and tell your son about it, but first wash yourself and anoint your face. Do not go about with your cheeks covered in tears; it is not right for you to grieve incessantly, for Telemachus, whom you always prayed you might live to see with a beard, is already grown."

"I know, Eurynome," replied Penelope, "that you mean well, but do not try to persuade me to wash and anoint myself; heaven robbed me of all my beauty the day my husband sailed. Nevertheless, tell Autonoe and Hippodamia that I want them with me when I am in the cloister; I will not go among the men alone; it would not be proper for me to do so."

With that, the old woman went out to summon the maids. Meanwhile, Minerva thought of another matter and sent Penelope into a sweet slumber; she lay down on her couch, her limbs heavy with sleep. The goddess then shed grace and beauty over her so that all the Achaeans would admire her. She washed her face with the ambrosial loveliness that Venus wears when she dances with the Graces; she made her taller and more commanding, and her complexion whiter than ivory. When Minerva finished, she went away, and the maids entered from the women's room, waking Penelope with their chatter.

"What an exquisitely delicious sleep I have had," she said, passing her hands over her face, "in spite of all my misery. I wish Diana would let me die so sweetly now, that I might no longer waste away in despair for my dear husband, who possessed every kind of good quality and was the most distinguished man among the Achaeans."

With these words, she came down from her upper room, attended by two maidens. When she reached the suitors, she stood by one of the posts supporting the roof of the cloister, holding a veil before her face, with a maidservant on either side. The suitors, upon seeing her, were so overwhelmed that they became desperately enamored, each praying he might win her as his own.

"Telemachus," she said to her son, "I fear you are no longer as discreet and well-mannered as you used to be. When you were younger, you had a better sense of propriety; now that you are grown, a stranger would take you for the son of a well-to-do father because of your size and good looks, but your conduct is not what it should be. What is this disturbance that has been going on? How could you allow a stranger to be so disgracefully mistreated? What would have happened if he had suffered serious injury while a suppliant in our house? Surely that would have been very discreditable to you."

"I understand your displeasure, dear mother," replied Telemachus, "and I know when things are not as they should be, which I didn't grasp when I was younger. However, I cannot always behave perfectly. One wicked person after another keeps driving me mad, and I have no one to stand by me. But this fight between Irus and the stranger didn't turn out as the suitors intended, for the stranger got the better of it. I wish Father Jove, Minerva, and Apollo would break the neck of every one of your suitors, some inside the house and some outside; I wish they might all be as limp as Irus is over there in the gate of the outer court. Look at him nodding his head like a drunken man; he's been thrashed so badly he can't stand or get back to his home, wherever that is, for he has no strength left."

As they conversed, Eurymachus approached and said, "Queen Penelope, daughter of Icarius, if all the Achaeans in Iasian Argos could see you at this moment, you would have even more suitors in your house by tomorrow morning, for you are the most admirable woman in the world, both in beauty and strength of understanding."

Penelope replied, "Eurymachus, heaven robbed me of all my beauty when the Argives set sail for Troy with my dear husband. If he were to return and look after my affairs, I would be more respected and present a better image to the world. As it is, I am burdened with care and the afflictions heaven has chosen to heap upon me. My husband foresaw it all, and when he left, he took my wrist in his hand—'Wife,' he said, 'we may not all come home from Troy, for the Trojans fight well with both bow and spear. They are excellent at fighting from chariots, and nothing decides a battle faster. I do not know if heaven will send me back to you, or if I may fall at Troy. In the meantime, look after things here. Take care of my father and mother as you do now, and even more so during my absence, but when you see our son grow a beard, then marry whom you will and leave this home.' This is what he said, and now it is all coming true. A night will come when I must yield myself to a marriage that I detest, for Jove has taken away all hope of happiness. This further grief cuts me to the heart. You suitors are not courting me according to our customs. When men are courting a woman they wish to marry, especially one of noble birth, they usually bring oxen and sheep to feast her friends and make her magnificent gifts, instead of eating up other people's property without payment."

Upon hearing her words, Ulysses was glad she was trying to get presents from the suitors, flattering them with words he knew she did not mean.

Then Antinous said, "Queen Penelope, daughter of Icarius, take as many presents as you wish from anyone who will give them; it is not wise to refuse a gift. But we will not go about our business or leave until you have married the best man among us, whoever he may be."

The others agreed with Antinous, and each sent a servant to fetch a present. Antinous's man returned with a large, lovely dress, exquisitely embroidered, with twelve beautifully made gold brooch pins to fasten it. Eurymachus immediately brought her a magnificent chain of gold and amber beads that gleamed like sunlight. Eurydamas's two men returned with earrings fashioned into three brilliant pendants that sparkled beautifully, while King Pisander, son of Polyctor, gave her a necklace of rare craftsmanship, and everyone else brought her beautiful gifts.

Then the queen went back upstairs, and her maids brought the presents after her. Meanwhile, the suitors took to singing and dancing, staying until evening. They danced and sang until it grew dark, then brought in three braziers to provide light, piling them high with old, dry firewood. They lit torches from the braziers, which the maids held up in turn. Then Ulysses said:

"Maids, servants of Ulysses, who has long been away, go to the queen inside the house; sit with her and entertain her, or spin and pick wool. I will hold the light for all these people. They may stay until morning, but they shall not beat me, for I can endure a great deal."

The maids looked at one another and laughed, while pretty Melantho began to mock him contemptuously. She was Dolius's daughter, but had been raised by Penelope, who had given her toys to play with and looked after her as a child; yet she showed no consideration for her mistress's sorrows, misconducting herself with Eurymachus, whom she loved.

"Poor wretch," she said, "have you lost your mind? Go sleep in a smithy or some gossip's place instead of prattling here. Aren't you ashamed to open your mouth before so many of your betters? Has the wine gotten into your head, or do you always babble this way? You seem to have lost your wits because you beat the tramp Irus; take care that a better man than he doesn't come and bash your head till you're bleeding out of the house."

"Vixen," replied Ulysses, scowling at her, "I will tell Telemachus what you've been saying, and he'll have you torn limb from limb."

With these words, he frightened the women, and they hurried into the house, trembling all over, thinking he would do as he said. Ulysses took his stand near the burning braziers, holding up torches and watching the people, brooding over what was sure to come.

But Minerva would not let the suitors cease their insolence, wanting Ulysses to grow even more bitter against them; she therefore inspired Eurymachus, son of Polybus, to mock him, which made the others laugh. "Listen to me," he said, "you suitors of Queen Penelope, that I may speak my mind. It is not for nothing that this man has come to the house of Ulysses; I believe the light is not coming from the torches, but from his own head—for he's bald!"

Turning to Ulysses, he continued, "Stranger, will you work as a servant if I send you to the fields and make sure you're well paid? Can you build a stone fence or plant trees? I will provide you food all year round and give you shoes and clothing. Will you go, then? Not you; you've fallen into bad ways and prefer to fill your belly by begging around."

"Eurymachus," Ulysses answered, "if you and I were to work against each other in early summer, when the days are long—give me a good scythe, and take another yourself, and let's see who can last longer mowing the grass from dawn till dark. Or if you want to plow against me, let's each take a yoke of strong, tawny oxen: turn me into a four-acre field, and see who can drive the straighter furrow. If war broke out today, give me a shield, a couple of spears, and a helmet fitting well upon my temples—you would find me first in the fray, and you'd stop your mockery about my belly. You are insolent and cruel, thinking yourself great because you live in a little world, and a bad one at that. When Ulysses returns, his doors will be wide, but you will find them narrow when you try to slip through."

Eurymachus was furious at this. He scowled at Ulysses and cried, "You wretch, I will soon make you pay for daring to speak to me like that, and in public too. Has the wine gotten into your head, or do you always talk this way? You seem to have lost your wits because you beat the tramp Irus." He grabbed a footstool, but Ulysses sought refuge at the knees of Amphinomus of Dulichium, fearing the worst. The stool struck the cupbearer on his right hand and knocked him down; the man fell with a cry, flat on his back, and his wine jug clattered to the ground. The suitors in the covered cloister were now in an uproar, and one turned to his neighbor, saying, "I wish the stranger had gone somewhere else; bad luck to him, for all the trouble he's causing us. We cannot allow such disturbance over a beggar; if such ill counsel prevails, we shall have no more pleasure at our feast."

Telemachus stepped forward and said, "Sirs, are you mad? Can't you carry your meat and drink decently? An evil spirit has possessed you. I do not wish to drive any of you away, but you've had your suppers, and the sooner you all go home to bed, the better."

The suitors bit their lips, marveling at his boldness; but Amphinomus, son of Nisus, replied, "Do not let us take offense; it is reasonable, so let us make no reply. Neither let us do violence to the stranger nor to any of Ulysses' servants. Let the cupbearer go round with drink offerings, so we may make them and go home to our rest."

Thus did he speak, and his saying pleased them well. Mulius of Dulichium, servant to Amphinomus, mixed a bowl of wine and water and handed it to each man, whereupon they made their drink offerings to the blessed gods. After making their offerings and drinking as they wished, they each went home to their own abodes.

BOOK 19:

Ulysses remained in the cloister, contemplating how he might, with Minerva's help, kill the suitors. He turned to Telemachus and said, "Telemachus, we need to gather the armor and take it down into the storeroom. When the suitors ask you why you've moved it, say you did so to keep it away from the smoke, as it has become soiled over time since your father left. Add that you're worried Jove might incite them to quarrel over their wine, leading to harm that would disgrace both their banquet and wooing, for the sight of arms can tempt people to use them."

Telemachus agreed with his father's plan, so he called nurse Euryclea and said, "Nurse, lock the women in their room while I take the armor my father left down to the storeroom. No one looks after it since my father is gone, and it has gotten filthy during my boyhood. I want to move it where the smoke cannot reach it."

"I wish, my child," answered Euryclea, "that you would take over the management of the house completely and look after everything yourself. But who will go with you and light your way to the storeroom? The maids would have done so, but you wouldn't let them."

"The stranger," said Telemachus, "will show me a light; those who eat my bread must earn it, no matter where they come from."

Euryclea followed his instructions and locked the women in their room. Ulysses and his son then hurried to bring the helmets, shields, and spears inside. Minerva went before them, holding a gold lamp that cast a soft, brilliant light. Telemachus exclaimed, "Father, my eyes behold a great marvel: the walls, rafters, and crossbeams are all aglow as if with a flaming fire. Surely some god is here, come down from heaven."

"Hush," answered Ulysses, "hold your peace and ask no questions; this is the way of the gods. Get to bed and leave me here to talk with your mother and the maids. In her grief, your mother will ask me all sorts of questions."

Telemachus then went by torchlight to his own room, where he lay in bed until morning. Ulysses was left in the cloister, pondering how, with Minerva's help, he might kill the suitors.

Penelope soon came down from her room, looking like Venus or Diana. They set her a seat inlaid with silver and ivory near the fire, in her accustomed place. It had been crafted by Icmalius and had a footstool integrated with the seat itself, covered with a thick fleece. She sat down as the maids joined her from the women's room. They began removing the tables at which the wicked suitors had been dining, clearing away leftover bread and the cups from which they had drunk. They emptied the embers from the braziers and piled on plenty of dry wood for light and heat.

But Melantho, ever the scornful one, began to rail at Ulysses again, saying, "Stranger, do you mean to plague us by lingering about the house all night and spying on the women? Be off, you wretch, and eat your supper outside, or you shall be driven out with a firebrand."

Ulysses scowled at her and replied, "Good woman, why are you so angry with me? Is it because I am not clean, and my clothes are in rags, forced to beg like a common tramp? I too was once a rich man with a fine house; in those days, I gave generously to many a beggar, no matter who they were or what they sought. I had countless servants and everything that people have who live well and are esteemed wealthy, but Jove has taken it all from me. Beware, woman, lest you lose your pride and position while you revel above your fellows. Have a care that you do not fall out of favor with your mistress, for Ulysses may yet return, and though you think him dead, he has left behind a son, Telemachus, who will notice anything amiss done by the maids in this house, for he is no longer a boy."

Penelope overheard this and scolded the maid, "Impudent baggage," she said, "I see how shamefully you are behaving, and you shall pay for it. You knew perfectly well that I intended to see the stranger and inquire about my husband, for whose sake I am in such continual sorrow."

Then she turned to her head maid, Eurynome, and said, "Bring a seat with a fleece upon it for the stranger to sit on while he tells his story and listens to what I have to say. I wish to ask him some questions."

Eurynome quickly brought the seat and set a fleece upon it. Once Ulysses was seated, Penelope began, "Stranger, I will first ask you who you are and where you come from. Tell me of your town and parents."

"Madam," Ulysses answered, "who on the face of the earth would dare to chide you? Your fame reaches to the heavens; you are like a blameless king who upholds righteousness as a ruler over a great and valiant nation. The earth yields its wheat and barley, trees are laden with fruit, ewes give birth to lambs, and the sea teems with fish because of his virtues, and his people do good deeds under him. Nevertheless, as I sit here in your house, please ask me something else and do not seek to know my race and family, or you will stir memories that will only deepen my sorrow. I am weighed down with grief, and I should not sit weeping and wailing in another's house; it is not well to grieve in this manner. I may soon have one of the servants or even you complaining about me, saying that my eyes swim with tears because I am heavy with wine."

Penelope replied, "Stranger, heaven has robbed me of all beauty, both of face and figure, since the Argives sailed for Troy with my dear husband. If he were to return and tend to my affairs, I should be more respected and present a better image to the world. As it stands, I am burdened with care and with the afflictions that heaven has chosen to lay upon me. The chiefs from all our islands—Dulichium, Same, and Zacynthus, as well as those from Ithaca itself—are wooing me against my will and ravaging my estate. I cannot give attention to strangers or suppliants or those who claim to be skilled artisans; I am always broken-hearted about Ulysses. They insist that I marry again at once, and I must devise schemes to deceive them. At first, heaven inspired me to set up a large loom in my room and begin working on a great piece of needlework. I told them, 'Sweethearts, if Ulysses is indeed dead, do not pressure me to remarry immediately; wait—let me finish this web as a tribute to the hero Laertes, to have it ready when death takes him. He is wealthy, and the women of the land will talk if he is laid out without a shroud.' This is what I said, and they agreed; so I worked at my great web all day long, but at night I would unpick the stitches by torchlight. I deceived them in this way for three years without them discovering my ruse. But now, in my fourth year, as the moons wane and many days pass, those good-for-nothing maids betrayed me to the suitors, who broke in upon me and caught me. They were furious with me, and I was forced to finish my work whether I wanted to or not. Now I see no further way to avoid this marriage. My parents are pressuring me greatly, and my son chafes at the destruction the suitors are wreaking on his estate, for he is old enough to understand and manage his affairs, blessed by heaven with an excellent disposition. Still, notwithstanding all this, tell me who you are and where you come from—surely you must have had parents; you cannot be the son of an oak or a rock."

Ulysses replied, "Madam, wife of Ulysses, since you persist in asking about my family, I will answer, no matter the cost: people must expect to feel pain when they have been exiles as long as I have and suffered as much among many peoples. Nevertheless, regarding your question, I will tell you all you ask. There is a fair and fruitful island in mid-ocean called Crete; it is thickly populated with ninety cities where people speak many different languages, for there are Achaeans, brave Eteocretans, Dorians of three-fold race, and noble Pelasgi. There is a great town there, Cnossus, where Minos reigned, who every nine years conferred with Jove himself. Minos was father to Deucalion, and I am his son, for Deucalion had two sons, Idomeneus and me. Idomeneus sailed for Troy, and I, the younger, am called Aethon; my brother, however, was both older and braver than I. It was in Crete that I met Ulysses and showed him hospitality when the winds brought him there as he was sailing to Troy, having been carried off course from cape Malea, landing him in Amnisus near the cave of Ilithuia, where the harbors are hard to enter and he could scarcely find shelter from the raging winds. Once he arrived, he went into the town to seek out Idomeneus, claiming to be an old and valued friend, but Idomeneus had already set sail for Troy ten or twelve days earlier. I took him to my house and offered him every kind of hospitality, for I had abundance of everything. I fed his men with barley meal from the public store, providing wine and oxen for sacrifices to satisfy their hearts. They stayed with me for twelve days, as a gale blew from the North, so strong that one could hardly keep one's feet on land. Some unfriendly god must have raised it, but on the thirteenth day, the wind dropped, and they were able to leave."

Ulysses spun a tale, and Penelope wept as she listened, her heart softened. Just as the snow melts on the mountain tops when the winds from the southeast and west warm it until rivers swell, so did her cheeks overflow with tears for the husband who sat beside her. Ulysses felt for her and sympathized, yet he kept his eyes as hard as horn or iron, restraining his tears. When she had wept and found some relief, she turned to him again and said, "Now, stranger, I shall put you to the test and see whether you truly did host my husband and his men, as you claim. Tell me, how was he dressed? What was he like to look at, and what of his companions?"

"Madam," Ulysses replied, "it has been so long that I can hardly say. Twenty years have passed since he left my home and went elsewhere, but I will tell you as best I remember. Ulysses wore a mantle of purple wool, double-lined, fastened with a gold brooch that had two catches for the pin. On the face of the brooch, there was a device showing a dog holding a spotted fawn between its paws, watching it as it lay panting on the ground. Everyone marveled at the craftsmanship of the gold, the dog looking at the fawn and strangling it while the fawn struggled to escape. His shirt, worn next to his skin, was soft and fit him like the skin of an onion, glistening in the sunlight to the admiration of all the women who beheld it. Furthermore, I swear, I do not know whether Ulysses wore these clothes when he left home or if one of his companions gave them to him during his voyage, or perhaps someone at whose house he was staying gifted them to him, for he had many friends and few equals among the Achaeans. I myself gave him a bronze sword and a beautiful purple mantle, double-lined, with a shirt that reached his feet, and sent him on board with every mark of honor. He had a servant with him, a little older than himself; I can tell you about him: his shoulders were hunched, he was dark, and he had thick curly hair. His name was Eurybates, and Ulysses treated him with greater familiarity than any of the others, as they were most like-minded."

Penelope was deeply moved by the undeniable proofs Ulysses presented, and when she found relief in her tears once more, she said to him, "Stranger, I was already inclined to pity you, but from now on you shall be honored and welcomed in my house. I gave Ulysses the clothes you mention. I took them out of the storeroom and folded them myself, and I also gave him the gold brooch to wear as an ornament. Alas! I shall never welcome him home again. It was by ill fate that he ever set out for that detested city whose very name I cannot bring myself to mention."

Ulysses replied, "Madam, wife of Ulysses, do not further disfigure yourself by grieving so bitterly for your loss, though I can hardly blame you for it. A woman who has loved her husband and borne him children would naturally grieve at losing him, even if he were worse than Ulysses, who they say was like a god. Still, cease your tears and listen to what I can tell you. I will hide nothing from you and can say with perfect truth that I have recently heard of Ulysses as being alive and on his way home; he is among the Thesprotians, bringing back much valuable treasure that he has collected from them. However, his ship and crew were lost as they left the Thrinacian island, for Jove and the sun-god were angry with him because his men slaughtered the sun-god's cattle, and they all drowned. But Ulysses clung to the ship's keel and was washed ashore on the land of the Phaeacians, who are almost like the immortals. They treated him as a god, giving him many gifts and wishing to escort him home safely. In fact, Ulysses would have returned long ago if he hadn't decided to travel from place to place gathering wealth; there is no one living who is as cunning as he is. King Pheidon of the Thesprotians told me this, swearing by making drink-offerings in his house that the ship was waiting by the water and that a crew was ready to take Ulysses home. He sent me off first on a Thesprotian ship sailing for Dulichium, but he showed me all the treasure Ulysses had gathered, and there was enough in King Pheidon's house to sustain his family for ten generations. The king said Ulysses had gone to Dodona to learn Jove's will from the sacred oak tree, to know whether he should return to Ithaca openly or in secret. So you can know he is safe and will be here shortly; he is close at hand and cannot remain away from home much longer. Nevertheless, I will confirm my words with an oath, calling upon Jove, the first and mightiest of all gods, as well as the hearth of Ulysses to which I have now come, that all I have spoken shall surely come to pass. Ulysses will return this very year; by the end of this moon and the beginning of the next, he will be here."

"May it be so," Penelope answered. "If your words come true, you shall receive such gifts and goodwill from me that all who see you will congratulate you; but I know very well how it will be. Ulysses will not return, nor will you get your escort home, for as surely as Ulysses ever was, there are no longer any masters in the house like him, to welcome honorable strangers or to further them on their way. And now, you maids, wash his feet for him, and make a bed with rugs and blankets, that he may be warm and comfortable until morning. Then at daybreak, wash him and anoint him again, so he may sit in the cloister and eat with Telemachus. It will be the worse for any of these hateful people who are uncivil to him; whether they like it or not, he shall have no more to do in this house. How, sir, shall you be able to learn whether I am superior to others of my sex in goodness of heart and understanding, if I allow you to dine in my cloisters squalid and ill-clad? Men live but for a little while; if they are hard and deal hardly, people wish them ill while they are alive and speak contemptuously of them when they are dead. But he who is righteous and deals righteously is praised among all lands, and many shall call him blessed."

Ulysses replied, "Madam, I have forsaken rugs and blankets since the day I left the snowy ranges of Crete for shipboard. I will lie as I have lain many sleepless nights before. Night after night I have passed in rough sleeping places, waiting for morning. Nor do I wish to have my feet washed; I shall not let any of the young hussies in your house touch my feet. However, if you have any old and respectable woman who has endured as much trouble as I have, I will allow her to wash them."

To this Penelope said, "My dear sir, of all the guests who have come to my house, there has never been one who has spoken with such admirable propriety as you do. There happens to be in the house a most respectable old woman—the same who received my poor dear husband in her arms the night he was born and nursed him in infancy. She is very frail now, but she shall wash your feet." "Come here," she called, "Euryclea, wash the feet of your master's age-mate; I suppose Ulysses' hands and feet are now much the same as yours, for trouble ages us all dreadfully fast."

At these words, the old woman covered her face with her hands, weeping and lamenting, saying, "My dear child, I do not know what to do with you. I am certain that no one has been more god-fearing than you, and yet Jove has forsaken you. No one in the whole world has ever burned him more thigh bones or offered finer hecatombs when you prayed that you might reach a green old age and see your son grow up to take after you. Yet look how he has prevented you alone from returning home. I do not doubt that the women in some foreign palace are mocking him as all these hussies here have mocked you. I do not wonder that you do not want them to wash you after how they have insulted you. I will wash your feet myself gladly, as Penelope has ordered. I will wash them both for Penelope's sake and for your own, for you have stirred deep feelings of compassion in me; and let me add this, which you should heed: we have had all kinds of distressed strangers come here before now, but I boldly say that none have ever yet come who resembles Ulysses so closely in figure, voice, and feet as you do."

"Those who have seen us both," Ulysses replied, "have always said we are remarkably alike, and now you have noticed it too."

The old woman then took the cauldron to wash his feet, pouring cold water into it and adding hot until the bath was warm enough. Ulysses sat by the fire but soon turned away from the light, fearing that when the old woman touched his leg, she would recognize a certain scar it bore, revealing the whole truth. As soon as she began washing his feet, she recognized the scar from the wild boar he had hunted on Mt. Parnassus with his grandfather Autolycus—who was known as the most skilled thief and liar in the world—and the sons of Autolycus. Mercury himself had endowed Autolycus with this gift, for he used to burn thigh bones of goats and kids to him, enjoying his company. It happened once that Autolycus visited Ithaca and found the child of his daughter just born. After supper, Euryclea set the infant on his knees and said, "Autolycus, you must find a name for your grandson; you greatly wished for one."

"Son-in-law and daughter," replied Autolycus, "call the child thus: I am greatly displeased with many people here and there; so name the child 'Ulysses,' or the child of anger. When he grows up and visits his mother's family on Mt. Parnassus, where my possessions lie, I will make him a present and send him on his way rejoicing."

Thus, Ulysses went to Parnassus to receive the gifts from Autolycus, who, along with his sons, welcomed him warmly. His grandmother Amphithea embraced him, kissing his head and both of his beautiful eyes, while Autolycus asked his sons to prepare dinner, and they did so. They brought in a five-year-old bull, flayed it, prepared it, and cut it into joints; these they spitted and roasted sufficiently to serve around. All day long, from dawn until sunset, they feasted, and every man had his fill until they were satisfied; when the sun set and darkness fell, they went to bed and enjoyed a good night's sleep.

When rosy-fingered Dawn appeared, the sons of Autolycus went out with their hounds to hunt, and Ulysses went too. They climbed the wooded slopes of Parnassus and soon reached its breezy valleys. As the sun began to warm the fields, rising from the depths of Oceanus, they came to a mountain dell. The dogs were in front, tracking the scent of the beast they were after, and the sons of Autolycus followed closely behind them, among whom was Ulysses, armed with a long spear. There, in some thick brushwood, lay a huge boar's lair, so dense that wind and rain could not penetrate it, nor could the sun's rays break through, and the ground was thick with fallen leaves. The boar heard the noise of the men's feet and the baying of the hounds as the hunters approached, and rushed from its lair, bristles raised on its neck, standing at bay with fire flashing from its eyes. Ulysses was the first to raise his spear and try to strike the beast, but the boar was too quick, charging him and ripping his leg above the knee with a deep gash that did not reach the bone. Ulysses struck the boar on the right shoulder, and the spear pierced through it, causing it to fall groaning in the dust until its life left it. The sons of Autolycus busied themselves with the carcass of the boar and bound Ulysses' wound, then after chanting a spell to stop the bleeding, they hurried home. When Autolycus and his sons thoroughly healed Ulysses, they made him splendid gifts and sent him back to Ithaca with warm goodwill. Upon his return, his father and mother rejoiced to see him and asked him about everything, including how he had received the scar; he told them how the boar had wounded him while hunting with Autolycus and his sons on Mt. Parnassus.

As soon as Euryclea had the scarred limb in her hands, she recognized it and dropped the foot at once. The leg fell into the bath, ringing out and spilling all the water; Euryclea's eyes filled with tears between her joy and grief, and she could not speak, but she caught Ulysses by the beard and said, "My dear child, you must be Ulysses himself; I did not know you until I touched and handled you."

As she spoke, she looked toward Penelope, wanting to tell her that her husband was in the house, but Penelope was unable to look that way and see what was happening, for Minerva had diverted her attention. Ulysses then caught Euryclea by the throat with his right hand, drawing her close, and said, "Nurse, do you wish to ruin me, you who nursed me at your breast, now that after twenty years of wandering I am at last come home? Since it has been revealed to you by heaven that you recognize me, hold your tongue and do not say a word about it to anyone else in the house; for if you do, I tell you—and it shall surely be—that if heaven grants me to take the lives of these suitors, I will not spare you, though you are my own nurse, when I am killing the other women."

"My child," Euryclea replied, "what are you talking about? You know very well that nothing can bend or break me. I will hold my tongue like a stone or a piece of iron; furthermore, let me add that when heaven has delivered the suitors into your hands, I will provide you with a list of the women in the house who have misbehaved and of those who are innocent."

Ulysses answered, "Nurse, you ought not to speak in that way; I am well able to judge one and all of them; hold your tongue and leave everything to heaven."

As he said this, Euryclea left the cloister to fetch more water, as the first had all been spilled. When she had washed him and anointed him with oil, Ulysses drew his seat nearer to the fire to warm himself and hid the scar under his rags. Then Penelope began speaking to him, saying, "Stranger, I would like to discuss something else briefly with you. It is nearly bedtime—for those, at least, who can sleep despite sorrow. As for me, heaven has given me such unending woe that even during the day, when I attend to my duties and oversee the servants, I am still weeping and lamenting. Then, when night comes, and we all go to bed, I lie awake, tormented by my thoughts. As the nightingale sings sweetly from her seat in the shadiest covert in early spring, lamenting the loss of her child Itylus, son of king Zethus, even so does my heart toss and turn in uncertainty whether I should stay with my son here, safeguarding my property, my bondsmen, and my home out of respect for public opinion and in memory of my husband, or if it is time for me to go with the best of these suitors who are wooing me and making me such splendid gifts. As long as my son was still young and unable to understand, he would not hear of my leaving my husband's house, but now that he is grown, he begs and prays me to do so, angered by how the suitors are consuming his property. Listen to a dream I had and interpret it for me if you can. I have twenty geese that eat mash from a trough, and I am exceedingly fond of them. I dreamed that a great eagle came swooping down from a mountain and dug his curved beak into each of their necks until he had killed them all. Then he soared into the sky, leaving them lying dead about the yard, causing me to weep in my dream until all my maids gathered around me, piteously grieving because the eagle had killed my geese. Then he returned, perching on a rafter, and spoke to me with a human voice, telling me to stop crying. 'Be of good courage, daughter of Icarius; this is no dream but a vision of good omen that will surely come to pass. The geese are the suitors, and I am no longer an eagle, but your own husband, who has returned to you and will bring these suitors to disgrace.' Upon waking, I looked out and saw my geese at the trough eating their mash as usual."

"This dream, madam," Ulysses replied, "can have but one interpretation, for had not Ulysses himself told you how it shall be fulfilled? The death of the suitors is foretold, and not one of them will escape."

Penelope answered, "Stranger, dreams are curious and unaccountable things, and they do not always come true. There are two gates through which these unsubstantial fancies pass; one is of horn and the other of ivory. Those that come through the gate of ivory are false, while those from the gate of horn mean something to those who see them. I do not believe that my dream came through the gate of horn, though I and my son would be grateful if it proves to have done so. Furthermore, I say—the coming dawn will usher in the ill-omened day that will sever me from Ulysses' house, for I am about to hold a tournament of axes. My husband used to set up twelve axes in the court, one in front of the other, like the stays upon which a ship is built; he would then go back and shoot an arrow through all twelve. I shall make the suitors try to do the same, and whichever of them can string the bow most easily and send his arrow through all twelve axes, him will I follow, and leave this house of my lawful husband, so rich and bounteous. But I do not doubt that I will remember it in my dreams."

Ulysses replied, "Madam, wife of Ulysses, you need not delay your tournament, for Ulysses will return before they can string the bow, no matter how they handle it, and send their arrows through the iron."

To this Penelope said, "As long as you sit here and talk to me, I can have no desire to go to bed. However, people cannot do without sleep, and heaven has appointed us dwellers on earth a time for all things. I will therefore go upstairs and recline upon that couch which I have never ceased to flood with tears since the day Ulysses set out for that hateful city."

She then went upstairs to her room, attended by her maidens, and when there, she lamented her dear husband until Minerva shed sweet sleep over her eyelids.

BOOK 20:

Ulysses slept in the cloister on an undressed bullock's hide, over which he threw several sheep skins from the suitors' feast, and Eurynome covered him with a cloak after he had settled down. There, Ulysses lay awake, brooding over how to kill the suitors. Before long, the women who had misconducted themselves with the suitors left the house, giggling and laughing among themselves. This angered Ulysses, and he debated whether to rise and kill each one of them right then or let them have one last night with the suitors. His heart growled with rage, and he felt a fury like that of a she-dog with puppies showing her teeth at a stranger. But he beat his breast, saying, "Heart, be still; you endured worse on the day when the terrible Cyclops devoured your brave companions. You bore it in silence until your cunning got you safely out of the cave, despite thinking you would be killed."

Thus he chided his heart, forcing it to endure, but he tossed about like something cooking on a fire, turning from side to side, contemplating how he could single-handedly kill such a large number of men as the wicked suitors. But then Minerva descended from heaven in the guise of a woman, hovering over him and saying, "My poor unhappy man, why do you lie awake like this? This is your house; your wife and son are safe inside it."

"Goddess," Ulysses replied, "what you say is true, but I am uncertain how I can kill these wicked suitors alone, given how many of them there are. Moreover, if with Jove's and your assistance I manage to kill them, I need to consider where I can escape from their avengers once it's over."

"For shame," Minerva said, "anyone else would trust a worse ally than me, even if that ally were mortal and less wise. Am I not a goddess, and have I not protected you throughout all your troubles? I assure you that even if fifty bands of men surrounded us, eager to kill us, you could take all their sheep and cattle and drive them away. Now go to sleep; it is bad to lie awake all night, and you will soon be out of your troubles."

As she spoke, she cast sleep over his eyes and then returned to Olympus.

While Ulysses sank into a deep slumber that eased the burden of his sorrows, his admirable wife awoke and sat up in bed, crying. After relieving herself with tears, she prayed to Diana, saying, "Great Goddess Diana, daughter of Jove, either drive an arrow into my heart and slay me, or let a whirlwind snatch me up and carry me through paths of darkness until I am dropped into the mouths of overflowing Oceanus, as the daughters of Pandareus were. They lost their father and mother, for the gods killed them, leaving them orphans. But Venus took care of them, feeding them on cheese, honey, and sweet wine. Juno taught them to excel all women in beauty and understanding; Diana granted them an impressive presence, and Minerva endowed them with every accomplishment. But one day when Venus went to Olympus to see Jove about getting them married (for he knows what shall happen and what shall not), a storm came and swept them away to become handmaids to the dread Erinyes. I wish the gods would hide me from mortal sight, or that fair Diana would strike me, for I would gladly go beneath the earth if I could do so while still looking towards Ulysses and without having to yield myself to a man worse than he. No matter how much people may grieve by day, they can endure it as long as they can sleep at night, for when the eyes are closed in slumber, they forget good and ill alike; whereas my misery haunts me even in my dreams. This very night I dreamed there was one lying beside me who looked like Ulysses as he was when he left with his host, and I rejoiced, believing that it was no dream, but the truth."

At this, day broke, but Ulysses heard the sound of her weeping, which puzzled him, for it seemed as though she already knew him and was by his side. He gathered up the cloak and fleeces on which he had lain, setting them on a seat in the cloister, and took the bullock's hide out into the open. He lifted his hands to heaven and prayed, saying, "Father Jove, since you have brought me over land and sea to my home after all the afflictions you laid upon me, give me a sign from someone inside the house, and let me have another sign from outside."

Thus he prayed. Jove heard his prayer and thundered high up among the clouds from the splendor of Olympus, and Ulysses was glad when he heard it. At the same time, inside the house, a miller-woman from nearby raised her voice and gave him another sign. There were twelve miller-women whose job it was to grind wheat and barley, the staff of life. The others had completed their task and gone to rest, but this one was not yet done, being weaker than the rest. When she heard the thunder, she stopped grinding and addressed her master. "Father Jove," she said, "you, who rule over heaven and earth, have thundered from a clear sky with no clouds in sight, which means something for someone. Grant the prayer of your poor servant who calls upon you, and let this be the last day the suitors dine in the house of Ulysses. They have worn me out with labor grinding meal for them, and I hope they may never dine anywhere again."

Ulysses was glad to hear the signs from the woman's words and the thunder, knowing they meant he would avenge himself on the suitors.

The other maids rose and lit the fire on the hearth, while Telemachus also got up and dressed. He girded his sword about his shoulder, bound his sandals onto his feet, and took a sturdy spear with a sharpened bronze tip. Then he went to the threshold of the cloister and said to Euryclea, "Nurse, did you make the stranger comfortable with bed and board, or did you let him shift for himself? My mother, though good, often pays great attention to second-rate people while neglecting those who are in reality much better."

"Do not find fault, child," Euryclea replied, "when there is no one to find fault with. The stranger sat and drank his wine as long as he liked; your mother asked him if he wanted more bread, and he declined. When he wanted to go to bed, she told the servants to prepare one for him, but he said he was such a wretched outcast that he would not sleep on a bed and under blankets; he insisted on having an undressed bullock's hide and some sheepskins laid out for him in the cloister, and I threw a cloak over him myself."

Then Telemachus went out to the place where the Achaeans were meeting in assembly; he had his spear in hand and was not alone, for his two dogs followed him. Euryclea called the maids, saying, "Come, wake up; sweep the cloisters and sprinkle them with water to settle the dust; put covers on the seats; wipe down the tables with a wet sponge; clean the mixing-jugs and cups, and go fetch water from the fountain at once; the suitors will be here directly, and they will come early since it is a feast day."

Thus she spoke, and they did as she said: twenty of them went to the fountain for water while the others busily worked about the house. The men who served the suitors also came up and began chopping firewood. Eventually, the women returned from the fountain, and the swineherd followed them with the three best pigs he could find. He let them feed around the premises, then said good-humoredly to Ulysses, "Stranger, are the suitors treating you any better now, or are they as insolent as ever?"

"May heaven," Ulysses answered, "repay them for the wickedness with which they act high-handedly in another man's house without any sense of shame."

Thus they conversed, when Melanthius the goatherd approached, bringing in his best goats for the suitors' dinner, accompanied by two shepherds. They tied the goats under the gatehouse, then Melanthius began to mock Ulysses. "Are you still here, stranger," he sneered, "to pester people with your begging about the house? Why can't you go elsewhere? You and I will not settle our differences until we've had a taste of each other's fists. You beg without a shred of decency; are there not feasts elsewhere among the Achaeans, as well as here?"

Ulysses said nothing, bowed his head, and brooded. A third man, Philoetius, joined them, bringing in a barren heifer and some goats. The boatmen had brought these over for those who needed assistance crossing. Philoetius secured his heifer and goats under the gatehouse, then approached the swineherd. "Who, swineherd," he asked, "is this stranger that has recently come here? Is he one of your men? What is his family? Where does he come from? Poor fellow, he seems to have once been a great man, but the gods give sorrow to whom they will, even to kings if it pleases them."

As he spoke, he walked over to Ulysses and greeted him with his right hand. "Good day to you, father stranger," he said. "You seem very poorly off now, but I hope better times await you. Father Jove, of all gods, you are the most malicious. We are your own children, yet you show us no mercy in our misery and afflictions. A sweat broke out over me when I saw this man, and tears filled my eyes, for he reminds me of Ulysses, who I fear is out there in just such rags, if he is still living. If he is dead and in Hades, then alas! for my good master, who made me his stockman when I was quite young among the Cephallenians, and now his cattle are countless; no one could have managed them better than I, for they have bred like ears of corn; yet I must keep bringing them in for others to eat, who take no heed of his son though he is in the house, and fear not heaven's wrath, but are already eager to divide Ulysses' property among themselves because he has been away so long. I have often thought of running away to some foreign country; bad as this would be, it is still harder to stay here and be ill-treated about other people's herds. My situation is intolerable, and I should have long since run away to put myself under the protection of some other chief, only I believe my poor master will yet return and send all these suitors flying out of the house."

"Stockman," Ulysses replied, "you seem to be a very reasonable man, and I can see that you are sensible. Therefore I will tell you, and will confirm my words with an oath. By Jove, the chief of all gods, and by the hearth of Ulysses to which I have now come, Ulysses shall return before you leave this place, and if you are so inclined, you will see him killing the suitors who now hold sway here."

"If Jove were to bring this to pass," the stockman replied, "you would see how I would do my utmost to help him."

In like manner, Eumaeus prayed that Ulysses would return home.

Thus they conversed, while the suitors plotted to murder Telemachus. But just then, a bird flew near them on their left hand—an eagle carrying a dove in its talons. Amphinomus said, "My friends, this plot to murder Telemachus will not succeed; let us go to dinner instead."

The others agreed, so they went inside, laying their cloaks on the benches and seats. They sacrificed sheep, goats, pigs, and the heifer, and when the inner meats were cooked, they served them around. They mixed wine in the mixing-bowls, and the swineherd gave every man his cup while Philoetius distributed bread from the baskets, and Melanthius poured the wine. Then they laid their hands upon the good things before them.

Telemachus purposely made Ulysses sit on the stone-paved part of the cloister; he gave him a shabby-looking seat at a small table to himself, having his portion of inner meats brought to him, along with his wine in a golden cup. "Sit there," he said, "and drink your wine among the great people. I will put a stop to the gibes and blows of the suitors, for this is no public house, but belongs to Ulysses and has passed from him to me. Therefore, suitors, keep your hands and tongues to yourselves, or there will be mischief."

The suitors bit their lips, marveling at the boldness of his speech; then Antinous said, "We do not like such language but we will put up with it, for Telemachus is threatening us in good earnest. If Jove had allowed us, we would have put an end to his brave talk by now."

Thus spoke Antinous, but Telemachus paid him no mind. Meanwhile, heralds brought the holy hecatomb through the city, and the Achaeans gathered under the shady grove of Apollo.

They roasted the outer meat, drew it from the spits, served each man his portion, and feasted to their hearts' content. Those who waited at the table gave Ulysses the same portion as the others, as Telemachus had instructed them.

But Minerva would not let the suitors drop their insolence for even a moment, wanting Ulysses to become even more bitter against them. Among the suitors was a rowdy man named Ctesippus from Same. Confident in his wealth, he paid court to Ulysses' wife and said to the suitors, "Listen to me. The stranger has already received as large a portion as any of us, which is right, for it's not fair to ill-treat any guest of Telemachus who comes here. I will, however, make him a present on my own account so that he may have something to give to the bath-woman or to some other servant of Ulysses."

As he spoke, he picked up a heifer's foot from the meat basket and threw it at Ulysses, but Ulysses turned his head aside, avoiding it with a grim smile, and it hit the wall instead. Telemachus then spoke fiercely to Ctesippus, saying, "It's a good thing for you that the stranger turned his head, or you would have hit him. If you had, I would have run you through with my spear, and your father would have had to arrange for your burial rather than your marriage in this house. So let there be no more unseemly behavior from any of you, for I am grown up now and understand good and evil. I have long seen you killing my sheep and making free with my corn and wine; I have tolerated this, for one man cannot match many, but do not give me any more violence. Still, if you wish to kill me, kill me; I would rather die than witness such disgraceful scenes day after day—guests insulted and men dragging the servant women about the house in a shameful manner."

They all fell silent until Agelaus, son of Damastor, finally spoke up, "No one should take offense at what has just been said; it is quite reasonable. Therefore, stop ill-treating the stranger or anyone else in the house. However, I would like to give a friendly word of advice to Telemachus and his mother, which I trust will commend itself to both. As long as you had hope that Ulysses would one day return, no one could blame you for waiting and suffering the suitors to stay in your house. It would have been better if he had returned, but it is now clear that he will never do so. Therefore, talk this over with your mother and tell her to marry the best man, the one who offers her the most advantageous deal. This way, you will manage your own inheritance and be able to eat and drink in peace, while your mother will look after another man's house, not yours."

To this, Telemachus replied, "By Jove, Agelaus, and by the sorrows of my unhappy father, who has either perished far from Ithaca or is wandering in some distant land, I place no obstacles in my mother's marriage; on the contrary, I urge her to choose whomever she likes, and I will give her many gifts besides. But I cannot insist that she leave the house against her own wishes. Heaven forbid that I should do such a thing."

Minerva made the suitors laugh uncontrollably, setting their wits in a spin, but they laughed with forced amusement. Their meat became smeared with blood; their eyes filled with tears, and their hearts were heavy with foreboding. Theoclymenus saw this and said, "Unhappy men, what is the matter with you? A shroud of darkness has descended upon you, your cheeks are wet with tears; the air is alive with wailing voices; the walls and roof-beams drip blood; the gate of the cloisters and the courtyard beyond are full of ghosts trooping down into the night of Hades; the sun is blotted out of heaven, and a blighting gloom hangs over all the land."

Thus he spoke, and they all laughed heartily. Eurymachus then said, "This stranger who has lately come here has lost his senses. Servants, throw him out into the streets, since he finds it so dark here."

But Theoclymenus said, "Eurymachus, you need not send anyone with me. I have my own eyes, ears, and feet, not to mention an understanding mind. I will take myself out of this house, for I see mischief hanging over you, and none of you who insult people and plot ill deeds in the house of Ulysses will be able to escape."

He left as he spoke and went back to Piraeus, who welcomed him, while the suitors continued to look at one another, mocking Telemachus and laughing at the strangers. One insolent fellow said to him, "Telemachus, you are not happy in your guests; first, you have this importunate tramp, who comes begging bread and wine and is useless for work or hard fighting, and now here is another fellow who is setting himself up as a prophet. Let me persuade you; it would be much better to put them on board a ship and send them off to the Sicels to sell for whatever they can fetch."

Telemachus ignored him, silently watching his father, expecting every moment that he would begin his attack on the suitors.

Meanwhile, wise Penelope, daughter of Icarius, had a rich seat placed for her facing the court and cloisters so she could hear everything being said. The dinner had been prepared amid much merriment; it was both good and plentiful, as they had sacrificed many victims. The supper was yet to come, and nothing could be conceived more gruesome than the meal a goddess and a brave man were about to lay before them, for they had brought their doom upon themselves.

BOOK 21:

Minerva inspired Penelope to challenge the suitors to try their skill with the bow and the iron axes, hoping this contest would lead to their destruction. She went upstairs, took the key to the store-room, and made her way to where her husband's treasures of gold, bronze, and wrought iron were kept, including his bow and a quiver full of arrows given to him by a friend he met in Lacedaemon—Iphitus, the son of Eurytus. Ulysses had met Iphitus while on a journey to recover sheep stolen by the Messenians. Iphitus was also there to reclaim his own stolen mares, but he was later killed by Hercules, who disregarded the laws of hospitality. This bow, gifted by Iphitus, had remained in Ulysses' home as a keepsake from a dear friend.

Penelope reached the oak threshold of the store-room, where the carpenter had meticulously crafted the doors. She unlocked it, and as she opened the doors, they creaked loudly, reminiscent of a bull bellowing in a meadow. Stepping onto the raised platform, she gathered the bow and wept bitterly as she took it from its case. After calming herself, she went to the cloister where the suitors were, carrying the bow and quiver filled with arrows. Accompanied by her maidens, she brought a chest containing much iron and bronze, trophies won by her husband. Standing by a post supporting the roof of the cloister, she held a veil before her face, with a maid on either side.

"Listen to me, suitors," she said, "who continue to abuse the hospitality of this house because its owner is long absent. As a prize for your contest, I will bring out Ulysses' mighty bow. Whomever can string it most easily and shoot an arrow through all twelve axes, I will follow and leave this house of my lawful husband, so rich and full of wealth. Yet I doubt I will forget this place in my dreams."

As she spoke, she instructed Eumaeus to present the bow and the pieces of iron before the suitors. Eumaeus wept as he did so, and the stockman joined him in mourning when he saw his master's bow. Antinous scolded them, saying, "You fools, why do you add to your mistress's sorrows? She has enough grief over her husband. Sit quietly and eat your dinners in silence, or step outside if you wish to cry, but leave the bow behind. We suitors will contend for it with all our strength, for it will not be easy to string such a bow as this. None among us is like Ulysses; I remember him well, even though I was just a child then."

While he spoke, he was confident that he could string the bow and shoot through the iron, unaware that he would soon be the first to taste the arrows from Ulysses' hands—arrows he had dishonored in his own house.

Then Telemachus exclaimed, "Great heavens! Jove must have robbed me of my senses. My dear mother speaks of leaving this house to marry again, yet here I am laughing and enjoying myself as if nothing is wrong. But suitors, since the contest is agreed upon, let it proceed. This woman is incomparable, and you all know it. What need have I to sing her praises? Let us see if you can string the bow. I too will give it a try; if I can string it and shoot through the axes, I will not allow my mother to leave this house with a stranger."

He jumped from his seat, threw off his crimson cloak, and took his sword from his shoulder. First, he arranged the axes in a row in a long groove that he had dug straight. The others were surprised by his orderly setup, as he had never seen such a contest before. He stepped forward to try the bow. He pulled at it three times with all his might but could not draw the string. Just as he attempted a fourth time, Ulysses signaled him to stop despite his eagerness. Telemachus said, "Alas! I am either always weak and ineffective, or I am still too young and have not reached my full strength. You others, therefore, who are stronger than I, take a turn with the bow and resolve this contest."

He then placed the bow down, leaning it against the door with the arrow resting against its tip. He returned to his seat, and Antinous suggested, "Let each of you try in turn, starting from the right where the cupbearer begins when serving wine."

The others agreed, and Leiodes, son of Oenops, was the first to rise. As the sacrificial priest to the suitors, he was seated near the mixing-bowl and had grown indignant at their behavior. He approached the bow to try it but found he could not string it; his hands were weak from lack of practice, and he soon grew tired. "Friends," he said, "I cannot string it; let another try. This bow will take the life and soul of many among us; it is better to die than to live and miss the prize we have long sought. Whoever hopes to marry Penelope should know that if he cannot string this bow, he might as well seek another bride."

He leaned the bow against the door, with the arrow resting against its tip, and returned to his seat. Antinous rebuked him, saying, "What nonsense are you speaking, Leiodes? Your words are intolerable. Why should the bow take the lives of many among us just because you cannot bend it? True, you were not meant to be an archer, but others will soon try their strength."

He then ordered Melanthius the goatherd, "Light a fire in the court and set a seat with a sheep skin next to it; bring a large ball of lard from what we have in the house. We will warm the bow and grease it, and then we can try again and finish this contest."

Melanthius obeyed, lighting the fire and setting a seat beside it. He brought a ball of lard, and the suitors warmed the bow again, but none of them were strong enough to string it. However, Antinous and Eurymachus, the leaders among the suitors, remained.

Meanwhile, the swineherd and the stockman left the cloister, and Ulysses followed them. Once outside the gates and into the outer yard, Ulysses quietly asked them, "What would you do if some god were to bring Ulysses back here suddenly? Would you side with the suitors or with Ulysses?"

"Father Jove," replied the stockman, "if you were to ordain it, I would fight for Ulysses with all my might."

Eumaeus echoed his sentiments, praying to the gods for Ulysses' return. When Ulysses saw their loyalty, he revealed himself, saying, "It is I, Ulysses, who am here. After twenty years of suffering, I have returned to my homeland. You two alone have wished for my return; I have heard none of the others praying for it. Therefore, to you two, I will reveal the truth. If heaven delivers the suitors into my hands, I will grant you both wives, land, and homes close to mine, and you shall be as brothers to me and friends to Telemachus. To prove my identity, look here at the scar from the wild boar that gored me while hunting on Mt. Parnassus with the sons of Autolycus."

As he spoke, he pulled back his rags to reveal the scar. When they recognized it, they both wept, embraced him, and kissed his head and shoulders, while Ulysses returned their affection. They would have mourned all day had Ulysses not interrupted them, saying:

"Stop your weeping, lest someone outside see us and tell those within. When you enter, do so separately; I will go first, and you follow. This will be our signal: the suitors will try to prevent me from taking the bow and quiver. Eumaeus, place it in my hands when you bring it, and tell the women to close the doors to their quarters. If they hear any commotion, they must not come out but stay quiet. Philoetius, fasten the doors of the outer court securely."

After issuing these instructions, Ulysses returned to the house and took his seat. The bow was now in the hands of Eurymachus, who warmed it by the fire but could not string it.

Sighing deeply, he lamented, "I grieve for myself and all of us; it pains me to think I will have to forgo the marriage. I do not mind the loss of the prize itself, for there are plenty of other women in Ithaca and elsewhere, but I feel ashamed that we cannot string this bow like Ulysses. This will bring disgrace upon us, even to those yet unborn."

"It shall not be so, Eurymachus," replied Antinous, "and you know it yourself. Today is the feast of Apollo throughout the land; who can string a bow on such a day? Let us set it aside for now. The axes can remain where they are; no one is likely to come and take them away. Instead, let the cupbearer serve wine, so we can make our drink-offerings and drop this bow matter for today. We can ask Melanthius to bring us some of the best goats tomorrow; then we can offer the thigh bones to Apollo, the mighty archer, and try the bow again to conclude the contest."

The others agreed with Antinous, and the servants poured water over the guests' hands while pages filled the mixing-bowls with wine and water. Once they had made their offerings and drunk as they desired, Ulysses craftily spoke up:

"Suitors of the illustrious queen, listen to me as I express my thoughts. I particularly address Eurymachus and Antinous, who has spoken with such reason. Cease your shooting for now and leave the outcome to the gods. In the morning, let heaven give victory to whom it will. For now, give me the bow so I can test my strength among you and see if I still possess the vigor I once had or if travel and neglect have taken their toll."

His words angered the suitors, who feared he might string the bow. Antinous rebuked him fiercely, saying, "Wretched creature, you lack sense. You should consider yourself fortunate to dine among your betters without receiving any less than we. You've been allowed to hear our private conversation—no other beggar or stranger has enjoyed this privilege. Surely the wine has clouded your mind, just as it did with the Centaur Eurytion when he stayed with Peirithous among the Lapithae.

Drunkenness drove him mad, leading to his shameful deeds that angered the heroes present, who then disfigured him and cast him out. Thus, I can tell you it will not go well for you if you manage to string the bow. You will find no mercy here; we shall ship you off to King Echetus, who kills everyone who comes near him. You won't escape alive, so drink and keep quiet; don't provoke men younger than yourself."

Penelope then interjected, "Antinous, it is wrong for you to mistreat any guest of Telemachus in this house. If the stranger can string Ulysses' mighty bow, do you think he would take me away and make me his wife? Surely he would not even think that, nor should any of you worry while you feast."

"Queen Penelope," Eurymachus replied, "we do not believe this man will take you away; it is impossible. Yet we fear that some lesser person, whether man or woman among the Achaeans, might say, 'These suitors are weak; they are courting the wife of a great man whose bow not one could string, while a beggarly tramp came in and strung it effortlessly.' This will reflect poorly on us."

"Eurymachus," Penelope answered, "those who consume the estate of a great chieftain and dishonor his home should not expect others to think highly of them. Why should you care if people speak ill of you? This stranger appears strong and well-built, and he claims noble birth. Give him the bow, and let us see if he can string it. I swear that if Apollo grants him the strength to do so, I will reward him with a cloak, a good shirt, a javelin to fend off dogs and thieves, a sharp sword, and sandals, and I will see him safely on his way wherever he wishes to go."

Telemachus then said, "Mother, I am the only man in Ithaca or in the islands opposite Elis who has the authority to let anyone have the bow or refuse it. No one shall force me, not even if I decide to give the stranger the bow outright and let him take it with him. Now go inside and attend to your daily tasks—your loom, your distaff, and managing your servants. The bow is a man's matter, and especially mine, for I am the master here."

Penelope went back into the house, pondering her son's words. She went upstairs with her handmaids and mourned for her dear husband until Minerva sent sweet sleep over her eyelids.

Meanwhile, Eumaeus took up the bow, intending to bring it to Ulysses, but the suitors shouted at him from all sides of the cloisters. One shouted, "You fool! Where are you taking the bow? Have you lost your wits? If the gods grant our prayer, your own dogs will get you into a quiet spot and worry you to death."

Frightened by their outcry, Eumaeus set the bow down. Telemachus, however, called out from across the cloisters and threatened him, saying, "Father Eumaeus, bring the bow despite them, or I will pelt you with stones back to the country, for I am stronger than you. I wish I were as strong as I am compared to you in order to send the suitors away sick and sorry, for they mean mischief."

His words made the suitors laugh heartily, putting them in a better mood toward Telemachus. Eumaeus then brought the bow and placed it in Ulysses' hands. After doing so, he called Euryclea aside and said, "Euryclea, Telemachus has instructed you to close the doors of the women's apartments. If they hear any groaning or fighting, they must stay inside and keep quiet while they work."

Euryclea complied and closed the doors to the women's quarters.

Philoetius then quietly exited and secured the gates of the outer court. Using a ship's cable made from byblus fiber, he bound the gates and returned, taking the seat he had left while keeping a watchful eye on Ulysses, who now held the bow, examining it closely to see if the worms had damaged its two horns during his absence. Some suitors turned to each other and commented, "This is a crafty old bow-fancier; either he has a similar one at home, or he wants to make one, for he handles it skillfully."

Another said, "Let's hope he is as unsuccessful in other matters as he will surely be in stringing this bow."

But Ulysses, having examined the bow thoroughly, strung it as easily as a skilled bard strings a new peg on his lyre, fastening the twisted gut at both ends. He took it in his right hand, testing the string, which sang sweetly under his touch like a swallow's song. The suitors were dismayed and lost color at the sound; at that moment, Jove thundered loudly above them as a sign, and Ulysses' heart rejoiced at the omen sent by the son of Saturn.

He took an arrow lying on the table—those that the Achaeans were soon to taste were still in the quiver—and placed it on the center of the bow. Drawing the arrow and string back, still seated, he took aim and released it, piercing all the handle-holes of the axes in order until it went through the outer courtyard. He then said to Telemachus:

"Your guest has not disgraced you, Telemachus. I did not miss my target, nor did it take long for me to string my bow. I am still strong, not as the suitors taunt me. Now, however, it is time for the Achaeans to prepare supper while there is still daylight and then to enjoy themselves with song and dance, the crowning ornaments of a banquet."

As he spoke, he raised his eyebrows, and Telemachus girded on his sword, grasped his spear, and stood armed beside his father's seat.

BOOK 22:

Then Ulysses tore off his rags and jumped onto the broad pavement with his bow and quiver full of arrows. He dropped the arrows at his feet and declared, "The mighty contest is over. Now I will see if Apollo grants me the skill to hit another target that no man has yet struck."

With that, he aimed a deadly arrow at Antinous, who was about to lift a two-handled gold cup to drink his wine. Antinous had no thought of death; who would expect a single man to stand alone among so many and kill him? The arrow struck Antinous in the throat, piercing clean through, and he fell over, dropping the cup from his hand as blood gushed from his nostrils. He kicked the table away, upsetting the food and spilling bread and roasted meats onto the ground.

The suitors erupted into chaos upon seeing one of their own hit. They jumped from their seats in dismay and searched for shields or spears on the walls, but found none. They angrily rebuked Ulysses. "Stranger," they shouted, "you will pay for shooting like that! You will face no other contest; you are a doomed man. The one you have killed was the foremost youth in Ithaca, and vultures will devour you for this."

As they spoke, they believed he had killed Antinous by mistake, unaware that death loomed over each of them. Ulysses glared at them and said, "Dogs, did you think I would not return from Troy? You have squandered my wealth, forced my servants to sleep with you, and pursued my wife while I was still living. You have shown no fear of God or man, and now you will die."

They turned pale at his words, each looking for a place to escape, but Eurymachus was the only one to speak. "If you are Ulysses," he said, "then what you say is true. We have done much wrong in your lands and your house. But Antinous, the chief instigator, lies dead. He had no desire to marry Penelope; his true goal was to kill your son and be the chief man in Ithaca. Now that he has met the death he deserved, spare the lives of the rest of us. We will make amends, paying you back for all we have consumed. Each of us will give you gifts worth twenty oxen, and we will continue to provide you gold and bronze until you are appeased. Until then, we can expect no complaint from you."

Ulysses glared at him again and replied, "Even if you offered me everything you have now and everything you ever will have, I will not stop until I have exacted full vengeance. You must either fight or flee for your lives, but I assure you, none of you will escape."

Fear sank into their hearts, and Eurymachus spoke again. "Friends, this man will not give us mercy. He will stand his ground and shoot us down until none are left. Let us fight back; draw your swords and use the tables as shields against his arrows. We must charge him, drive him away from the doorway, and then we can escape into the town and raise an alarm to stop his shooting."

With that, he drew his sharp bronze blade and rushed at Ulysses. But Ulysses instantly shot an arrow into his breast, striking him at the nipple and piercing through to his liver. He dropped his sword, fell over the table, and struck the ground with his forehead as his cup and food spilled out, his body wracked with the agonies of death.

Then Amphinomus drew his sword and charged at Ulysses, aiming to push him away from the door. But Telemachus was quicker, striking him from behind. The spear pierced him between the shoulders and went through his chest, causing him to fall heavily to the ground, his forehead hitting the earth. Telemachus fled from him, leaving his spear lodged in the body, fearing that if he stayed to retrieve it, one of the Achaeans might attack him with a sword. He ran to his father's side and said, "Father, let me fetch you a shield, two spears, and a brass helmet for your head. I will arm myself too and bring armor for the swineherd and the stockman, for we should be better prepared."

"Go and get them," Ulysses replied, "while I still have arrows left. Once they are gone, they may overpower me at the door."

Telemachus did as his father instructed, heading to the store-room for the armor. He quickly chose four shields, eight spears, and four brass helmets with horse-hair plumes. He brought them back to Ulysses and armed himself first, while the stockman and the swineherd also donned their armor, taking their positions beside Ulysses. Meanwhile, Ulysses had continued to shoot the suitors one by one, causing them to fall thickly on one another. When his arrows ran out, he leaned the bow against the wall of the house by the doorpost and slung a four-hide shield over his shoulders. He set a well-crafted helmet on his head, adorned with a crest of horse-hair that nodded menacingly above him, and grasped two formidable bronze-shod spears.

There was a trap door on the wall, and at one end of the pavement, an exit leading to a narrow passage closed by a sturdy door. Ulysses instructed Philoetius to guard this door, as only one person could attack it at a time. Agelaus shouted, "Can someone go up to the trap door and alert the townspeople? Help would come quickly, and we could end this man and his shooting."

"That may not happen, Agelaus," replied Melanthius, "the mouth of the narrow passage is dangerously close to the outer court. One brave man could easily hold off many from entering. But I know what to do; I'll go fetch you arms from the store-room, for I believe that's where Ulysses and his son have hidden them."

With that, Melanthius went through back passages to Ulysses' store-room. There, he chose twelve shields, as many helmets and spears, and hurried back to give them to the suitors. Ulysses' heart began to fail him when he saw the suitors arming themselves and brandishing their spears. Recognizing the danger, he said to Telemachus, "Someone among the women is aiding the suitors against us, or it may be Melanthius."

Telemachus replied, "Father, the fault is mine alone; I left the store-room door open, and they have kept a sharper lookout than I have. Eumaeus, go and close the door, and see if it's one of the women helping them, or if it's Melanthius, as I suspect."

As they spoke, Melanthius was making another trip to the store-room for more armor, but the swineherd spotted him and said to Ulysses, "Noble son of Laertes, that scoundrel Melanthius is headed to the store-room, just as we suspected. Should I kill him if I can overpower him, or bring him here so you can take your revenge for all the wrongs he has done in your house?"

Ulysses answered, "Telemachus and I will hold these suitors at bay, no matter what they do. You both go back and bind Melanthius' hands and feet behind him. Throw him into the store-room and lock the door. Then, fasten a noose around his body and hang him from the rafters so that he will linger in agony."

They did as he instructed, heading to the store-room before Melanthius noticed them. He was busy searching for arms in the innermost part of the room, allowing them to take their positions on either side of the door and wait. When Melanthius emerged, helmet in one hand and an old, rotten shield in the other, which Laertes had used when he was young, they seized him, dragged him back by the hair, and threw him down. They bound his hands and feet behind his back tightly and painfully, as Ulysses had instructed, then they strung him up from a high pillar until he was close to the rafters. Eumaeus taunted him, saying, "Melanthius, you will pass the night on a soft bed as you deserve. You will know it's morning when the streams of

Oceanus flow, and it's time for you to bring in your goats for the suitors to feast on."

They left him there in cruel bondage and, donning their armor, closed the door behind them, returning to stand by Ulysses. The four of them stood in the cloister, fierce and ready for battle, while those in the court were still brave in numbers. Then Jove's daughter Minerva approached them, taking on the voice and form of Mentor. Ulysses was glad to see her and said, "Mentor, lend me your aid; do not forget your old comrade or the many good deeds he has done for you. You are my age-mate."

But Ulysses was certain it was Minerva. The suitors on the other side raised an uproar upon seeing her. Agelaus was the first to reproach her, "Mentor," he called, "do not allow Ulysses to deceive you into siding with him against us. Here's our plan: once we have killed father and son, we will kill you too. You will pay with your life, and when we are done with you, we will take all you possess, inside or out, adding it to Ulysses' property. None of your children will remain in your house, nor will your wife live on in the city of Ithaca."

Minerva became even angrier at this, scolding Ulysses fiercely. "Ulysses," she said, "your strength and valor are no longer what they were when you fought for nine long years among the Trojans for the noble lady Helen. You killed many men in those days, and it was through your cleverness that Priam's city fell. How can you now be so lamentably less brave on your own ground, face to face with the suitors in your own home? Come on, my good fellow, stand by my side and see how Mentor, son of Alcimus, shall fight your foes and repay the kindnesses you have conferred upon him."

With that, Ulysses felt renewed courage, standing tall with the bow and ready to face his enemies. As he took aim, he knew that victory was near and that with Minerva's support, he would reclaim his home and his honor. The suitors, now fully aware of the gravity of their situation, braced themselves for the impending confrontation, realizing too late that they had underestimated the strength of the man they had wronged. The clash that was about to unfold would determine their fate and the future of Ithaca itself.

This made Minerva even angrier, so she scolded Ulysses fiercely. "Ulysses," she said, "your strength and bravery are not what they used to be when you fought for nine long years against the Trojans over the noble lady Helen. You killed many men back then, and it was your cleverness that helped bring down Priam's city. Why is it that you are so much less brave now, standing on your own ground, facing the suitors in your own house? Come on, my friend, stand by my side and see how Mentor, son of Alcimus, will fight your enemies and repay the kindness you have shown him."

But she would not give him full victory yet, as she wished to further test his prowess and that of his brave son. So she flew up to one of the rafters in the cloister and sat upon it in the form of a swallow.

Meanwhile, Agelaus son of Damastor, Eurynomus, Amphimedon, Demoptolemus, Pisander, and Polybus son of Polyctor were the bravest among the suitors still fighting for their lives; they were the most valiant, for the others had already fallen under Ulysses' arrows. Agelaus shouted to them, "My friends, he will soon have to stop, for Mentor has gone away after doing nothing but brag. They stand at the doors without support. Do not all aim at him at once; let six of you throw your spears first and see if you can win glory by killing him. Once he has fallen, we need not worry about the others."

They threw their spears as he instructed, but Minerva made them all miss. One hit the door post; another struck the wall; and still another hit the door. The only success came when Amphimedon grazed Telemachus's wrist and Ctesippus nicked Eumaeus's shoulder above his shield. But the spear fell to the ground, and then Ulysses and his men aimed again, hitting their marks. Ulysses killed Demoptolemus, Telemachus struck Euryades, Eumaeus hit Elatus, while the stockman took down Pisander. They all fell, and as the remaining suitors retreated into a corner, Ulysses and his men rushed forward to reclaim their spears from the bodies of the slain.

The suitors aimed a second time, but once again, Minerva made most of their weapons ineffective. One struck a bearing post, another hit the door, and yet another lodged in the wall. Amphimedon did manage to slice the top of Telemachus's wrist, and Ctesippus grazed Eumaeus's shoulder, but the spear fell to the ground. Ulysses and his men retaliated and struck back, with Ulysses hitting Eurydamas, Telemachus taking down Amphimedon, and Eumaeus hitting Polybus. The stockman then struck Ctesippus in the breast and taunted him, "Foul-mouthed son of Polytherses, do not be foolish enough to speak wickedly again. Let heaven guide your words, for the gods are stronger than men. I offer you this advice in return for the foot you gave Ulysses when he was begging in his own house."

Thus spoke the stockman, and Ulysses struck the son of Damastor with a spear in close combat, while Telemachus hit Leocritus, son of Evenor, in the belly, piercing him through so that he fell forward onto the ground. As Ulysses's men continued to press the attack, Minerva raised her deadly aegis, causing the hearts of the suitors to quail. They fled to the far end of the court, like cattle driven mad by the gadfly in early summer when the days are longest. Like eagle-beaked, crook-taloned vultures swooping down on smaller birds that cower in flocks, Ulysses and his men fell upon the suitors, striking them down and causing them to groan as their lives were taken.

Leiodes then caught the knees of Ulysses, pleading, "Ulysses, I beseech you to have mercy on me and spare my life. I have never wronged any of the women in your house, either in word or deed, and I tried to stop the others. I saw their folly, but they would not listen, and now they are paying for it. I was their sacrificing priest; if you kill me, I shall die unjustly, without thanks for the good I have done."

Ulysses looked sternly at him and replied, "If you were their priest, you must have prayed many times for my absence and that you might marry my wife. Therefore, you shall die."

With those words, he picked up the sword that Agelaus had dropped and struck Leiodes on the back of his neck, severing his head from his body as he spoke.

The minstrel Phemius, son of Terpes, who had been forced by the suitors to entertain them, now tried to save himself. He stood near the trap door with his lyre in hand, uncertain whether to flee to the altar of Jove in the outer court or embrace Ulysses's knees. Ultimately, he chose to approach Ulysses and grasp his knees, saying, "Ulysses, I beg you, have mercy on me and spare my life. You will regret it if you kill a bard who can sing for both gods and men. I compose all my own songs, and heaven inspires me with every kind of brilliance. I would sing for you as if you were a god; do not rush to cut my head off. Telemachus can tell you that I did not wish to sing for the suitors, but they were too many and too strong for me."

Telemachus heard him and quickly approached his father. "Hold!" he cried. "The man is innocent; do not harm him. Spare Medon too, who was kind to me when I was young, unless Philoetius or Eumaeus has killed him or he has fallen in your path during your rampage."

Medon heard Telemachus and emerged from his hiding place beneath a seat, throwing off a freshly flayed heifer's hide. He grasped Telemachus's knees and said, "Here I am, my dear sir; stay your hand and tell your father, or he will kill me in his anger at the suitors for having wasted his estate and disrespected you."

Ulysses smiled at him and said, "Do not fear; Telemachus has saved your life so you may know how greatly better good deeds prosper than evil ones. Go outside the cloisters to the outer court and stay away from the slaughter—you and the bard—while I complete my work here inside."

The two men hurried to the outer court, seeking refuge at Jove's great altar, looking around in fear, still expecting to be killed. Ulysses carefully searched the entire court for any hidden survivors but found only the dead, all sprawled in the dust and soaking in their blood, like fish caught by fishermen and thrown upon the shore, gasping for water until the sun's heat claims them. So were the suitors lying, all huddled together.

Then Ulysses said to Telemachus, "Call nurse Euryclea; I have something to say to her."

Telemachus went and knocked at the door of the women's room. "Hurry," he called, "you old woman set over the other servants. Come out; my father wishes to speak with you."

Euryclea heard this, unlocked the door, and came out, following Telemachus. When she saw Ulysses among the corpses, bespattered with blood like a lion that has just devoured an ox, she began to cry for joy, realizing a great deed had been accomplished. But Ulysses stopped her, saying, "Old woman, rejoice quietly; do not raise your voice. It is unholy to boast over the dead. Heaven's judgment and their own wicked deeds have brought these men to ruin; they showed no respect for anyone who came to them, neither rich nor poor, and they have met a bad end as punishment for their folly. Now, tell me which women in the house have misbehaved and which are innocent."

"I will tell you the truth, my son," answered Euryclea. "There are fifty women in the house who do tasks such as carding wool and all kinds of household work. Of these, twelve in all have misbehaved and shown disrespect to me and to Penelope. They did not disrespect Telemachus, as he has only recently grown up, and his mother never permitted him to give orders to the female servants. Let me go upstairs to tell your wife all that has happened; some god has sent her to sleep."

"Do not wake her yet," replied Ulysses, "but summon the women who have misbehaved to come to me."

Euryclea went to call the women, and soon they came, weeping and wailing bitterly. First, they carried the dead bodies out, propping them against each other in the gatehouse. Ulysses ordered them around, urging them to work quickly. When they had finished, they cleaned the tables and seats with sponges and water, while Telemachus and the others shovelled the blood and dirt from the ground, and the women carried it away and disposed of it outside. Once they had made the place clean and orderly, they took the women into the narrow space between the wall of the domed room and the outer court, ensuring they could not escape. Telemachus then said to the others, "I will not let these women die easily, for they were insolent to me and my mother and lay with the suitors."

With that, he fastened a ship's cable to one of the supporting posts of the domed room and secured it high enough that none of the women's feet could touch the ground. As thrushes or doves struggle against a net set for them in a thicket just as they are about to nest, and face a terrible fate, so the women were forced to put their heads in nooses one after another, dying most miserably. Their feet kicked convulsively for a short while, but soon stopped.

As for Melanthius, they dragged him through the cloister to the inner court, where they cut off his nose and ears. They drew out his insides and fed them to the dogs raw, then in their rage, they cut off his hands and feet.

After finishing their grim work, they washed their hands and feet and returned to the house, for all was now over. Ulysses said to the dear old nurse Euryclea, "Bring me sulphur, which cleanses all pollution, and also fire so I may burn it and purify the cloisters. Go, and tell Penelope to come here with her attendants and all the maidservants in the house."

"All that you have said is true," answered Euryclea, "but let me bring you some clean clothes—a shirt and cloak. Do not keep these rags on your back any longer; it is not right."

"First light me a fire," replied Ulysses.

She brought the fire and sulphur as he had instructed, and Ulysses purified the cloisters and both the inner and outer courts. Then she went inside to call the women and inform them of what had happened. Soon they came from their apartment with torches in hand, gathering around Ulysses to embrace him, kissing his head and shoulders and taking hold of his hands. It made him feel as if he might weep, for he remembered each of them.

BOOK 23:

Euryclea now went upstairs, laughing, to tell her mistress that her dear husband had come home. She felt young again with joy and moved quickly to her mistress, bending over her to speak. "Wake up, Penelope, my dear child," she exclaimed. "See with your own eyes what you have long desired. Ulysses has indeed returned home and has killed the suitors who have caused so much trouble in his house, consuming his wealth and mistreating his son."

"My good nurse," replied Penelope, "you must be mad. The gods sometimes drive sensible people insane and make foolish ones sensible. This must be what they've done to you, for you were always reasonable. Why would you mock me when I have enough trouble as it is—talking such nonsense and waking me from a sweet sleep? I haven't slept so soundly since the day my poor husband went to that ill-fated city. Go back to the women's room; if it were anyone else waking me with such absurd news, I would have scolded her severely. As it is, your age protects you."

"My dear child," said Euryclea, "I am not mocking you. It is true that Ulysses has come home. He was the stranger they all mistreated in the cloister. Telemachus knew all along that he was back but kept it a secret to take his revenge on those wicked men."

Then Penelope sprang from her couch, threw her arms around Euryclea, and wept for joy. "But, my dear nurse," she said, "explain this to me: if he has really come home, how did he manage to overcome all those wicked suitors alone, considering how many there were?"

"I was not there," Euryclea answered, "and do not know; I only heard their groans while they were being killed. We sat crouched in a corner of the women's room with the doors closed until your son came to fetch me because his father sent him. Then I found Ulysses standing over the corpses lying all around him, one on top of another. You would have enjoyed it if you could have seen him there, covered in blood and filth, looking just like a lion. But the bodies are now piled up in the gatehouse of the outer court, and Ulysses has lit a great fire to purify the house with sulphur. He sent me to call you, so come with me, and you will both be happy together at last; your husband is home to find both wife and son alive and well, and to take revenge in his own house on the suitors who treated him so poorly."

"My dear nurse," replied Penelope, "do not rejoice too confidently over this. You know how delighted everyone would be to see Ulysses home—especially myself and our son—but what you tell me cannot be true. It is some god angry with the suitors for their wickedness who has brought this about; they have respected no one in the world, neither rich nor poor, and they have met a bad end for their iniquity. Ulysses is dead far from Achaea; he will never return home again."

Euryclea said, "My child, what are you talking about? You've made up your mind that your husband will never return, but he is in the house and by his own fireside at this very moment. I can give you another proof: when I was washing him, I noticed the scar the wild boar gave him, and I wanted to tell you, but in his wisdom he clapped his hand over my mouth. Come with me, and I will make you this bargain: if I am deceiving you, you can have me killed by the most cruel death you can think of."

"My dear nurse," Penelope replied, "however wise you may be, you can hardly fathom the counsels of the gods. Nevertheless, we will go to search for my son, so I may see the suitors' corpses and the man who killed them."

With that, she came down from her upper room, considering whether to keep her distance from her husband and question him, or to embrace him at once. As she crossed the stone floor of the cloister, she sat down opposite Ulysses by the fire, against the wall, while Ulysses sat near one of the bearing-posts, looking down and waiting to see what his brave wife would say to him. For a long time, she sat in silence, lost in amazement. At one moment, she looked him in the face, but then again, misled by his shabby clothes, she failed to recognize him until Telemachus began to reproach her.

"Mother—but you are so hard that I cannot call you by that name—why do you keep away from my father? Why do you not sit by him, ask him questions, and talk to him? No other woman could bear to stay away from her husband after twenty years apart, especially after all he has endured; yet your heart is always as hard as a stone."

Penelope replied, "My son, I am so lost in astonishment that I can find no words to ask or answer. I cannot even look him straight in the face. Still, if he really is Ulysses come back, we will understand one another better, for there are tokens known only to us."

Ulysses smiled at this and said to Telemachus, "Let your mother put me to any test she likes; she will come to understand in due time. She rejects me for now and thinks I am someone else because I am covered in dirt and in rags. But let us consider what we should do next. When one man has killed another—even if he wasn't someone who would leave many friends to take up his cause—the killer must still say goodbye to his friends and flee the country. We have just killed the chief of a whole town, the best of Ithaca's youth. I want you to consider this matter."

"Leave it to you, father," answered Telemachus, "for they say you are the wisest of all men, and no other mortal can compare with you. We will follow your lead and not fail you as far as our strength holds out."

"I will tell you what I think is best," Ulysses replied. "First, wash and put on your tunics; tell the maids to do the same. Phemius will then play a dance tune on his lyre, so that if anyone outside hears it, or a neighbor happens to notice, they will think there is a wedding in the house, and no rumors of the suitors' deaths will spread through the town before we can escape to the woods on my land. Once there, we can decide which of the paths heaven gives us will seem the wisest."

Thus he spoke, and they did as he said. First, they washed and put on their tunics, while the women got ready. Then Phemius took his lyre and made them long for sweet song and stately dance. The house echoed with the sound of men and women dancing, and people outside said, "I suppose the queen has finally gotten married. She ought to be ashamed for not keeping her husband's property safe until he returns."

This is what they said, unaware of the true events that had transpired. The upper servant Euryclea washed and anointed Ulysses in his own house and dressed him in a shirt and cloak, while Minerva made him look taller and stronger than before; she also made his hair grow thick and curl down like hyacinth blossoms. She glorified him about the head and shoulders just as a skilled craftsman enriches a piece of silver plate with gold. He emerged from the bath looking like an immortal and sat down opposite his wife on the seat he had left. "My dear," he said, "heaven has given you a heart harder than any woman's. No other woman could stay away from her husband after twenty years apart, especially after all he has endured. But come, nurse, get a bed ready for me; I will sleep alone, for this woman has a heart as hard as iron."

"My dear," Penelope answered, "I have no wish to set myself up or to put you down; but I do not recognize you, for I remember what kind of man you were when you sailed from Ithaca. Nevertheless, Euryclea, take his bed outside the chamber he built. Bring the bed outside and lay it with fleeces, good covers, and blankets."

She said this to test him, but Ulysses was very angry and replied, "Wife, I am displeased by what you have just said. Who has taken my bed from the place I left it? It must have been a hard task, no matter how skilled the worker, unless some god helped him shift it. There is no man alive, however strong, who could move it from its place, for it is a marvel that I made with my own hands. There was a young olive tree growing in the courtyard, stout and healthy, about as thick as a bearing-post. I built my room around it with strong stone walls and a roof, then made the doors strong and well-fitting. I cut off the top boughs of the olive tree and left the stump standing. I dressed it roughly from the roots and worked it with carpenter's tools, straightening it and making it into a bed-post. I bored a hole down the middle, using it as the center-post of my bed, and finished it by inlaying it with gold and silver; after that, I stretched a hide of crimson leather from side to side. So you see, I know all about it, and I want to learn if it is still there or if someone has removed it by cutting down the olive tree."

When Penelope heard the sure proofs Ulysses gave her, she broke down, flew to his side, flung her arms around his neck, and kissed him. "Do not be angry with me, Ulysses," she cried. "You are the wisest of mankind. We have both suffered. Heaven has denied us the happiness of spending our youth and growing old together; do not be aggrieved or take it amiss that I did not embrace you the moment I saw you. I have been trembling with fear that someone might come and deceive me with a lying story; there are many wicked people about. Jove's daughter Helen would never have yielded herself to a man from a foreign country if she had known that the sons of Achaeans would come after her to bring her back. Heaven put it in her heart to do wrong, and she did not consider that sin, which has been the source of all our sorrows. Now, however, that you have convinced me by showing that you know all about our bed—

only you and I, and a single maidservant, the daughter of Actor, who was given to me by my father on my marriage and who keeps the doors of our room—though I have been hard to believe, I can mistrust no longer."

Then Ulysses melted in turn and wept as he embraced his dear and faithful wife. As the sight of land is welcome to men swimming toward the shore after Neptune has wrecked their ship with the fury of his winds and waves, so was her husband welcome to her. She could not tear her fair arms from around his neck. Indeed, they would have continued indulging their sorrow until rosy-fingered dawn appeared, had not Minerva determined otherwise, holding back the night in the far west and preventing dawn from leaving Oceanus or yoking the two steeds, Lampus and Phaethon, that carry her to break the day upon mankind.

Finally, Ulysses said, "Wife, we have not yet reached the end of our troubles. I have an unknown amount of toil still ahead of me. It is long and difficult, but I must go through with it, for thus the shade of Teiresias prophesied when I went down to Hades to ask about my return and that of my companions. But now let us go to bed so we may lie down and enjoy the blessed boon of sleep."

"You shall go to bed whenever you please," replied Penelope, "now that the gods have sent you home to your good house and country. But since you have mentioned it, tell me about the task that lies before you. I should hear about it later, so it is better to know at once."

"My dear," answered Ulysses, "why should you press me to tell you? Still, I will not conceal it from you, even though you may not like it. I do not like it myself, for Teiresias told me to travel far and wide, carrying an oar, until I came to a land where the people have never heard of the sea and do not even mix salt with their food. They know nothing about ships or oars that are like the wings of a ship. He gave me this certain token which I will not hide from you. He said that a wayfarer would meet me and ask whether it was a winnowing shovel that I had on my shoulder.

On this, I was to plant my oar in the ground and sacrifice a ram, a bull, and a boar to Neptune; after which, I was to go home and offer hecatombs to all the gods in heaven, one after the other. As for myself, he said that death would come to me from the sea, and that my life would ebb away gently when I was full of years and at peace of mind, and my people would bless me. All this, he said, would surely come to pass."

And Penelope said, "If the gods are going to grant you a happier time in your old age, you may hope then to find some respite from misfortune."

Thus did they converse. Meanwhile, Eurynome and the nurse took torches and made the bed ready with soft coverlets. Once they had laid them, the nurse went back into the house to rest, leaving the bedchamber woman Eurynome to show Ulysses and Penelope to bed by torchlight. When she had conducted them to their room, she left, and they joyfully approached the rites of their old bed. Telemachus, Philoetius, and the swineherd stopped dancing and made the women do the same. They then lay down to sleep in the cloisters.

When Ulysses and Penelope had their fill of love, they began talking with one another. She told him how much she had endured seeing the house filled with wicked suitors who had killed many sheep and oxen on her account and drunk many casks of wine. Ulysses, in turn, recounted his sufferings and how much trouble he had caused others. He told her everything, and she listened with delight, never going to sleep until he had finished his whole story.

He began with his victory over the Cicons, how he then reached the fertile land of the Lotus-eaters. He recounted his encounter with the Cyclops and how he punished him for ruthlessly eating his brave comrades, then on to Aeolus, who received him hospitably and aided his journey. Yet he could not reach home, for to his great grief, a hurricane carried him out to sea again; he described the Laestrygonian city of Telepylos, where the people destroyed all his ships with their crews, leaving only himself and his own ship alive. He told of cunning Circe and her craft, and how he sailed to the chill house of Hades to consult the ghost of the Theban prophet Teiresias, how he saw his old comrades in arms, and his mother who bore him and raised him as a child. He told of the wondrous singing of the Sirens, his perilous journey past the wandering rocks, terrible Charybdis, and Scylla, whom no man had ever passed safely; how his men then ate the cattle of the sun-god and how Jove struck the ship with his thunderbolts, leading to the death of all his men, with only himself left alive. Finally, he reached Ogygia, the island of the nymph Calypso, who kept him in a cave, feeding him and wanting him to marry her. If he did, she would make him immortal so he would never grow old, but he could not be persuaded. After much suffering, he found his way to the Phaeacians, who treated him as a god and sent him back in a ship to his own country with gifts of gold, bronze, and raiment in abundance. This was the last thing he recounted before a deep sleep overtook him, easing the burden of his sorrows.

Then Minerva thought of another matter. When she deemed that Ulysses had enjoyed the company of his wife and had rested enough, she bade gold-enthroned Dawn rise out of Oceanus to shed light upon mankind. Ulysses then rose from his comfortable bed and said to Penelope, "Wife, we have both had our share of troubles, you here lamenting my absence, and I prevented from returning home despite my longing. Now that we have finally come together, take care of the property in the house. I will take many of the sheep and goats by force from others and compel the Achaeans to make good the rest until they fill my yards. I am going to the wooded lands to see my father, who has been grieving for me so long. I will give you these instructions, though you hardly need them. At sunrise, it will get out that I have been killing the suitors; so go upstairs and stay there with your women. Do not see anyone and ask no questions."

As he spoke, he donned his armor. He then roused Telemachus, Philoetius, and Eumaeus, telling them to arm themselves as well. They did, and when they were armed, they opened the gates and sallied forth, with Ulysses leading the way. It was now daylight, but Minerva concealed them in darkness and led them quickly out of the town.

BOOK 24:

Then Mercury of Cyllene summoned the ghosts of the suitors, holding the fair golden wand that he uses to put men to sleep or wake them at will. With this wand, he roused the ghosts and led them, as they followed him whining and gibbering. Just like bats squeal when one falls from the cluster in which they hang in the dark of a great cave, so did the ghosts whine and squeal as Mercury, the healer of sorrow, led them down into the dark abode of death. After they passed the waters of Oceanus and the rock Leucas, they reached the gates of the sun and the land of dreams, arriving at the meadow of asphodel where dwell the souls and shadows of those who can labor no more.

There, they found the ghost of Achilles, son of Peleus, along with those of Patroclus, Antilochus, and Ajax, the finest and handsomest of all the Danaans after Achilles himself. They gathered around the ghost of the son of Peleus, and Agamemnon's ghost joined them, sorrowing bitterly. The ghost of Achilles spoke first.

"Son of Atreus," it said, "we used to say that Jove loved you more than any other hero from first to last, for you were captain over many brave men when we fought together before Troy. Yet the hand of death, which no mortal can escape, fell upon you too soon. It would have been better for you to have fallen at Troy, at the height of your glory, for the Achaeans would have built a mound over your ashes, and your son would have inherited your good name. Now, instead, you meet a most miserable end."

"Happy son of Peleus," answered Agamemnon's ghost, "for dying at Troy far from Argos, while the bravest of the Trojans and the

Achaeans fell around you, fighting for your body. You lay there in a cloud of dust, heedless of your chivalry. We fought the whole day long, and we should have continued if Jove had not sent a hurricane to stop us. When we had borne you to the ships from the battle, we laid you on your bed and cleansed your fair skin with warm water and ointments. The Danaans tore their hair and wept bitterly around you. Your mother came with her immortal nymphs from the sea when she heard, and a great wailing went out over the waters so that the Achaeans quaked with fear. They would have fled in panic to their ships had not wise old Nestor, whose counsel was ever true, checked them saying, 'Hold, Argives, do not flee, sons of the Achaeans, for this is his mother coming from the sea with her immortal nymphs to view her son's body.'

"Thus he spoke, and the Achaeans feared no more. The daughters of the old man of the sea stood around you weeping bitterly and clothed you in immortal raiment. The nine muses came as well, lifting their sweet voices in lament, calling and answering one another; there was not an Argive who did not weep for pity at the dirge they sang. Days and nights, seven and ten, we mourned you, mortals and immortals alike, but on the eighteenth day, we gave you to the flames. Many fat sheep and oxen did we sacrifice around you. You were burned in the raiment of the gods, with rich resins and honey, while heroes, both horse and foot, clashed their armor round the pyre as you were burning, creating the sound of a great multitude. When the flames of heaven had done their work, we gathered your white bones at daybreak and laid them in ointments and pure wine. Your mother brought us a golden vase to hold them—a gift from Bacchus and the work of Vulcan himself. In this, we mingled your bleached bones with those of Patroclus, who had gone before you, and separately enclosed the bones of Antilochus, who had been closer to you than any other comrade after Patroclus was no more.

"Over these, the host of the Argives built a noble tomb on a point jutting out over the open Hellespont, that it might be seen from far out at sea by those now living and those who shall be born hereafter. Your mother begged prizes from the gods and offered them to be contended for by the noblest of the Achaeans. You must have been present at the funeral of many a hero when young men gird themselves and prepare to compete for prizes on the death of some great chieftain, but you never saw such prizes as silver-footed Thetis offered in your honor, for the gods loved you well. Thus even in death your fame, Achilles, has not been lost, and your name lives on among all mankind. But as for me, what solace had I when the days of my fighting were done? For Jove willed my destruction upon my return, by the hands of Aegisthus and those of my wicked wife."

As they conversed, Mercury approached with the ghosts of the suitors who had been killed by Ulysses. The ghosts of Agamemnon and Achilles were astonished at their presence and went to them at once. Agamemnon recognized Amphimedon, son of Melaneus, who lived in Ithaca and had been his host, and began to talk to him.

"Amphimedon," it said, "what has happened to all you fine young men—all of an age too—that you have come down here under the ground? You could not pick a finer group of men from any city. Did Neptune raise his winds and waves against you while at sea, or did your enemies end you on the mainland while you were cattle-lifting or sheep-stealing, or fighting in defense of their wives and city? Answer my question, for I have been your guest. Do you not remember how I came to your house with Menelaus to persuade Ulysses to join us with his ships against Troy? It took a whole month before we could resume our voyage, for we had a hard time persuading Ulysses to come with us."

Amphimedon's ghost answered, "Agamemnon, son of Atreus, king of men, I remember everything you have said and will tell you fully and accurately how our end was brought about. Ulysses had been long gone, and we were courting his wife, who did not say outright that she would not marry again, nor bring matters to an end, for she meant to bring about our destruction. This was the trick she played on us. She set up a great loom in her room and began to work on a huge piece of fine needlework. 'Sweethearts,' said she, 'Ulysses is indeed dead, but do not press me to marry again immediately; wait—for I would not have my skill in needlework perish unrecorded—until I have finished a pall for the hero Laertes, when death takes him. He is very rich, and the women of the place will talk if he is laid out without a pall.' This is what she said, and we agreed; we could see her working on her great web all day long, but at night she would unpick the stitches by torchlight. She fooled us in this way for three years without us finding out, but as time wore on and she was now in her fourth year, with many moons completed, one of her maids who knew what she was doing told us, and we caught her in the act of undoing her work. She had to finish it whether she wanted to or not; when she showed us the robe she had made, after it had been washed, its splendor was like that of the sun or moon.

"Then some malicious god conveyed Ulysses to the upland farm where his swineherd lives. There, his son also returned from a voyage to Pylos, and they both came to town after hatching their plot for our destruction. Telemachus came first, and then after him, accompanied by the swineherd, came Ulysses, clad in rags and leaning on a staff as though he were some miserable old beggar. He came so unexpectedly that none of us knew him, not even the older ones among us, and we reviled him and threw things at him. He endured both being struck and insulted without a word, though he was in his own house; but when the will of Aegis-bearing Jove inspired him, he and Telemachus took the armor and hid it in an inner chamber, bolting the doors behind them. Then he cunningly made his wife offer his bow and a quantity of iron to be contended for by us ill-fated suitors; and this was the beginning of our end, for not one of us could string the bow—or even come close. When it was about to reach

Ulysses's hands, we all shouted out that it should not be given to him, no matter what he said, but Telemachus insisted he should have it. When he got it in his hands, he strung it easily and sent his arrow through the iron. Then he stood on the floor of the cloister and poured his arrows on the ground, glaring fiercely around him. First, he killed Antinous, and then, aiming straight before him, he let fly his deadly darts, and they fell thick upon one another. It was plain that some god was helping them, for they fell upon us mightily throughout the cloisters, and there was a hideous sound of groaning as our brains were battered in, and the ground seethed with our blood. This, Agamemnon, is how we came by our end, and our bodies lie uncared for in the house of Ulysses, for our friends at home do not yet know what has happened, so they cannot lay us out and wash the black blood from our wounds, making moan over us according to the rites due to the departed."

"Happy Ulysses, son of Laertes," replied Agamemnon's ghost, "you are blessed in possessing such a wife, endowed with rare excellence of understanding, and so faithful to her wedded lord as Penelope, daughter of Icarius. The fame of her virtue shall never die, and the immortals shall compose a song welcome to all mankind in honor of Penelope's constancy. How far otherwise was the wickedness of the daughter of Tyndareus, who killed her lawful husband; her song shall be hated among men, for she has brought disgrace upon all womankind—even the good ones."

Thus they conversed in the house of Hades, deep within the earth. Meanwhile, Ulysses and the others passed out of the town and soon reached the fair, well-tilled farm of Laertes, which he had reclaimed with great effort. Here was his house, with a lean-to running around it, where the slaves who worked for him slept, sat, and ate. Inside the house, an old Sicilian woman looked after him on this country farm. When Ulysses arrived, he said to his son and the others:

"Go to the house and kill the best pig you can find for dinner. Meanwhile, I want to see if my father will recognize me after so long an absence."

He then took off his armor and gave it to Eumaeus and Philoetius, who went straight to the house, while he turned toward the vineyard to test his father. As he walked down into the great orchard, he did not see Dolius, nor any of his sons or other bondmen, for they were all gathering thorns to make a fence for the vineyard, at the place where the old man had instructed them. Thus, he found his father alone, hoeing a vine. He wore a dirty old shirt, patched and very shabby; his legs were bound with thongs of oxhide to protect them from the brambles, and he also had leather sleeves on; a goat skin cap sat on his head, and he looked very worn and sorrowful. When Ulysses saw him so aged, old, and full of sorrow, he paused beneath a tall pear tree and began to weep. He hesitated whether to embrace him, kiss him, and reveal that he had come home, or first to question him and see what he would say. In the end, he decided to be crafty, so he approached his father, who was bent down and digging around a plant.

"I see, sir," said Ulysses, "that you are an excellent gardener—what pains you take with it, to be sure. Not a single plant, not a fig tree, vine, olive, pear, nor flower bed, but bears the trace of your attention. I trust, however, that you will not be offended if I say you take better care of your garden than of yourself. You are old, unkempt, and very poorly clad. It cannot be that you are idle; your master takes poor care of you. Your face and figure do not speak of a slave but proclaim you of noble birth. I should say you are one of those who should wash well, eat well, and sleep comfortably at night, as old men have a right to do. But tell me, whose bondman are you, and in whose garden are you working? Also, tell me about another matter. Is this place that I have come to truly Ithaca? I met a man just now who said so, but he was dull and did not have the patience to hear my story when

I asked about an old friend of mine, whether he is still living or is already dead and in the house of Hades. Believe me when I tell you that this man came to my house once when I was in my own country, and never yet did any stranger come to me whom I liked better. He said his family came from Ithaca and that his father was Laertes, son of Arceisius. I received him hospitably, welcoming him to all the abundance of my house, and when he left, I gave him all customary presents: seven talents of fine gold, a cup of solid silver with flowers chased upon it, twelve light cloaks, as many pieces of tapestry, twelve cloaks of single fold, twelve rugs, twelve fair mantles, and an equal number of shirts. To all this, I added four good-looking women skilled in all useful arts, and let him take his choice."

His father shed tears and replied, "Sir, you have indeed arrived in the land you named, but it has fallen into the hands of wicked people. All these gifts you mention have been given to no purpose. If you had found your friend alive in Ithaca, he would have entertained you hospitably and would have richly rewarded you upon your departure, as was only right. But tell me, how many years has it been since you entertained this guest—my unfortunate son? Alas! He has perished far from his own country; the fishes of the sea may have eaten him, or he may have fallen prey to birds and wild beasts of some distant land. Neither his mother nor I, his father, could embrace him and wrap him in his shroud, nor could his excellent wife, Penelope, bewail him as was natural upon his deathbed, closing his eyes according to the rites due to the departed. Now, tell me truly, for I want to know—who are you and where do you come from? Tell me of your town and parents. Where is the ship that brought you and your men to Ithaca? Or were you a passenger on some other man's ship, and those who brought you here have gone on their way and left you?"

"I will tell you everything," answered Ulysses, "truly. I come from Alybas, where I have a fine house. I am the son of King Apheidas, who is the son of Polypemon. My name is Eperitus;

heaven drove me off course as I was leaving Sicania, and I have been carried here against my will. As for my ship, it lies over yonder, off the open country outside the town. It has been five years since Ulysses left my country. Poor fellow, yet the omens were good for him when he departed. The birds all flew on our right, and both he and I rejoiced at their sight as we parted, for we had every hope of meeting again and exchanging gifts."

A dark cloud of sorrow fell upon Laertes as he listened. He filled both hands with dust from the ground and poured it over his grey head, groaning heavily as he did so. Ulysses was moved, and his nostrils quivered as he looked upon his father. Then he sprang towards him, flung his arms around him, and kissed him, saying, "I am he, father, about whom you are asking—I have returned after twenty years. But cease your sighing and lamentation—we have no time to lose, for I must tell you that I have been punishing the suitors in my house for their insolence and crimes."

"If you truly are my son Ulysses," replied Laertes, "and have returned, you must give me such clear proof of your identity as shall convince me."

"First, observe this scar," answered Ulysses, "which I got from a boar's tusk while hunting on Mt. Parnassus. You and my mother had sent me to Autolycus, my mother's father, to receive the presents he had promised to give me when he was last here. Furthermore, I will point out to you the trees in the vineyard that you gave me, about which I asked you when I followed you around the garden. We examined them all, and you told me their names and what they were. You gave me thirteen pear trees, ten apple trees, and forty fig trees; you also promised me fifty rows of vines; there was corn planted between each row, and they yield grapes of every kind when the sun shines upon them."

Laertes' strength failed him as he heard the convincing proofs Ulysses provided. He threw his arms around him, and Ulysses had to support him, or he would have fainted. But as soon as he regained his senses, he said, "O father Jove, then you gods are still in Olympus after all, if the suitors have truly been punished for their insolence and folly. Nevertheless, I fear that all the townspeople of Ithaca will soon gather here, sending messengers throughout the cities of the Cephallenians."

Ulysses replied, "Take heart and do not trouble yourself about that; let us go into the house near your garden. I have already told Telemachus, Philoetius, and Eumaeus to go there and prepare dinner as soon as possible."

As they spoke, the two made their way towards the house. Upon arriving, they found Telemachus with the stockman and the swineherd cutting up meat and mixing wine with water. The old Sicilian woman took Laertes inside, washed him, and anointed him with oil. She dressed him in a fine cloak, and Minerva approached him, enhancing his presence, making him taller and sturdier than before. When he returned, his son was surprised to see him looking like an immortal and said, "My dear father, someone of the gods has made you much taller and better-looking."

Laertes responded, "Would, by Father Jove, Minerva, and Apollo, that I were the man I was when I ruled among the Cephallenians and took Nericum, that strong fortress on the foreland! If I were still what I was then and had been in our house yesterday with my armor on, I could have stood by you and helped against the suitors. I would have killed many of them, and you would have rejoiced to see it."

Thus did they converse, but the others, having finished their work and with the feast ready, ceased their tasks and took their proper places on the benches and seats. They began to eat, and soon old Dolius and his sons left their work and came up, for their mother, the Sicilian woman who looked after Laertes in his old age, had sent for them. Upon seeing Ulysses and recognizing him, they stood there, lost in astonishment. Ulysses playfully scolded them, saying, "Sit down to your dinner, old man, and do not worry about your surprise; we have wanted to begin for some time and have been waiting for you."

Dolius then reached out both hands and approached Ulysses. "Sir," he said, seizing his master's hand and kissing it at the wrist, "we have long wished for your return: and now heaven has restored you to us after we had given up hope. All hail, therefore, and may the gods prosper you! But tell me, does Penelope already know of your return, or shall we send someone to tell her?"

"Old man," answered Ulysses, "she knows already, so you need not trouble about that." With this, he took his seat, and the sons of Dolius gathered around Ulysses to greet and embrace him one after another; then they took their seats in due order near their father.

While they were busy preparing their dinner, word spread through the town, and news of the terrible fate that had befallen the suitors reached every quarter. As soon as the people heard of it, they gathered from all around, groaning and shouting before Ulysses' house. They took away the dead, burying each man where he belonged, and put the bodies of those from elsewhere on board fishing vessels, to be returned to their respective homes. They then met angrily in the assembly, and Eupeithes rose to speak. He was overwhelmed with grief for the death of his son Antinous, who had been the first man killed by Ulysses, and he said, weeping bitterly, "My friends, this man has wronged the Achaeans greatly. He took many of our best men away with him in his fleet and has lost both ships and men; now, moreover, upon his return, he has been killing all the foremost men among the Cephallenians. Let us rise up and act before he can escape to Pylos or to Elis, where the Epeans rule, or we will be ashamed of ourselves forever after. It would be a disgrace if we do not avenge the murder of our sons and brothers. For my part, I would rather die at once than live with this shame. Let us rise up, then, and pursue them before they can cross over to the mainland."

He wept as he spoke, and every one felt pity for him. But Medon and the bard Phemius had now awakened and came to them from Ulysses' house. They were astonished to see them, but they stood in the middle of the assembly, and Medon said, "Hear me, men of Ithaca. Ulysses did not act alone; it was not against the will of heaven. I myself saw an immortal god take the form of Mentor and stand beside him. This god appeared before him, encouraging him, and then went through the court, attacking the suitors, and they fell upon one another."

At this, a pale fear laid hold of them, and old Halitherses, son of Mastor, rose to speak, for he was the only man among them who knew both the past and the future. He addressed them plainly and sincerely, saying,

"Men of Ithaca, it is all your own fault that things have turned out as they have; you would not listen to me or to Mentor when we urged you to check the folly of your sons, who were doing much wrong in the wantonness of their hearts—wasting the estate and dishonoring the wife of a chieftain whom they thought would not return. But now, let it be as I say, and do as I tell you: Do not go out against Ulysses, or you may find that you have brought evil down upon your own heads."

This caused more than half to raise a loud shout and leave the assembly at once. But the rest stayed, for Halitherses' speech displeased them, and they sided with Eupeithes; they hurried off for their armor, and when they had armed themselves, they gathered in front of the city, led on by Eupeithes in their folly. He thought he would avenge his son's murder, but in truth, he would perish in his attempt.

Then Minerva said to Jove, "Father, son of Saturn, king of kings, what do you propose to do? Will you set them fighting further, or will you make peace between them?"

And Jove replied, "My child, why do you ask me? Was it not by your own design that Ulysses returned and took his revenge upon the suitors? Do as you please, but I will suggest what I believe to be the most reasonable course of action. Now that Ulysses has avenged himself, let them swear to a solemn covenant, whereby he shall continue to rule, while we cause the others to forgive and forget the slaughter of their sons and brothers. Let them all become friends as they were before, and let peace and abundance prevail."

This was what Minerva was already eager to bring about, so she swiftly descended from the heights of Olympus.

After Laertes and the others had finished their dinner, Ulysses began, "Some of you go out and see if they are drawing near." One of Dolius's sons did as he was told. Standing at the threshold, he could see them coming close, and he reported to Ulysses, "Here they are! Let us put on our armor at once."

They hurriedly donned their armor—Ulysses, his three men, and the six sons of Dolius. Laertes and Dolius also donned their armor—warriors by necessity, despite their gray hair. Once they were all armed, they opened the gate and rushed out, Ulysses leading the way.

Then Jove's daughter Minerva approached them, having taken on the form and voice of Mentor. Ulysses was pleased to see her and said to his son Telemachus, "Telemachus, now that you are about to engage in a battle that will reveal every man's courage, make sure not to disgrace your ancestors, who were renowned for their strength and bravery throughout the world."

"You speak truly, my dear father," replied Telemachus, "and you will see that I have no intention of bringing shame upon your family."

Laertes rejoiced to hear this. "Good heavens," he exclaimed, "what a wonderful day this is! I truly rejoice. My son and grandson are competing with each other in valor!"

Then Minerva drew close to him and said, "Son of Arceisius—my best friend in the world—pray to the blue-eyed goddess and to Jove her father; then take your spear and throw it."

As she spoke, she infused him with renewed strength, and after he prayed to her, he raised his spear and hurled it. He struck Eupeithes' helmet, and the spear pierced it, for the helmet did not stop it, and it rang as it fell heavily to the ground. Meanwhile, Ulysses and his son attacked the front line of the enemy, striking them with their swords and spears. Indeed, they would have slain every one of them and prevented their return home, had not Minerva raised her voice and called out, "Men of Ithaca, cease this dreadful war and settle the matter at once without further bloodshed."

At her words, a pale fear seized them; they were so terrified that their weapons fell from their hands to the ground at the sound of the goddess' voice, and they fled back to the city for their lives. But Ulysses let out a great cry, gathering himself and swooping down like a soaring eagle. At that moment, the son of Saturn sent a thunderbolt that fell just in front of Minerva, and she said to Ulysses, "Ulysses, noble son of Laertes, stop this violent strife, or Jove will be angry with you."

Thus spoke Minerva, and Ulysses obeyed her gladly. Then Minerva assumed the form and voice of Mentor and soon established a covenant of peace between the two opposing parties.

Made in the USA
Las Vegas, NV
21 March 2025

9475f5d9-460c-4d44-a851-9c45447539afR01